THE GOOD GIRLS

ALSO BY SARA SHEPARD

The Good Girls

A **PERFECTIONISTS** NOVEL

SARA SHEPARD

HARPER TEEN

An Imprint of HarperCollinsPublishers

Produced by Alloy Entertainment
1700 Broadway, New York, NY 10019

Library of Congress Control Number: 2015932004

ISBN 978-0-06-207452-2
ISBN 978-0-06-239115-5 (int. ed.)

Design by Liz Dresner

15 16 17 18 19   CG/RRDH   10 9 8 7 6 5 4 3 2 1

First Edition

THE GOOD GIRLS

PROLOGUE

"HE DESERVES TO BE PUNISHED."

That's how it starts—with a simple statement like that. You might say it about a boyfriend who broke your heart when he kissed that skanky new girl. Or that former best friend who lied about you to save his ass. Or about a bully who went too far. You're angry and hurt, and deep down, all you want is to *get even.*

That doesn't mean you do it, of course. You might *fantasize* about fulfilling your darkest wishes . . . but you're a good person. You wouldn't actually go through with it. But as five girls learned, sometimes even *thinking* about revenge can lead to danger—and murder.

In other words, be careful what you wish for. Because you might get exactly what you want.

* * *

In a normal-seeming classroom in a normal-seeming high school in the normal-seeming town of Beacon Heights, Washington, thirty teenagers sat in darkness as the words *The End* flashed across the flat-screen TV before them. They had just watched *And Then There Were None*, an old black-and-white movie about justice, punishment, and murder. This was film studies class, a popular senior elective at Beacon High that was taught by the well-liked—and, at least according to most of the girls, totally gorgeous—Mr. Granger.

When Granger flicked on the lights, he had a smug, I'm-handsome-and-smart-and-you-should-worship-me smile on his face. "Amazing, right?" He swiftly divided the class into groups. "Discuss. What do you think this movie is truly about? Get some ideas for your papers." Granger assigned an open-themed paper on every film they watched. It might seem easier that way, but his grading scale was brutal, in line with every *other* class at ultra-competitive Beacon High, so group discussions to come up with paper topics were key.

At the back of the room, Julie Redding sat in a group of girls who were, mostly, relative strangers to her. But she knew them in passing: There was musical genius Mackenzie Wright—word had it she'd played onstage with Yo-Yo Ma. Gorgeous Ava Jalali sat across from them, who'd done some small-time modeling gigs and apparently was snapped as a "trendsetter on the street" in *Glamour*. There was soccer star Caitlin Martell-Lewis, who was twitchy as a caged animal. Next to Julie sat the only one she knew well—her best friend, Parker Duvall, whose only talent these days was being a pariah. And of course, there was Julie herself, the most popular girl at school.

The girls didn't know each other very well—yet. But soon enough, they would.

At first they talked about the movie, which was about killing people who had done terrible things—was that simply punishment, or murder? Suddenly Parker took a deep breath. "I know it's kind of sick," she said, her voice low, "but sometimes I think the judge in the movie was right. Some people deserve to be punished."

There was a shock wave through the group, but then Julie spoke up, always quick to come to Parker's defense. "Right?" she chimed in. "I mean, *I* know some people who deserve punishment. Personally, first on my list would be Parker's dad. The judge let him off too easy." She *hated* Parker's dad for what he'd done to Parker. The scars of it were still all over her face, and ever since that night, Parker had gone from the most popular girl in school to . . . well, a damaged outsider. Parker hadn't even tried to regain the friends she'd pulled away from, though maybe it was easier to hide than to reveal exactly how broken she was.

Parker nodded at Julie, and Julie gave her friend's hand a squeeze. She knew it was always hard for Parker, talking about her dad. "Or what about Ashley Ferguson?" Parker offered, and Julie winced. Ashley was a junior girl who tried way too hard to be like Julie, buying the same exact clothes, retweeting everything she posted, even dying her hair the same color as Julie's. It was starting to feel a little creepy.

The other girls in the group shifted. They weren't sure they liked where this was going, but they also felt the all-too-familiar tug of peer pressure.

Mackenzie cleared her throat. "Um, I would pick Claire, I guess."

"Claire *Coldwell*?" Ava Jalali's eyes widened. The others were just as surprised—wasn't Claire Mackenzie's best friend? But Mackenzie just shrugged. She must have had her reasons for choosing Claire, Julie thought. Everyone had secrets.

Ava tapped her bright red nails on the desk. "I'd go for my father's new wife, Leslie," she decided. "She's . . . *awful*."

"But how would you do it?" Parker pressed, leaning forward. "For example, Ashley. She could trip in the shower, while she's washing her copycat hair. If you were going to commit the perfect crime, what would you do?" Her eyes traveled to each of the girls in turn.

Ava's brow knitted in concentration. "Well, Leslie's always drunk," she said slowly. "Maybe she could fall off her balcony after she finishes her nightly bottle of chardonnay."

Parker looked at Mackenzie. "And you? How would you take out Claire?"

"Oh," the musician squeaked. "Well . . . maybe a hit-and-run. Something totally accidental." She reached for her water bottle and took a nervous swig, then glanced around the classroom. Claire was *in this class* . . . but she seemed to be paying no attention. Only Mr. Granger was looking at them from his desk. But when Mackenzie met his stare, he smiled at her and looked back down at a yellow legal pad, his paper of choice.

"Parker's dad could get his ass kicked in the prison yard," Julie volunteered in a small voice. "That happens all the time, doesn't it?"

Caitlin, who hadn't said a word, inched her chair closer to the others. "You know who I'd get rid of?" she said suddenly. She glanced across the room, her gaze cutting through group one and then Mr. Granger, who was peering at them again, until it finally landed on a guy in group three. The hottest guy in the room, actually. But his handsome mouth was twisted into a cruel smile, and his eyes narrowed dangerously.

Nolan Hotchkiss.

"*Him*," Caitlin said gravely.

Each girl sucked in a breath. It was clear why Caitlin hated Nolan so much—her brother's tragic death said it all—he'd been tormented to his breaking point by Nolan.

Each girl's own frustrations with Nolan began to surface. He'd started nasty rumors about Ava after she had broken up with him last year. Mackenzie felt her cheeks redden as she thought of how she'd fallen for his Casanova act—and sent him some seriously embarrassing pictures. Julie hated Nolan for the same reason Parker did—if he hadn't drugged Parker that night, maybe her dad would never have hurt her like this. Maybe Parker would still be her old self, glittery and happy and full of life.

It was true, each of them thought: The world *would* be a much better place without Nolan. He was a monster, not just to them, but to Beacon as a whole. But even *thinking* these things felt dangerous. Nolan could ruin any of them with a snap of his fingers—and he had.

"How would you do it?" Ava asked, looking down. "If you were going to kill him, I mean?"

And so they talked it through—just for fun. They hypothesized a way to kill him, with cyanide, like in all the old movies. Not that they'd ever do that.

But then they came up with something they *would* do: prank Nolan. They could use Oxy, his drug of choice, to spike his beer. And then when he was passed out, they would write embarrassing messages on his face in Sharpie and post the pictures online. They'd make a fool out of him, just like he'd done to all of them.

At one point during the discussion, Nolan looked up

at the girls, an eyebrow raised. His gaze flicked to each of them in turn, and then he rolled his eyes and looked back at his group. It was clear he thought he didn't have a thing to worry about.

But that was just it. He did. Because a week later, Nolan was dead—of cyanide poisoning. Exactly the way the girls had originally planned.

After Nolan's death, the girls called one another and spoke in panicked whispers. What had happened? All they did was prank Nolan, with a single Oxy pill and some dumb stuff written on his face. How had *cyanide* ended up in his system? This wasn't their fault, they told one another. They were good girls, every last one of them. Not killers.

But they couldn't help wondering: Had someone heard them in class and decided to take advantage of their plan? Someone else who hated Nolan, too, maybe? That was *truly* the perfect crime—Nolan was dead, and the girls were built-in suspects.

At first the girls thought it was Mr. Granger. Hadn't they noticed him watching them carefully in class that day? But when Granger turned up dead, too, they were back to square one. The killer was someone else.

But how far would that someone go? What about all the *other* names on the list?

What if one of them was next?

CHAPTER ONE

ON SUNDAY MORNING, MACKENZIE WRIGHT stood outside the Beacon Heights police station, staring morosely at the curb. Storm clouds hung low in the sky. Six squad cars were lined up in the parking lot. The other girls from film studies had all already left, either with their parents—Mac's would be there any minute now—or on their own.

As if summoned by her thoughts, her parents' sedan turned into the parking lot. Mac's stomach flipped. She'd caught a ride with Ava here this morning, but after the cops had called her parents, they'd insisted on coming to get her. Mac couldn't imagine how her family was reacting to the news that she'd broken into the house of a teacher who'd been killed last night—stabbed with his own *kitchen knife*. She, Mackenzie Wright, first chair cello, was a murder suspect.

The car slowed, and her mother bolted out of the passenger seat, enveloping Mackenzie in a firm hug. Mac stiffened, surprised. "Are you okay?" Mrs. Wright said into Mac's shoulder, her voice tinged with sobs.

"I guess so," Mac said.

Her father had jumped out of the car, too. "We came as soon as we could. What *happened*? The police said you broke into a house? And there'd been a *murder*? What's happening to this town?"

Mac took a deep breath, saying the words she'd rehearsed for the past five minutes. "It was a big mix-up," she said slowly. "A few friends and I thought we had some information on Nolan Hotchkiss's death. That's why we came to the police station. But then . . . well, then things got kind of confusing."

Her father frowned. "Did you or did you not break into a teacher's house?"

Mac swallowed hard. She'd been dreading this part. "We thought he was home. The door was open. We had some questions for him, about Nolan's death."

She lowered her eyes. Her parents had known who Nolan Hotchkiss was even before he'd died—everyone did. The Hotchkisses were wealthy and powerful, even in the influential, glamorous, perfect world of Beacon Heights. What her parents didn't know was what Nolan had meant to *Mac*. Not so long ago, he'd taken Mac out on a couple of dates. Wooed her, made her feel good, lit up her life. When he'd asked for a few pictures, she hadn't even flinched, posing behind her cello and snapping away.

Turns out he'd only wanted the pictures for a bet—which Mackenzie realized when he drove by her house with his friends, laughing and throwing money at her. Can you say *humiliating nightmare*?

Worse, the police had *found* those pictures on Nolan's phone, which to them was as good a motive as any for Mac to have murdered Nolan. They didn't have proof of anything yet, but still, it wasn't good.

That was why Mackenzie and the other girls had gone to Granger's house—to try to clear their own names. They knew that Nolan had something on Granger—something big—and thought maybe Granger killed him to keep him quiet.

Mrs. Wright held Mac at arm's length. "You honestly thought your teacher had something to do with Nolan's death? What kind of teacher was he?"

"Not a good one." Mac squirmed at the thought of Granger fooling around with quite a few of his students—the Something Big that Nolan had known about. They'd discovered that when Ava found a threatening message from Nolan on Granger's phone. Oh, and Granger had hit on Ava, too.

After they snooped through Granger's house and found hard evidence that Nolan was blackmailing the teacher, they'd all gone to the police station together. But they hadn't exactly gotten the warm welcome they'd expected. Granger had died just moments after they fled the scene. Ava's boyfriend—or maybe ex-boyfriend—had seen them leaving Granger's house and called the cops.

The mind-boggling discussion she'd just had with her friends flashed through Mackenzie's mind. *Is Granger Nolan's killer?* Caitlin had asked. *Or did Nolan's killer kill Granger, too—and make it look like us* again? No one had an answer for that. It had all made sense when they thought Granger killed Nolan, but now it was clear that everything was more complicated than they'd realized.

Her father slung his arm around her and pulled her in close, yanking Mac back to the present. "Well, we believe you, and we'll get this worked out," he said. "I already have a call in to an old friend who's a lawyer. I'm just sorry it happened, especially in light of all the good things going on right now."

It took Mac a moment to realize what he was referring to: She was supposed to be celebrating her unofficial acceptance to Juilliard in New York. She'd gotten the call from her mom's friend—who had inside information from the admissions office—two days ago, but they hadn't really gotten to enjoy the moment. Not that Mac felt much like celebrating, since the victory was tainted by the fact that Claire Coldwell had gotten in, too.

Her dad guided her into the backseat of the car. "I'm just glad you're okay. What if you'd been inside that house with some maniac holding a knife?"

"I know, I know," Mac mumbled into her chest. "And I'm sorry." But that made her wonder: If they'd remained on Granger's property, a safe distance away, for a little while longer, would they have seen who'd snuck into his house and killed him?

She was just about to get into the car when she heard a snicker behind her. Standing across the street in her front yard was Amy something-or-other, a sophomore she knew from school. Amy was leaning against a tree, a cup of coffee in her hands, just . . . staring.

Mac put her head down. How long had the girl been watching? Had she heard about Granger? How much did she know?

Sighing, Mac scooted into the seat next to her younger sister, Sierra. Sierra looked at Mac a little cautiously, almost as if she were afraid of her. Mac stared straight ahead, pretending she didn't notice, but when she heard Nolan's name on the local news radio, she flinched. *The search is still on for the person who poisoned Mr. Hotchkiss on the night of . . .*

"Enough of that," Mrs. Wright said sharply, her hand shooting forward to adjust the dial to the classical station, which was playing Beethoven. Nobody spoke for the short ride home. Mac leaned back and closed her eyes, feeling deeply, painfully tired. The silence was only broken when they pulled into the driveway and Mrs. Wright cleared her throat. "Looks like you have a visitor, Mackenzie."

Mac's eyes popped open, and she followed her mother's gaze. Her first thought was that it must be Claire, her ex–best friend. Dread filled her. After Claire's attempts to sabotage Mac's Juilliard audition, Mac never wanted to see her again. The fact that she'd have to spend the next four years with her—at the school they'd both devoted their lives to getting accepted to—felt like some sort of cosmic joke.

But then her vision adjusted. It wasn't Claire sitting on the family's front porch, slowly turning the shiny fronds of a pinwheel that was jammed into the flower bed. It was Claire's boyfriend—and the boy Mac had loved quietly for years. *Blake.*

Blake's head shot up as the car pulled to a stop. There was a desperate, searching look in his eyes. His mouth opened, but no words came out, and he snapped it shut again. Mac felt a tug in her heart. His shaggy hair and long-lashed pale blue eyes still knocked the wind out of her. And he looked so . . . sad, like he missed hanging out with her.

Then she noticed something in his lap. It was a confection box from his sister's bakery in town along with a square white envelope. A memory suddenly struck her: meeting Blake at the bakery last week so they could rehearse songs for his band. It felt like ages ago. Mac had kept her distance from Blake for so long—ever since Claire started dating him even though she clearly knew how Mac felt about him. But that day in the bakery, they'd . . . connected, just like old times.

She closed her eyes, flooded with the memory of how their lips had met. It had felt so wrong and so *right*, all at once.

But the soft spot inside Mac quickly turned iron-hard. She thought of the next time she'd seen Blake at the bakery: finding him and Claire after the Juilliard audition. They'd stood together, hand-in-hand, a united front. *I told Blake to hang out with you,* Claire had teased. *I knew you'd drop everything, even practicing for your audition. Oh, and all your confessions to Blake? He told me everything. Including that you were playing Tchaikovsky.* She'd looked at Mac with so much anger and hate in her eyes. *And we aren't broken up. We're stronger than ever.*

Blake hadn't been able to look at Mac when she asked him if it was true. But he hadn't needed to. His downcast eyes and guilty expression had said it all.

Now Mac turned and followed her parents into the house through the garage. "I don't want to talk to you," she snapped.

Blake leaped off the porch and ran down the driveway. "I'm sorry, Macks. Seriously. I am so, *so* sorry."

14

Mac stopped short. She might have whimpered. Her mother touched her arm. "Honey? Are you okay?"

"Yeah," Mac said weakly. She hadn't told her mom about the Blake-Claire drama—they didn't exactly have that sort of relationship. She gave her mom her bravest smile. "I just need a sec, if that's okay?"

"A few minutes," Mrs. Wright said, glancing cautiously in Blake's direction before stepping inside.

Mac turned and looked at Blake. He reached out a hand toward her arm. She reflexively tried to pull away, but then wilted. The warm smell of cupcake batter and powdered sugar wafted off him.

"I'm sorry," Blake began.

"I don't want to hear it," Mac said, feeling tired, but Blake pressed on.

"Macks. It's true that Claire *did* ask me to start hanging out with you." He winced. "But once I realized how you felt—and I felt—I wanted to put a stop to it. You're the one that I've always wanted. I didn't mean to hurt you. I felt terrible about it—all of it."

Mac scoffed. "That didn't stop you from carrying out your plan." Telling Claire that she was playing Tchaikovsky, so that Claire could practice the same piece and play it first. Trying to distract her before the most important audition of her life. "You almost ruined everything."

"I know, and I'm an asshole." Blake kicked at a pebble

on the ground. "Just so you know, I broke up with Claire. For good this time. I want to be with you . . . if you'll have me."

In Mac's darkest moments over the past few days, she'd imagined a scene just like this one, where Blake came crawling on hands and knees to beg her forgiveness. But now that it was actually happening, she didn't feel nearly as satisfied as she'd thought she would. She stared at him now, somewhat shocked. He screwed her over and then had the nerve to ask her out?

"Here," Blake said, his voice jittery. He pushed the cake box and envelope at her. "For you . . ."

Mac knew he wouldn't leave until she opened the lid. Inside was a single cupcake with a violin shaped out of gummy worms. The icing was sloppy—it was clear Blake had crafted it himself. Briefly, Mac tried to picture it: him standing over a mixing bowl, then checking on the cupcake in the oven, then carefully positioning the gummies just so. That seemed like a lot of effort for someone he'd tried to sabotage.

"Congrats on Juilliard," Blake said gently. "I'm so proud of you."

Mac's head shot up. "How did you know I got in?"

Blake blinked. He looked caught. That was when Mac understood: He knew because Claire had told him. Which meant they were *still talking*.

"I heard it from Claire, but that was the last thing we talked about before we broke up," Blake said quickly, as if he could sense Mac's thought process. "It's awesome, Macks. You so deserve it." He shifted closer. "What will it take for you to forgive me? Do I have *any* chance?"

Mac could feel her eyes filling with tears. Just a few days ago, she would have given anything to hear Blake say that—to say that he wanted her, he chose *her*. For so long he'd been the guy on a pedestal, the one she wanted so badly but couldn't have.

But now he wasn't any of those things. He was just Blake the backstabber. Blake, the guy who truly didn't get it. How could she ever trust him again after what he'd done? How could he ever be that perfect, ideal Blake she'd fantasized about for so long?

She closed the bakery box. "There's no chance," she blurted, grabbing the unopened envelope and walking inside.

And when she shut the door, she shut all thoughts of Blake firmly behind her.

CHAPTER TWO

"JULIE?" A HOARSE CRY SOUNDED through Julie Redding's bedroom door on Monday.

Julie rolled over, pulled the covers all the way over her head, and willed herself back to sleep. It was quiet for a moment, but then, "Julie? *Julie!*" This call was more urgent.

With a grunt of frustration, Julie kicked off her crisp white duvet and sat up in her hospital-cornered bed. Her silk camisole felt smooth against her skin. Soft morning sunlight streamed through the gauzy curtains. Lilting birds welcomed the day outside, and a gentle breeze washed over her face through the open window. Her room was in perfect order, just as she had left it the night before. Except for her crumpled James jeans and gray cashmere cardi—both from last season, bought secondhand—which she'd peeled off and let fall to the floor before collapsing into bed.

All around her, the day was dawning beautifully, perfectly . . . but Julie felt only darkness and grief. She heard the mewling and scratching of cats—hordes and hordes of cats—outside her bedroom door. And her mother's desperate voice.

"JULIE!"

Julie bolted from the bed and stomped across her room, past the extra twin bed where her best friend, Parker, usually slept. Parker hadn't come here last night—again.

She flung open the door. The precious, invaluable, beloved door, the only thing that separated her world from her mother's. The only thing that kept the moldering mess at bay, protecting Julie's domain from the contamination on the other side. As the door opened, the pungent stew of mildewed newspapers, food-caked dishes, crusted tins of cat food, and wet fabric wafted over her. She swallowed hard to suppress her gag reflex.

"What?" she growled at her mother, who stood in the crowded hallway. Guilt spiked through Julie when Mrs. Redding's fleshy face crumpled, but she pushed it away. The last thing she could handle on top of everything else was her mother. Julie rubbed both hands over her face, trying to will her brain into some form of Zen state. No luck. The best she could muster was a calm exterior. She took a couple of deep breaths. "I mean, yes, Mom?" she said, her voice now neutral and controlled.

Mrs. Redding pushed a strand of greasy hair out of her eyes. "School's already started, you know," she barked. "But since you're already late, you might as well pick me up some Diet Sprite and cat litter for later."

Julie set her jaw. "I can't. I'm never going out again."

"Why not?"

Julie looked away. *Because of you, actually. Because of a horrible email that someone sent around to the whole student body about* you.

She could practically see the taunting looks on her classmates' faces; they'd surely read Ashley Ferguson's email by now. She already knew the catchy nicknames they'd scrawl on her locker: *JULIE ROTTING, DROOLY JULIE,* and the one she dreaded most, *PUSSY GALORE.* It was what the kids at her old school had called her, after all.

So there was no way she was going back, ever. Julie hated to admit it, but Ashley had even outdone Nolan Hotchkiss in the I'm-going-to-make-your-life-hell department. And, oh yeah, there was also all that bullshit about Granger's murder. The story had broken on the news yesterday afternoon; no doubt Beacon would be buzzing with it. What if kids also knew that Julie and the others were suspects? In Beacon, things had a way of getting around even when they were supposed to be private. She could just hear the whispers. *Not only does Julie Redding live in a trash pit, she also killed Nolan Hotchkiss and her teacher! Didn't you hear she was arrested?*

The Granger thing was really messing with her mind. Just when she and the others thought they'd found Nolan's killer, he turned up dead. Did the same person who killed Nolan—the same person, in other words, who set them up the first time—kill Granger, too? But who could that be? Individually, Julie and the other film studies girls had made a few enemies—like Ashley Ferguson. But who hated them *collectively*?

She sighed, realizing she hadn't answered her mom's question about skipping school. "Because I'm not welcome at school any longer," she said emptily. "Because everything is ruined."

Her mother shrugged, seeming to accept this as an answer. "Well, I still need some cat litter and Diet Sprite," she said simply. "Surely you can go out for that."

God forbid she'd ever ask Julie what could possibly be wrong. *One, two, three* . . . Julie counted, using her fallback technique to calm herself. Then she felt something soft and slinky brush her legs and almost screamed. One of her mother's mangy beasts was trying to get into her room. "Get away," Julie muttered, half kicking it back into the hallway. The cat yowled and disappeared into a stack of boxes that another cat, a black one her mother always called Twinkles, was standing on top of. A third cat, a matted thing with one eye, stood in a random litter box halfway down the hall, staring at them.

Then Julie turned back to her mother. She'd had it. "Sorry," she said. "No Diet Sprite. No litter. Get it yourself."

Mrs. Redding's mouth fell open. "Excuse me?"

Julie twitched slightly. It had been a long, long time since she'd told her mom no. Ever since her mom's hoarding had started in full force, she'd always found it easier to just comply. But look where that had gotten her: She'd spent years scurrying around, trying her damnedest to make sure no one ever saw where she lived. She'd tried to make herself absolutely, unimpeachably perfect, so that no one would ever know the truth. But now the brunt of her resentment poked through, making her seethe.

"I said get it yourself," Julie repeated firmly. "In case you're interested, Mom, I can't show my face to the world. Everyone knows now." She waved her hand in the air wildly. "About this . . . this place."

She narrowed her eyes, a newfound power flooding through her. Suddenly, she was ready to say all the things she'd kept pent up. And anyway, what was the point of holding back now that she was probably going to jail?

She looked at her mom again. "They know about you. And now they'll hate me again, just like they did in California." It felt good to say it out loud. Julie felt a thousand pounds lighter, like she was floating. "Oh, and one more thing," Julie continued. "I also feel a little uncomfortable going out because I'm *wanted* for a murder I didn't commit. Is that a good enough excuse for you?"

Mrs. Redding looked at Julie blankly. After a long moment, her eyes narrowed. "How *dare* you not help me!" she screeched. She stepped toward her daughter, her eyes bulging out of her reddening face.

Julie took one step back. With a jolt of panic, she realized that her mother had crossed over the threshold . . . and *was in her room.* Mrs. Redding had never set foot in there. Even through her illness, she seemed to understand that this was a sacred space. Julie's heart thudded against her ribs, and she choked back a sob. With her stringy hair and frayed housecoat, her mother looked even more unkempt against the backdrop of spare furnishings and a spotless rug.

"What the hell good are you?" Mrs. Redding sputtered, thrashing her arms around like a maniac. "You were a useless child, and now you're a useless teenager. You just take and take and take, and you never do anything for *me.*" Her eyes spun around. "Your father knew how useless you were."

Julie froze. "Stop." She didn't want her mom to go down this road.

But Mrs. Redding knew she had her. "That's why he left, you know. The first time he held you, he turned to me and he said, 'Well, maybe we'll get it right next time.' He saw right through you. *You're* the reason he abandoned us. You were never good enough for him."

"Please," Julie said weakly, shriveling into herself, the rush of confidence she had felt just moments before vanishing. This was always her mom's secret weapon. And it was always the thing that decimated Julie completely.

"So you're not going to school today, huh?" Mrs. Redding challenged. "I'm not surprised. Your father always said you weren't smart enough. You're a piece of nothing. A worthless, no-good, piece of nothing. Of course you're accused of a murder! You probably did it, you stupid bitch!"

She said more than that, way more, but the words soon blurred together, washing over Julie as they had since she was a little girl. Her mother had always been mean, even before she snapped. Julie remembered crying so hard when she was little, once even asking, "What can I do to make you love me?" To which her mother had just laughed and said, "Become someone else."

That was when Julie became . . . well, *Super Julie*. Even as a six-year-old, she'd scuttled around doing everything her mother asked—anticipating her every need, bringing her slippers, a case of Diet Sprite, her favorite weekly tabloids. It was why she studied harder than anyone else in her class, dressed neater, brushed her auburn hair until it was the shiniest of all the girls in her grade.

But it had never been enough. No matter what Julie did or how she did it, her mother despised her. Julie often felt like the barrage of words was worse than the sea of trash lapping at her bedroom door.

When they moved to Beacon Heights, she'd thought she could start fresh, and for a little while, she'd gotten away with it. But maybe her mother was right. Maybe Julie *was* the problem. If she had just tried harder to keep her secret from Ashley, no one else at school would have found out. If she had just tried harder to fix her mother, then there wouldn't have been a secret in the first place. And if Julie had just tried harder to stop herself and the others from drugging Nolan, if she'd done a better job of disguising her handwriting so the cops wouldn't recognize it on Nolan's face, if she just hadn't broken into Mr. Granger's house, maybe she and the others wouldn't be suspects. If Julie were smarter, better, stronger, then she would be able to figure out who had snuck back in after they left and killed him. Because right now she didn't have the faintest idea, and unless she figured it out fast, she was going to jail.

Maybe it *was* all her fault.

Somewhere in the distance, Julie thought she heard a bell. Mrs. Redding halted mid-word. Julie heard it again—this time more clearly. It was the doorbell.

Julie's mom turned back to her. "Well, are you going to get that or not?"

Julie, who had flung herself on her bed and curled into

a tight fetal ball, slowly sat up and blinked. "Uh, sure," she said weakly.

"Good." Mrs. Redding hefted herself up from Parker's bed and trudged out the door, leaving a cyclone of cat hair swirling behind her. "And after you do, you can get my cat litter and Diet Sprite."

"Okay," Julie said in a tiny voice.

The doorbell chimed again. Julie rubbed her eyes, sensing how red they probably were. What if it was Ashley? The girl materialized in her thoughts, her red-gold hair the same shade as Julie's, her clothes so carefully copied, her smile so saccharine and evil. Ever since the email, Julie had had nightmares about Ashley ambushing her at every turn. Ashley popped out of a cake at a birthday party, poked her head into a private bathroom stall, even interrupted Julie at a waxing appointment. "Do you know the truth?" Ashley giggled every time. "She's a disgusting freak! She lives in a trash heap! Her clothes are made of cat hair!" And whoever else was in the dream—a friend, an acquaintance, even a stranger—would look at Julie in horror, understanding her true nature.

Then again, maybe it was just Parker at the door. Parker needed her now. And Julie had wondered where her friend had disappeared to after the police station yesterday—after they'd spoken about who could be after them, Parker had taken off through the woods, insisting she wanted to be alone. Julie should have followed her. Parker was too fragile to be alone.

She slipped from her bed and wrapped a plush terry cloth robe around herself. Slowly, she wedged her way down the hall, following the square beacon of light that streamed in through the one small window set high in the front door.

Just as Julie was a few feet from the door, the light went dark. A face blocked the window, peering in. She froze in her tracks, her heart leaping into her throat. She recognized the olive-green eyes, the beautiful dark skin: It was Carson Wells. The new guy in town, whom she'd been foolish enough to go on a few dates with before everything went down.

A small cry escaped her lips. Wasn't her disgrace complete already?

She jumped as the doorbell rang again. Slowly, she edged backward, pressing herself against the stack of boxes—maybe she could just slip away and pretend no one was home.

The face at the window moved in closer to the glass. Carson's hands shaded his eyes as he pressed his nose to the window. "Julie," he yelled, his Australian accent sharpening the vowels in her name. "Julie, I know you're in there. Open the door."

Julie shrank backward another step. She started to hyperventilate.

"You can't hide in there forever. I just want to talk to you."

Tears rolled down her cheeks. Yeah, *right*. He wanted to tease her. Or maybe cut her apart for not telling the truth. Whatever he was going to say, she didn't want to hear it.

Carson was silent for a moment, watching her through the small window.

"Please talk to me."

She looked up. His voice was so sweet, so sincere. Something in her turned. She desperately *wanted* someone to help her, soothe her, especially after the police and Ashley and her mother's cruel words.

She forced herself to take one step forward, then another. She felt like she'd walked a mile when her fingers finally closed over the knob. The door swung open, and the fresh air washed over her like a spring shower. Julie took in the dewy grass, the cars still beaded with last night's rain, the newspaper on her neighbor's stoop. And Carson.

She slipped out onto the porch and shut the door firmly behind her. She couldn't look at him directly but instead kept her eyes focused on the collection of empty boxes, soda cans, cat food tins, and half-used sacks of bird feed littering the porch. "What do you want?"

"I just wanted to see how you were doing," Carson said gently. "I tried to text you, but your phone was off."

Julie shrugged. She'd turned her phone off after Ashley's email went out. She couldn't face the aftermath.

"And you weren't at school."

Julie sniffed sarcastically. "It's pretty obvious why, isn't it?"

He scoffed. "I just want to be with you, Julie. I don't care what people think."

She stared at him, confused. "But what about that picture of you and Ashley?"

He cocked his head. "What picture?"

"At the Pike Place Fish Market. Ashley said, *This is what Carson thinks of you now.* You looked . . ." She trailed off. He'd looked, well, totally disgusted.

Carson narrowed his eyes. "The Pike Place . . ." Then he brightened. "I was in a picture with Ashley there, yeah. We were there for a class trip a few weeks ago."

"A few weeks ago?" Julie repeated.

Carson nodded. "James West shot it, and he told us to make a crazy face. Ashley grabbed my hand, and I just went with it." He shook his head in disbelief. "Wait, she sent it to you now? That girl is horrible."

"I know," Julie exploded, and she suddenly erupted into fresh tears.

Carson put his arms around Julie's shoulders and pulled her in. She stiffened, but then relaxed into his chest, breathing in the fresh-laundry scent of his flannel shirt.

But then she leaned back. "How could you not care about the truth about me?" she asked. "Because it *is* true,

Carson. All of it—well, at least the stuff about my mom, anyway." She squeezed her eyes shut, reliving the awful things her mom had just said to her. "It's disgusting. *I'm* disgusting."

Carson gently pulled back so he could see her face again. "You, Julie Redding, are beautiful. And smart. And funny. There is nothing about you—not even your pinky toe—that could be considered disgusting."

Then, amazingly, Carson tipped his head forward and brushed her lips with his. Julie didn't even believe it was happening until a few seconds in, when her numbness subsided and she actually felt his lips on hers. They were kissing. Really *kissing*.

And then it hit her: This was her first kiss, *ever*. Not quite how she pictured it, of course—in her bathrobe, on her wretched front porch, in full view of the broken patio furniture and multitudes of Christmas decorations and even a couple of random cat scratching posts on the lawn. But it was a pure, sweet, sensual kiss all the same.

When it was over, Carson leaned back and smiled graciously at her. "Thank you," he breathed.

"I should be thanking *you*," Julie said. "Are you sure about this? About . . . *me*? Because, I mean, you have no idea how cruel people can be. It's going to be brutal. It's okay if you don't want to be associated with me. I understand."

He waved his hand. "I don't care."

She blinked hard. "You're . . . *sure?*"

"Well," he said with mock seriousness, "that depends. It's my understanding that *you yourself* are not the Crazy Cat Lady of Beacon Heights. Is that correct?"

Julie couldn't help but laugh out loud. "That's correct," she replied with a weak smile. "I'm simply an innocent bystander to the cat collecting."

"Then it's settled. You are officially absolved of all responsibility for this"—Carson pointed at the house behind her, his eyebrows bunched together as he searched for the appropriate word—"um . . . situation. . . . And you are officially my girlfriend—if you want to be, that is. Anyone who has a problem with that can take it up with me."

Julie beamed at him. She couldn't believe her eyes, her ears . . . or her heart. And just like that, every horrible thing her mother had said to her receded into the background. Maybe, just maybe, she wasn't damaged goods after all. Maybe she was okay—someone worth caring for. Someone worth loving, even.

More than anything on earth, Julie wanted to believe Carson was right.

CHAPTER THREE

MONDAY AFTERNOON, CAITLIN MARTELL-LEWIS PULLED into a lot that was empty except for a boatlike green Cadillac under a canopy of trees. When she got out of her own car, her ears rang with the peaceful silence, and her nose twitched with the scent of freshly cut grass and newly planted flowers. She looked beyond the wrought iron gates and into the rolling hills peppered with tombstones. Suddenly she heard a sound behind a tree, and her heart seized. For some reason, she felt like she was being tailed . . . maybe by the cops. *Was* she? Were they following all of them around, trying to find something that might link them to Granger's death?

But then she looked again. It was just a squirrel.

Sighing, Caitlin locked her car, pocketed her keys, and made her way to her brother's grave. She could probably do it blindfolded at this point—pass the headstone with the big angels on top of it, a right at the guy who was buried next to his two Italian greyhounds, and then up the little hill and under the tree. *Hey, Taylor,* began the monologue in her head. *It's me again. Your crazy sister, skipping soccer practice, here to vent about how crazy my life has become.*

There was so much she had to tell Taylor, who'd passed away at the end of last year . . . and so much she wished he could tell her, stuff she would never get to know. Like how much he suffered at Nolan Hotchkiss's hands, or why he'd decided it would be easier to die than to show his sweet face at school for just one more day. Had there been a final straw? Caitlin would probably never forgive herself for not seeing the signs in him sooner. If she had, would he still be here?

She rounded a tree. Her brother's grave was ahead— and a new *Dragon Ball Z* figurine rested atop his headstone. Caitlin stopped, confused. She was the only person who placed new action figures on his grave. Well, she and . . .

Her thoughts halted as a figure appeared from behind another tree. It was Jeremy Friday. The only other person who cared enough to leave Taylor little tokens.

Jeremy turned and saw Caitlin at the same time. His eyebrows shot up, and his eyes softened. His expression looked hopeful, which filled Caitlin with all kinds of emotions—love, relief, excitement, and anxiety, too. She took in his lanky frame, holey *Star Wars* T-shirt, and dark jeans. If you'd asked her even a few weeks ago if she'd go for someone like Jeremy, Caitlin would've laughed. But he was perfect. A diamond in the rough. He'd been under her nose this whole time, and she hadn't seen how special he was.

And what was even more perfect? That Jeremy was smiling at her instead of scowling. The last time she'd seen him was two nights ago in the Fridays' basement, when all the Granger stuff had gone down. Josh, her ex-boyfriend and Jeremy's brother, had caught them together, and instead of standing up for their new relationship, Caitlin had just kind of . . . *bolted*. She'd assumed Jeremy hated her for that.

But when she stepped toward him, he pulled her into a hug. "I'm sorry," Caitlin blurted, overwhelmed. "About *everything*. I'm sorry I just ran like that. I just . . . I don't know."

"It's okay." Jeremy kissed the top of her head. "You were caught off guard."

"That's an understatement," Caitlin said emphatically.

"But, well," Jeremy faltered, playing with her hair. "*Do you still want to be with me? I mean*—I understand that it's really complicated, so . . ."

In reply, Caitlin stood up on her tiptoes and kissed him, cutting him off. "Does that answer your question?" she breathed, when they broke apart.

He rested his forehead against hers. "That pretty much tells me everything I need to know."

They looked down at Taylor's grave. Caitlin wondered what Taylor would think about this turn of events—her now being with quirky, kinda-geeky Jeremy, her younger brother's best friend, instead of popular ultrajock Josh. It had happened unexpectedly: Caitlin had run into Jeremy at Taylor's grave a few weeks ago, when she was going through a particularly tempestuous time—she wasn't sure if she wanted to continue playing soccer, she didn't know if she was with the right guy, she was still so mixed up and angry about Taylor, and she and the others had just pulled that prank on Nolan. They'd got to talking, and Caitlin had realized how easily she connected with Jeremy. *And* how much he understood what she was going through. Josh never even asked about Taylor. He seemed to think that avoiding uncomfortable issues was the answer.

Jeremy shifted his weight. "So have you talked to Josh at all?" he asked, as if there was a big sign over Caitlin's head broadcasting what she was thinking.

Caitlin stiffened. "Yeah," she said vaguely, making a face.

"That good of an experience, huh?"

She kicked up a divot of grass. She'd run into Josh that morning at school—which had been weird enough because of the whole Granger thing. Girls were literally *sobbing* because Granger was gone, placing bouquets of flowers in his doorway and meeting during lunch to pray about him around the flagpole. Caitlin had been amazed that even the girls who'd turned up on Granger's phone—like Jenny Thiel—had been in the tight knots of sobbing kids or had been one of the distraught teens slipping into the guidance counselors' offices during class. It was like they had blinders on regarding what a jerk the guy was. And though the lawyer Caitlin had spoken with said the police were under obligation to keep her involvement with Granger's death a secret since they weren't yet officially charged, Caitlin was almost positive Beacon kids had caught wind of the rumor all the same. She'd gotten vicious looks all day, like everyone believed she was guilty. Even girls on her soccer team were looking at her funny—but then again, no one brought it up, so maybe she was just paranoid.

It was halfway through the morning when she ran into Josh. He'd been standing by his locker with Guy Kenwood and Timothy Burgess, his buddies from the soccer team. They'd locked eyes, and Caitlin had frozen in her tracks, knowing she'd look like an asshole if she turned around and went the other way. By the daggers Guy and Timothy were shooting her, it was clear they'd found out that Caitlin was now with Josh's brother. Caitlin had wondered, for a split second, how exactly Josh had told them. Having your less popular younger brother steal your girlfriend wasn't exactly something to brag about, after all.

"Well, at first he didn't look at me," Caitlin told Jeremy, shoving her hands in her pockets. "But then I pulled him aside and tried to explain."

Jeremy winced. "I'm sure *that* went over well."

"I told him we hadn't been connecting for a while, and it was just a matter of time, you know?" She swallowed hard, thinking of Josh's tight, furious expression as soon as Caitlin had said all that. "He was pretty blindsided. And hurt. But then . . . well, I don't know. He was okay, in the end."

"Really?" Jeremy looked curious. "What did he say?"

Caitlin took a breath. "He just said that if that's what I wanted, then he wanted me to be happy," she explained. She'd been astonished when Josh had said it, actually—it was so gracious and mature. *I'm not going to be one of those pathetic guys who can't deal. I'm not thrilled that you're into Jeremy, but I guess I can't stop you, can I?*

"I expected him to be so angry," Caitlin concluded, pecking at Jeremy. "It was nice that he wasn't."

Jeremy nodded. "Well, he's been ignoring me for days. Although that's better than him insulting me, which I figured he'd be doing in full force. Maybe our boy is growing up."

"Maybe." Caitlin smiled weakly. Then she was hit with

a pang. Every good thing in her life, she realized, was offset by something sad or bad. Here she was with Jeremy, but at Taylor's grave—and with Josh so hurt. Here she was, happier than she was in years, but she was also an accused murderer. Nothing came easy.

She looked up at Jeremy, Granger now on her mind. "So I guess you've heard about Mr. Granger—and my involvement. It's not what it seems, though."

Jeremy waved his hand. "Please. I know that. But why were you at his house?"

She shrugged, feeling uncomfortable. She couldn't totally tell Jeremy the truth. "It's a long story. But it has to do with Nolan. Some friends of mine and I thought Granger was the one who killed him."

Jeremy widened his eyes. "Really?"

"Well, maybe not anymore," Caitlin said faintly. Finding Nolan's threat to Granger seemed like perfect proof—of course Granger would want Nolan dead to protect his reputation. But what if Granger was killed because he knew something *else*, something about Nolan's murderer? There still could be all kinds of secrets out there.

An elderly couple appeared at the top of the hill and walked with stooped backs down the path. Suddenly feeling like they no longer had the place to themselves, Caitlin turned to Jeremy. "Pizza?"

"Sure," he said, a grin breaking out on his face.

They headed to Gino's, a mom-and-pop place near the cemetery that was blissfully empty at that time of the day. Over slices of white pie, they talked about normal things— Jeremy's participation in the next science fair, shows they liked on TV, and how Caitlin's soccer team was voting on captain this week. Caitlin was still on the fence about what soccer meant to her, but deep down, she couldn't help feeling jittery over the election. Captain was something she'd wanted forever, and it felt weird to just let it go when she actually, *finally*, had a chance.

There wasn't a single mention of Josh, Granger, Nolan, or the police—a welcome change. An hour later, after a kiss at Caitlin's car, Jeremy climbed on his Vespa and roared off into the distance, promising to call her later. Feeling much more contented, Caitlin headed home. She'd hoped to have a few hours to herself, but when she pulled into the driveway, her moms' cars were already there, both of them home from work.

Sigh.

She put the car in park, grabbed her soccer bag and backpack, and girded herself for whatever was going to come next. NPR was on in the kitchen—a news story about raising backyard chickens. She could hear the steady *chop chop chop* of a knife hitting a cutting board and water running in the sink. She could tell from the familiar and comforting assortment of sounds that Sibyl and Mary Ann, her two moms, were cooking together. Caitlin tiptoed as quietly as she could toward the stairs, but too late—Mary Ann looked up and saw her. "Honey?" she called out.

Caitlin sighed. So much for getting a few minutes to herself. "Uh, hey," she said, remaining where she was by the stairs.

Mary Ann's eyes were sad. "Want to help us prep?"

Not really, Caitlin thought, but she knew refusing would mean one of her moms would follow her upstairs and ask even more plaintive, intrusive questions than the ones she'd get down here. So she trudged into the kitchen and accepted a cutting board and a bell pepper Sibyl offered.

"So how was your day?" Sibyl asked cautiously, her eyes flicking from Caitlin back to her own chopping work.

"Fine," Caitlin answered.

She felt her moms exchange a glance. She knew they wanted more. Mary Ann cleared her throat. "Did they, um, talk about that teacher?"

Caitlin carefully cut the top off the pepper. "Yeah. A lot."

Another exchanged glance. Caitlin's moms had been silent and worried when they'd gotten the call on Sunday that she'd potentially been part of a murder plot. She'd told them again and again that it was just an unfortunate coincidence, but she wasn't entirely sure they believed her. Just like she wasn't sure they believed her about Nolan—Mary

Ann had made pointed comments about Caitlin's Oxy supply, after all, begging her to get rid of the stash. And though it came back that it was cyanide that had killed Nolan, not Oxy, there was Oxy in his blood, too. As the cops hadn't dragged them back into the station yet, the subject had been momentarily dropped, but Caitlin knew it was swimming just below the surface, ready to erupt at a moment's notice.

"And did you talk to Josh?" Mary Ann asked.

She looked up. Her moms were looking at her eagerly. Clearly, they *wanted* her to talk to Josh. Sibyl Martell and Mary Ann Lewis were best friends with the Friday parents, and though they hadn't said it outright, it was clear that Caitlin's dumping Josh for Jeremy had put a crimp in their social schedule. Their normal Saturday antiquing with the Fridays had been canceled for this weekend. So had Sunday brunch, which they did the first of every month, and their regular weekly Wednesday dinners. And Caitlin had heard the two of them whispering in their bedroom the night it happened—*before* she'd been fingerprinted for sneaking into Granger's house, when Josh was all they'd had to worry about. *Why do you think she's doing this?* they'd said in low murmurs. *Is she acting out against us? Maybe this has something to do with Taylor?* And: *Poor Josh. He must be crushed.*

She hated the *Poor Josh* part. What about poor *her*?

Caitlin must have sniffed angrily, because Sibyl put down her knife. "Honey. If you think we're mad at you for the Josh and Jeremy thing, we're not."

"We're just trying to understand," Mary Ann broke in. "Whoever you like, it's fine. But the two boys are just so . . . *different*. We're not sure what you have in common with Jeremy is all."

Caitlin looked up, her eyes flashing. "I have nothing in common with *Josh*."

Her moms looked puzzled. "But you two have soccer. And you like doing the same things. And you have so much history."

Caitlin scoffed. "Like that's everything?" She shoved her half-sliced pepper away. "You know, if you actually got to know me a little better, you'd understand why Josh and I have nothing to say to each other anymore. But you just want me to be the same, predictable Caitlin as ever." She started out of the room.

"Honey!" Mary Ann called after her. "Don't be like that!"

"We support you!" Sibyl cried.

"Whatever," Caitlin called over her shoulder. She wanted it to be true—hell, as a same-sex couple with an adopted South Korean daughter, acceptance should be their thing, right? But they sounded like they were trying to say the right lines without actually meaning them.

"Come back!" Mary Ann shouted plaintively. "We haven't even talked about Mr. Granger!"

"I didn't do it," Caitlin said as she started up to her room. "That's all you need to know."

She glanced down for a split second. Her moms were standing at the foot of the stairs, looking so sad and confused and helpless. Caitlin knew she was putting a wall up. It was probably the same wall Taylor had put up, too. And yet, well—she just couldn't explain herself. Not about Jeremy, because they wouldn't get it.

And not about Granger . . . because they couldn't know.

CHAPTER FOUR

SOMETHING SHARP SCRATCHED PARKER DUVALL'S cheek. She swatted at it, but it just bounced back and jabbed at her again. She opened her eyes and saw the world sideways, but before she could figure out why she was lying down— and why she was in what looked to be a field—her head began to spin wildly.

She clamped her eyes shut to stop the woozy motion and suddenly felt the urge to puke. *Aha. I've been drinking.* Just a little clue to the puzzle.

Slowly, carefully, she tried to open her eyes again. This time she was able to keep the spins at bay and take in her surroundings. It was light out, the sun halfway up the sky. Dry, spiky stalks of half-dead grass jutted out of the ground as far as she could see. Off in the distance, a massive building loomed. Where the hell was she?

Finally, Parker managed to prop herself up on one elbow. Moving as slowly as she could, she eased herself to a sitting position. Stale cigarette smoke wafted off her hoodie. *So, I've been drinking* and *smoking.* Must have been a crazy night.

She hadn't been hungover in forever. But back when she was Beacon Heights's golden girl, when her arrival at any party meant the event was a true hit, she'd been a pro. Downing booze with the rest of them. Matching the boys shot for shot. Waking up the next morning feeling like shit, but laughing it off, knowing she'd had an awesome time.

It was easy to reminisce about the golden days: She'd been blond and beautiful, with a gaggle of friends and an even bigger bevy of hangers-on. She'd aced all her classes without even having to try. She had Nolan Hotchkiss's seal of approval—they were tight, one of those platonic friendships that was even closer and cooler than any couple's. And she had a wonderful best friend in Julie Redding, their bond strong and meaningful in a sea of superficial relationships.

Her life was perfect, right? Except, oh yeah, her family. A mom that hated her. And a dad that beat the crap out of her. But whatever. Maybe that's what made her so good at being the life of the party—because at home, she was better off dead. She would have kept up that life, too, if it hadn't been for Nolan . . . and her father's wrath. And now, everything had changed. Her father was locked up for life. She didn't have a home to go to anymore. And she'd become a different girl—a harder, edgier, angrier girl, a Bizarro Parker. No one invited her to any parties anymore. Well, screw them all.

Parker shivered, suddenly realizing how cold she was. The air had a distinct morning chill, and it felt like it was going to start raining any minute. Gradually, the building in the distance came into focus—a low, wide, cheap stucco structure in dirty beige with evenly spaced brown metal doors. A teenage boy in a bright orange uniform and wearing an apron and a paper hat stepped out of one of the doors with a giant garbage bag. He tossed it into a Dumpster and headed back inside. So a strip mall, maybe? Someplace with a bunch of crappy little take-out places? But how had she *gotten* here?

She shut her eyes and tried to think. The last thing she remembered, though, was leaving the police station with Julie. *Welcome to Parker 2.0,* she thought. *Complete with scars, sullen moods, and memory blanks!*

Parker looked down at herself. At least she was in the same clothes, even though they were caked with dirt. She patted her pockets. Her hand knocked against a hard lump in her hoodie, and she fumbled for her cell phone. *Tuesday, October 25,* it said at the top of the screen, as well as the time: 10:04 AM. Okay, so she'd only missed one night—she remembered parts of Monday. She quickly dialed Julie, but it went straight to voice mail.

Parker swallowed hard. It was rare that Julie didn't pick up her phone. Had something else happened? Something to do with the Granger investigation? All at once, she remembered the serious-looking file she'd found at Granger's house when they were looting it for clues. It had said *JULIE REDDING* across the envelope, and it didn't look like a folder full of old essays. Did it have something to do with her mom's hoarding, their quick and shameful exodus from California? It was a secret Parker had known for a while, something she'd worked hard to keep safe. Before Parker had realized what she was doing, she'd slipped the file out of Granger's drawer and stuffed it into her pocket.

Or had it been about something else? Parker was sure she'd read the file—while still in Granger's house, in fact— but she had no memory of what it said. *Typical,* she thought, patting her pockets, wishing she had the file with her now, though she'd undoubtedly left it back at Julie's place. Her brain only worked half the time and remembered the least important of details, courtesy of her dad's last beating.

She stood up and started to walk to the front of the strip mall, her legs feeling heavy and useless. The shops were open for business, their lights on, a little easel advertising a daily deal sitting in front of the Verizon store at the end of the strip. Then, she jammed her hands into the pockets of her sweatshirt and felt a stiff scrap of paper in the left-hand side. It was Elliot Fielder's business card, with his cell phone number scrawled on the back. *Call me anytime,* he'd said to her at their first meeting, which was also Parker's first-ever visit with a therapist.

But that was before she'd caught him stalking her. And that was before she confronted him and he grabbed her arm roughly, saying she needed to listen. *Listen to what?* Julie had hissed in Parker's ear when they left. And Parker had felt like an idiot—she'd let Fielder into her inner circle, decided she'd trust him, and told him everything about her life. And then he'd betrayed that trust by *following* her.

Parker turned the business card over in her hands. *Call me anytime.* His words tugged at her. She remembered his caring voice. But she couldn't call. No freaking way.

Someone gasped, and Parker looked up. A pimply guy in his early twenties in a Subway tee stood just outside the door, smoking a cigarette. He stared at Parker, then looked away. Parker gritted her teeth and turned around, heading in the opposite direction—but not before her reflection in the nail salon next door caught her eye. She was dressed in dingy black jeans and a dirty black hoodie pulled tightly around her head. Her blond bangs had grown out and fell over her eyes. Then her gaze traveled to the taut, ropy knots of a scar on her cheekbone. It was just like all the others that formed a disgusting web back and forth across her face.

Shame welled up in her throat, and she choked back a sob. No wonder that Subway worker had flinched: She looked like a monster. Then again, everyone looked at her that way these days—like she had no business being here on earth, like she should just crawl back under the rock from which she'd come. It hurt every time. Only two people in the world didn't flinch when they saw her: Julie . . . and Fielder.

Ducking around the corner and out of view, Parker pulled out her phone and looked at the keypad. Mustering up her courage, she punched Fielder's number into her cell phone and hit SEND. Julie would be so pissed, but she needed to talk to someone.

The phone rang once, and Parker's breath came fast and shallow, her heart pounding.

The phone rang a third time. Finally, the line clicked, and she heard a familiar voice on the other end. "Is this . . . Parker?" Elliot Fielder said, sounding surprised.

Parker blinked. She hadn't expected him to recognize her number. "Um, yeah," she said. "Hi."

"Hi," Fielder answered. "Are you . . . *okay?*"

Parker drew her bottom lip into her mouth. Suddenly she felt ridiculous for reaching out to someone she barely knew—and someone who had tricked her. She would find her own way back to Julie's, then they would figure everything out together. "You know what," she decided. "Never mind. I'm cool."

"Listen, Parker—I know why you're calling."

She almost dropped the phone and looked around. Had he followed her *here*, to this crappy strip mall? She tried to spot him in the distance, but she didn't see anyone around.

"I know about your dad."

The hair on the back of her neck stood up. "What about him?" she asked harshly.

Fielder exhaled slowly. "Wait, you don't know?"

"Don't know what?" There was a long pause. "Don't know *what?*" Parker practically growled.

His voice was shaky when he finally spoke. "I didn't think I'd have to be the one to tell you. Parker—" He paused. "There was an accident in the prison yard. Your father . . . well, he's dead."

CHAPTER FIVE

TUESDAY EVENING, AS AVA JALALI sat at the kitchen table, agonizing over her physics homework—she was in AP, much to the amazement of her only-interested-in-their-looks, fashionista friends. The problem sets were just getting harder and harder with each unit. What was also making the work practically impossible was that she was out in the open so her father and stepmother could keep an eye on her—their idea, not hers. After her latest scrape with the police, they'd kept eyes on her almost 24-7, as if she was a ticking, juvenile-delinquent time bomb.

Not that her father or her stepmother, Leslie, was watching her particularly closely. Her father was reading some work documents at the island while sipping tea. And Leslie was hurrying back and forth through the room, her bouncy, Drybar-styled curls barely shifting as she moved, and her cashmere dress floating gracefully around her knees. First she opened this cabinet, then that. Took out some candlesticks, frowned, then rifled through a drawer for some place mats. Amazingly, Leslie was doing all this while carefully balancing a glass of chardonnay in her hand. By Ava's count, this was glass number three—and it wasn't even five o'clock yet. *Classy*.

"Damn it," Leslie muttered under her breath as the Vitamix blender she was trying to pin with one hand and her chin—God forbid she put the glass of wine down—almost slipped from her grasp. She shoved it inside a different cabinet and shut the door with such force that Ava jumped in her chair, her pencil scribbling across her physics homework. Ava tried to meet her father's gaze, but Mr. Jalali was doing a really good job of feigning oblivious-ness. What the hell was Leslie so worked up about, anyway? Wasn't wine supposed to relax you?

Leslie clomped into the dining room, still muttering. She returned balancing a stack of silverware in one hand, her wine glass clenched in the other. "These need to be polished," she barked at Mr. Jalali.

He shifted uncomfortably on his stool. Clearly he real-ized she was acting like a freak, right? And yet all he said was, "I'll let the housekeeper know."

"Maybe you can have Ava do it." Ava could feel Leslie's eyes on her. "Silver polishing is a useful skill."

Mr. Jalali put a hand on his wife's shoulder. "Darling, we have almost a week to prepare. There's plenty of time."

Ava couldn't help but look up from her problem sets. "Prepare for what?"

Ava's father smiled kindly. "Leslie's mother is visiting us from New York. She'll be staying with us for a few days, and Leslie has decided to throw a party here at the house."

"And I want everything to be perfect." Leslie barged in, flicking at a crumb on the countertop with a crimson, talon-like fingernail. Then she shot Ava a look. It said, very clearly, *Which means I don't want any trouble from* you.

Ava shrugged, though inside she was seething. Leslie had never shown her an ounce of kindness, and after Ava's recent trip to the police station for Granger's murder, she'd become downright witchlike. Ava glanced at her father, but he was looking at his newspaper again as if he didn't sense the tension. Ava was astonished at how different her father had become in this woman's presence. In the old days—the *good* days—he and her mother used to care about her deeply. There was so much laughing and cheer in the house. None of this frantic cleaning. None of these dirty, hateful looks.

The phone rang, and Mr. Jalali excused himself from the kitchen to answer it in his office. Leslie began counting wine glasses, pulling down a few and placing them roughly in the sink. She mumbled something under her breath about them being too spotty. She looked like she was going to have a brain hemorrhage right then and there.

Ava shut her textbook and looked at Leslie. "I'm sure everything is going to be perfect for your mom."

Bad idea. Leslie whipped around and stared at her, her nostrils flaring. "*You* don't have the right to speak right now."

Ava pressed her pencil nub into her paper. "I'm just trying to help. Too much stress can make you sick."

Leslie moved closer to Ava in one swift movement. Ava could smell the fermented grapes on her breath. "I rush around to make things perfect because they are so *imperfect*. And I'm talking about you, first and foremost." She waved her hand at Ava. "You dress like a whore." She gestured at Ava's skinny jeans and, yes, maybe *slightly* revealing top. "No wonder no one respects you. What were you really doing in that teacher's house before you killed him, getting him off?"

Ava shot to her feet. First, she hated that Leslie knew about the rumor Nolan had passed around about Ava trading sex favors with teachers for As. She also hated that the cops had included Leslie in the conversation they'd had with her father about why she was under suspicion for killing Granger. "I didn't touch him!" she protested.

Leslie rolled her eyes. "Yeah, *right*."

Ava couldn't believe it. Nor could she take this another

second. She slammed her textbook closed, grabbed her notebook and pencil, and ran upstairs, where she threw herself onto her bed and pounded the Persian silk bedcover with her fists. It had been a gift from her parents after their last trip to Iran, not long before her mother died.

Ava missed her mom. And she couldn't stand living under the same roof as this woman. Why did she hate Ava so much? Was she jealous?

Downstairs, she heard the muffled sounds of her father speaking to Leslie. He was probably asking where Ava had gone, and Leslie probably made up some story about how Ava had made a sassy, bitchy remark and then fled upstairs like the spoiled brat she was. After a moment, Ava heard the front door open and close, then the sound of Leslie talking nonstop in harsh tones in the driveway. There was a car door opening and closing, and then the rumble of an engine. Ava peeled back the curtain and watched as her father's Mercedes pulled out of the driveway. They were gone.

She sighed and rolled over, staring at the ceiling. All at once, she felt suddenly and painfully alone. Who could she turn to? Not Dad, who'd been her rock for so many years. Not Alex, the boyfriend she loved—they hadn't spoken since that night he saw her leave Granger's and called the police on her.

Alex. She still couldn't believe he'd done such a thing.

Yeah, she knew what it had looked like—he'd seen her run out of Granger's house, disheveled and flushed, her dress half-buttoned.

It pained her that Alex would assume exactly what Leslie did—that she'd gone to Granger's for a booty call. Alex knew Granger had hit on her, and that he'd actually hooked up with his other students. Why couldn't he have just asked her what was going on? She would have told him. Not the whole truth, maybe—but close to it, perhaps. Even about what they'd done to Nolan.

That was the thing, though: Alex hadn't asked. He'd just called the police and told on her. Her *boyfriend*. She didn't know whether to be hurt or angry or both. Did he really think she was capable of killing someone? Did he know her at all?

She wanted so badly to ask him why he had done such a terrible thing. Because underneath all the hurt and betrayal, she *missed* Alex, so badly it ached. Not talking to Alex, not seeing him—it felt so weird. It was like she'd lost half of herself.

Her phone bleated, and she jumped up. Maybe it was from Alex. She'd texted him twice asking to talk, but he hadn't answered.

But it was only from Mackenzie. *School has been weird, huh?*

Ava heaved a breath. *That* was an understatement. Everywhere she turned, kids were sobbing in the halls.

Granger's door was festooned in flowers, and a couple of hippieish girls sat in front of it *all day long,* playing songs on their guitars and tambourines about flowers and meadows and Heaven—and the Beacon staff, who was usually so anal about attendance, *let them.* There had been several announcements for prayers around the flagpole—why the flagpole, Ava never knew, but the prayer sessions always seemed to gravitate there—and announcements had already been made that Granger's funeral would be Thursday, and attendance was mandatory. Worst of all, kids at Beacon had to know *something*—maybe just that Ava was at Granger's before he died, or maybe the whole enchilada—that she was under suspicion for killing him. Some bitch had trashed her gym locker, spilling out all the makeup, deodorant, and hair products she stashed there. She was left high and dry after running around the track and had to spend the rest of the day looking like a sweaty mess.

Weird is an understatement, she wrote back.

Have you heard from the cops? Mac asked.

Nope, Ava said. *You?*

Mac said she hadn't, either. Ava had to admit she was surprised—she'd expected another visit by now for sure. Especially if they found out about Ava's history with Granger—she'd met him at his house not so long ago for help on her paper, and he'd come on to her. She'd sat nervously all through school today, waiting for an officer to appear in the classroom doorway, but no one ever had.

She sighed, her thoughts returning to Alex again. If only he'd text her back. If only he'd *explain*—and she could explain, too. She turned her phone over in her hands. She needed to talk to him, but calling him wouldn't yield any results. He hadn't answered a single one of her calls or texts—why would he start now?

So, she decided, she would go to his house.

As she stood up, Ava caught a glimpse of herself in the mirror and nearly burst out laughing. Her hair jutted out in all directions, her normally glowing, caramel-colored skin looked sallow and worn, and bags had taken up residence under her eyes. She must have lost some weight, because her skinny jeans sagged on her hips, and her boobs didn't quite fill out her shirt. But she didn't have the energy to transform herself into her normal, perfect self—the girl who was smart *and* beautiful. Alex would have to see her like this. Perhaps it would show him exactly how much she was suffering because of what he'd done.

Taking the car out would probably get her into more trouble, so Ava pulled her old ten-speed from the garage and threw her leg over the bar. As she pedaled, she rehearsed what she was going to say to Alex when she saw him—*if* she saw him. *I know what it looked like, but it wasn't true,* she'd start off with. But what if Alex saw her doing that striptease for Granger through the window? What would she say—*I was trying to save my friends' lives because we'd broken into his house and thought he was a murderer?*

God, she felt nervous. And that was new, too—she hadn't felt nervous in front of Alex, *ever*.

Alex's house was only a few neighborhoods away, but she was winded by the time she got there, and damp from a drizzle that had begun to fall. She sucked in her breath as she turned onto Alex's block—which was Granger's block, too. Granger's house was still surrounded in yellow police tape. Technicians in matching jackets that said CRIME SCENE streamed in and out of Granger's front door, and a news van idled at the curb, its giant antenna jutting from the top. Ava twitched nervously, wondering what they were finding inside. Did Granger actually know something about Nolan's murder that cost him his life? Or were the forensic people just digging up more evidence against *her*?

She hit the brakes a few houses away. It was probably a terrible idea to return to the scene of the crime. The cops might see her and assume she was here to laugh at them or something.

She squinted at Alex's house. Strangely, it was surrounded by cops, too. Two police cars with doors flung open blocked the driveway. And there on the stoop stood four officers, their bodies tense. It looked like they were shouting at someone.

Ava edged up behind a neighbor's oak, not sure what she was looking at. But when an officer moved slightly to the side, she realized that the person on the porch they were shouting at was *Alex*. He was waving his hands wildly. Then, before Ava's eyes, two policemen grabbed Alex by the arms and spun him around. He kicked and struggled and tried to pull away, but the cops pressed his face against the front of the house.

Ava gasped. "No!" It pained her to see the boy she loved being treated so brutally. Why on earth were they doing this?

Then one of the officers began to cuff Alex. Ava let her bike fall to the ground and walked across the grass, no longer afraid of showing her face. She weaved through the throng of investigators, reporters, and rubbernecks from the neighborhood. "No!" she cried again. "Stop!"

Alex was struggling to get free. "Get off me!" he screamed. "I told you I didn't do anything!"

"You have the right to remain silent," one of the cops was telling him in a loud voice. "Anything you say can and will be used against you in a court of law."

Ava's mouth fell open. They were reading him his *rights*?

She had reached the front walkway. She pushed around a few random people until she had a clear view of the porch.

"Alex!" she called out before she could properly think the situation through. "Alex, it's me!"

Alex turned his head sharply and met her gaze. His mouth fell open. Suddenly, an officer touched Ava's shoulder. "We need you to stay back. This guy could be dangerous."

Dangerous? Alex was the type of guy who let spiders outside instead of squashing them. He had been the one who'd held off on having sex, saying he wanted to wait until it was absolutely and positively special and right. "Why is he being arrested?" Ava cried. Then she looked at Alex. "Alex, what's going on?"

Alex just stared through her. The cops pushed him across the lawn, holding him by the arms. And as they shoved him into the squad car, a strange thought began to take hold in Ava's mind. *This guy could be dangerous.* She thought of Alex's blank look as they led him away. Whatever had happened, Alex couldn't explain it to her.

The cop closed the car door on Alex, then made his way around to the front. The lights were already blaring, and as he opened his door, the reporters descended on him. "Officer!" they cried. "What's the nature of that boy's arrest? Can you tell us?"

Ava leaned forward, heart pounding.

The cop touched the walkie-talkie on his belt, then

looked into the camera. "All I can tell you is what I know," he said gruffly, his hand on the top of the door. "Which is that as of now, Alex Cohen is under arrest for the murder of Lucas Granger."

CHAPTER SIX

JULIE PULLED INTO THE JUDY'S DINER parking lot on Tuesday night. It was pouring down rain, but the lights of the diner were warm, and the people inside looked happy and relaxed. Suddenly, a flash of auburn hair inside the diner caught her eye, and her heart seized in her chest. Was that *Ashley*? Julie hadn't seen her enemy since before the email went out, and she was still dreading the inevitable showdown.

But then she looked again. It was just another girl with similar-colored hair. She spooned what looked like rice pudding into her mouth and smiled at the guy she was sitting with. Julie breathed out. She so wasn't ready to see Ashley yet.

Someone tapped on her window, and she looked up with a start. It was Parker—the reason Julie had come to the diner—and she was soaked. Julie hit UNLOCK, and Parker threw herself into the passenger seat. "Didn't you see me waving?" she asked, sounding annoyed. "You could have pulled closer to the curb."

"Sorry," Julie said. "I thought I saw someone inside."

"Ashley?"

That was the thing about Parker—she knew Julie far too well. "Maybe," Julie muttered.

Parker gritted her teeth. "I hate that girl. Like, really, *really* hate her."

"I know. I do, too."

"Yeah, but you're just rolling over and taking the abuse. Then again . . ." Parker homed in on Julie, staring at her pink blouse, dark-wash skinny jeans, and high ponytail. "You have actual clothes on. You don't even seem that upset."

Julie wanted to tell Parker that it was because of Carson—he'd called her that day to check in, and they'd talked for almost two hours. But sometimes it was hard to tell Parker happy things, considering Parker's own troubled life. So she just shrugged. "I'm trying to cope."

"I think we should do something to Ashley in retaliation," Parker growled.

"Like what?" Julie asked as she pulled out of the lot. "Let air out of her tires? Post some mean stuff on Facebook? It'll just look like we're stupid high school girls trying to get revenge."

Parker slumped down in the seat and muttered some-thing Julie couldn't hear. Julie stared at her friend for a moment. Parker was pale, and she looked exhausted and upset, probably for something more serious than Ashley.

The windshield wipers swished noisily. "So . . . where have you been anyway?" Julie had no idea where Parker had been sleeping. Before she'd received Parker's call this evening saying she was at the diner and needed a ride, Julie had almost been ready to report her to Missing Persons. Sure, Parker had disappeared before, but never for this long, and never without telling Julie where she was going.

Then again, they hadn't ever been wanted for murder before.

Parker shrugged. "Around."

Julie paused at a stop sign. "Just . . . around?" She won-dered if that meant Parker didn't remember. A shot of fear spiked through her chest. "Do you want to talk about it?" she asked tentatively.

"Not really."

Julie shut her eyes. She *wished* Parker would talk about it—about anything. It seemed like her friend was retreat-ing more and more into herself, especially after Nolan's death. If only the therapist she'd found for her had worked out. Instead, whenever Julie even thought of Elliot Fielder and what he'd done to Parker, she was seized with such crushing guilt she could barely breathe. She had made a lot of mistakes with Parker, horrible mistakes she couldn't undo. She would have to be very, very careful to take care of her from now on, she promised herself.

"So where are we going again?" Parker asked languidly, staring out the window at the passing redwood trees.

"Ava's," Julie answered. "She called a little while ago. Her boyfriend was arrested for Granger's murder."

Parker raised an eyebrow. "Wait. Ava's boyfriend, the guy who turned us in?"

"Yeah. Weird, huh?"

"Definitely weird," Parker said quietly as they turned onto Ava's street. Then she cleared her throat. "Wanna know something else that's weird? I found out this morning that someone killed my dad."

Julie unwittingly slammed on the brakes in the middle of the street. "*What?*"

"Yup. He died in the prison yard. They cremated him already. Good riddance, right?"

Parker's voice was robotic and toneless, and for a moment, Julie thought she was joking. But there was pain behind her eyes. And Parker wouldn't joke about that.

Julie clutched Parker's hand hard. "Oh my god," she whispered. "I'm sorry. But maybe we should be happy?"

Parker pulled her hoodie tighter around her face. "I know." She looked Julie square in the eye, something she rarely did anymore, considering her scars. "I mean, I was always talking about how I wanted him dead—and now he *is*. It's like my wish came true."

"My wish, too," Julie said faintly. But strangely, Markus Duvall's death didn't give her much satisfaction. It couldn't undo what he'd done to Parker.

Julie shut off the car as they pulled up in front of Ava's house and glanced worriedly at her friend. "Are you sure you want to go in there right now? We can skip it."

Parker nodded. "I'm fine. Really."

Julie gave her hand a reassuring squeeze. "Well, if you get uncomfortable, we can leave, okay? And it's movie night in my room tonight. Your choice. Even something with Ben Affleck."

They got out of the car and started up the walk. Just before they could ring the bell, the door swung open. Ava's stepmother, Leslie, stood in the foyer. Her eyes were cold, the corners of her mouth turned down, and she swayed back and forth. When the wind shifted, Julie could smell white wine on her breath.

"*More* of you," she said bitterly, looking at Julie and Parker with disdain. "Everyone's in her bedroom. Please try not to trash the place, okay?"

Julie just nodded, but Parker glared at the woman, puffing up her chest. "Actually, I was planning on setting fire to the house, thanks. And maybe doing heroin in your bathroom. That cool?"

"*Parker!*" Julie said, elbowing her. Parker was never great with authority figures. Her dad used to prey on that.

Ava's stepmother looked from girl to girl, clearly irritated. "*Who* are you again?" she asked, her words slightly slurred.

"Come on," Julie said, grabbing Parker's arm and dragging her upstairs. No wonder Ava bitched about that woman. She had the demeanor of a snake ready to strike.

Upstairs, Ava's door was ajar. Ava sat on her bed, while Caitlin and Mac were sprawled on the floor. Everyone looked stricken, but Ava's beautiful face was a teary mess.

Julie gave her a tight hug. "Are you okay?"

Ava shrugged, grabbing a Kleenex. "Not really. What about *you*? I haven't seen you in school since that horrible email." She looked Julie over, then smiled and flicked Julie's chandelier earrings. "Those are pretty."

Julie ducked her head. "Thanks. And I'm . . . getting there," she said quietly. "I might even go back to school soon." That was thanks to Carson, of course. He'd bolstered her so much she actually thought she could face the onslaught.

"You should totally come back," Caitlin said gently. "Don't let 'em see you sweat. And we'll support you."

"That's right," Mac echoed. "We'll be with you every step of the way."

Julie wanted to hug all of them. In the terrible pain of

her secret getting out, this knowledge—that she had new friends, girls she had barely known just weeks ago, who wouldn't judge her—felt like a gift. Whatever happened, they had one another's backs. They were in this together.

Ava shut her bedroom door firmly behind them, and they all stared at one another for a moment. Then Caitlin took a deep breath. "So. *Alex.*"

"I can't believe it." Julie looked at Ava. "You were really there when he was arrested?"

Ava nodded, looking tormented. "They dragged him out of the house and shoved him into the car. It was brutal."

"So do you think he . . . *did* it?" Julie asked Ava cautiously.

Ava pulled her bottom lip into her mouth. "No way. He wouldn't stab anyone."

Mac cleared her throat. "But what about this?" She pulled up a website on her phone. A newscaster from the local station appeared on the screen. *"The newest suspect in the Granger murder case, Alex Cohen, has a history of violence,"* the reporter said in a grave voice. *"We spoke to Lewis Petrovsky, a student who knew Alex at his old school in Monterey, California."*

A guy with wild curly hair and freckles popped up. "We all know about Alex here," he said. "He had this ex-girlfriend, Cleo, that he just couldn't get over. Practically stalked her. And one night he hurt Cleo's new boyfriend, Brett, really badly. Brett was hospitalized for a month." His mouth wobbled. "Brett's my best friend. I was so worried about him."

The newscast cut to the reporter again. "Channel 11 tried to contact Cleo Hawkins and Brett Greene's parents for questioning, but they couldn't be reached at this time."

Ava's mouth dropped open. She stared at Mac's phone. "How can this be true?"

Julie felt a pang. It was clear Ava hadn't heard this piece of the puzzle, not from her own lawyer, and certainly not from Alex. She looked like someone had just slapped her hard.

Mac winced. "I'm sorry you had to hear it like this."

Ava said nothing. She pressed PLAY, and the video started over. "Alex isn't like that," she said after it finished.

"It fits, though," Parker piped up. "He sees you doing a striptease for Granger, and he snaps and kills him."

Ava glared at her through tear-blurred eyes. "Alex isn't the type who *snaps*."

Caitlin bounced her balled fists on her knees. "Actually, my attorney told me the same story about the kid from his old school. Apparently the cops found a text from Alex to Granger saying 'Stay away from my girlfriend or I'll kill you.'"

Ava was growing paler and paler by the second. "*What?*"

"Alex sent it after you confessed that Granger hit on you," Caitlin said in a small voice. She peeked at Ava. "Your lawyer didn't tell you any of this?"

Ava made a face. "I haven't even *heard* from my lawyer yet. And he's supposed to be the best." She looked down. "Even with a verbal threat and a motive, and a *supposedly* violent history." She said *supposedly* as if she didn't fully believe it. "It still doesn't seem like enough to arrest Alex."

Caitlin coughed awkwardly. "Well, Alex's prints are all over Granger's doorknob, too."

"Wow," Mac exhaled.

"Why didn't I know any of this?" Ava exclaimed, her voice shaky.

"Maybe your lawyer or your parents were trying to protect you?" Julie volunteered.

Ava shook her head, looking shocked. "I just don't understand."

Julie looked around at the others. "But this means that we're no longer suspects, right?"

"That's what my lawyer told me," Caitlin said quietly.

Julie had to admit she felt relieved. If she never visited that police station again, it would be too soon. Still, Ava's face made the victory bittersweet. "So, if Alex killed Granger," she began, working something out in her mind, "and if he did it for jealousy reasons, does that mean Granger *did* kill Nolan? And the two murders are unrelated?"

"Maybe." Mac pulled her knees into her chest. "Maybe it's all cleared up after all."

No one spoke for a moment. Julie looked away from

Ava. Then Parker cleared her throat. "Someone else was killed recently, too."

Everyone looked at her. Suddenly, Parker couldn't speak. Julie took a breath, having a feeling she knew what Parker wanted to talk about. "Parker's dad was killed," she said.

The others gasped. "Oh my god," Ava said. "How?"

Parker cleared her throat, regaining her voice. "He was stabbed in the prison yard. They haven't figured out who did it yet, but obviously it was another inmate."

"Wow." Mac ran her fingers along the stitching on Ava's comforter. "There's a lot of death going around."

Caitlin cocked her head. "You don't think that's an awfully weird coincidence?"

"How so?" Mac asked.

Caitlin looked at Julie. "Julie, you said you wanted him dead in that same film studies conversation about Nolan. And now . . . he *is*."

Julie suddenly remembered what Caitlin was talking about. Before they'd plotted how to kill and then prank Nolan, they'd each gone around and named someone they would kill, and how they would do it. Julie's pick had been Parker's dad. And, come to think of it, hadn't she said, *he could be stabbed to death in the prison yard?*

"I don't want to be paranoid, but the timing of it is eerie," Caitlin said quietly. "First Nolan dies exactly how we planned, and then Parker's dad does, too?"

"Guys get killed in prison all the time, though," Mac said, looking around the room.

"Yeah," Ava seconded. "They're probably not connected."

"But let's play devil's advocate a minute," Caitlin argued. "Let's say it *isn't* a coincidence. Say someone . . . I don't know, *heard* that conversation." She looked at Julie again. "I wish we still had those notes Granger had written about our conversation. Do you remember what they said?"

Julie flinched. She'd found a yellow legal pad in Granger's office, which had notes that were clearly from their conversation that day. She looked at Parker to confirm.

Parker nodded. "It said 'Nolan—cyanide.' If Granger killed Nolan, then that's how he got the cyanide idea— and how he knew he could frame us."

"Did he have *all* of our other names on it?" Ava asked.

"I think so," Julie said. "There was something about Leslie, and Claire . . ."

Mac pitched her gaze to the ceiling. "I said Claire." Her cheeks turned red.

"And Parker's dad," Julie added. "Granger had written all of them down."

"Not Ashley Ferguson, though," Parker added, and Julie nodded. That was true. But maybe he just hadn't known who Ashley was at the time. She didn't take film studies.

"Do you think it's possible someone else heard us, too?" Caitlin interrupted. "Aside from Granger, I mean?"

Julie frowned. "Someone else in the classroom?"

Caitlin shrugged. "I don't know. Probably."

"Even if they did, what are you saying? That person snuck into the prison yard of a maximum-security prison and stabbed a guy to death?"

"Maybe? Let's just go over it. Who else was in the room that day?"

Ava shut her eyes. "Ursula Winters. Renee Foley. Alex, but he was all the way on the other side of the room, talking to Nolan."

"Oliver Hodges, Ben Riddle, and Quentin Aaron," Mac added. "James Wong—"

"His dad's a congressman, and he's a lock for Harvard early admission," Ava interrupted. "He wouldn't do anything that stupid. Cross him off the list."

"Oh, like *we* wouldn't do anything as stupid as pranking someone, because we're headed for Juilliard and soccer scholarships and all?" Mac said.

Ava paled. "Okay," she admitted. "James Wong could have heard us, too."

"Claire was there," Mac added. "So maybe it's her? If she heard me say I wanted her dead, she'd be the type who'd get revenge."

Caitlin tapped her lips. "What about Ursula? She wants to beat me at all costs."

"By *killing* people?" Parker looked at them skeptically.

Julie had to admit it sounded pretty extreme. No one said anything.

Julie shut her eyes, realizing what they sounded like. "Guys, this is crazy. No one heard us talking except for Granger. And I saw that legal pad with my own two eyes. Even if the cops find it, our names aren't on it. It doesn't prove anything."

"What happened to the legal pad?" Caitlin asked. "Do you know?"

Julie tried to think, but they'd been in such a rush to get out of there when Mr. Granger surprised them by returning home so soon. "I'm not sure," she admitted.

Parker looked confused, too. "I thought I grabbed it, but I have no idea where it could have gone."

"Which means it's still out there somewhere." Ava looked worried. "The police could have found it in Granger's house. Or someone else could have it now. The person who actually *killed* Granger."

Mac had flopped back onto the bed while they talked, her dirty blond hair splayed out around her. "Guys," she said, "we're getting worked up over nothing. Parker's dad's death has nothing to do with this—with us. He was probably a prime target considering what he did to Parker. I mean, aren't people who hurt their kids usually ganged up on in prison? This is the last thing we should worry about. And how impossible would it be for someone in high school to arrange to have a *prisoner* killed?"

"She's probably right," Julie said.

"Yeah." Caitlin pulled her arms inside her sweatshirt and hugged herself. "Sorry I brought it up."

"It's fine," Mac said, squeezing her arm. "It's good to think about all the angles. But right now, we should be looking at the bright side in all this. It sucks that Alex was arrested, but it means *we're* okay. We can put this all behind us."

"You're right," Julie said softly. They *should* be thrilled and happy and relieved right now, not worrying about random, crazy theories that didn't make sense. They weren't going to jail. Parker was still with her. She had good friends, too—friends who cared about her, no matter what.

And maybe that was all they needed right now. But as she sat back, she couldn't help saying one more thing. "Coincidence or not, I'm really glad Markus Duvall is dead."

CHAPTER SEVEN

WEDNESDAY NIGHT, MAC STOOD IN front of her bedroom mirror, holding up a brand-new dress patterned with splashy vibrant peonies. Her mother had presumably bought it that afternoon, and she'd laid it on her bed with a note that said, *Wear me tonight!* Mac wrinkled her nose. With Mac's chunky, dark-framed glasses and wild, untamed blond hair, it made her look half librarian, half *Little House on the Prairie*—in other words, totally not cool. Why couldn't she just wear jeans? Was the Juilliard party *that* fancy?

But maybe it was. It was the official Juilliard welcome event for Washington State, after all. And she was excited about meeting some of her new classmates.

She was less excited about coming face-to-face with Claire.

Mac hadn't seen Claire all week. She'd been avoiding

her at school, going down different hallways if she knew their paths would cross, opting for the library during lunch. She'd even considered ditching orchestra, but strangely, Claire hadn't been there at all. Normally it would have been a big deal, but practice was optional this week, since the orchestra was just learning a series of new pieces and not really rehearsing for anything in particular. Mac wondered if Claire was avoiding her, too.

And she'd been avoiding Blake, as well—every time she saw him in the halls, she ducked into a classroom so they wouldn't have to see each other. As for that gummyworm cupcake, she'd let Sierra eat it, never telling her where it had come from. She'd watched numbly as Sierra licked the icing off her finger, declining even the tiniest bite. And that card Blake had given her? Mac had thrown it in the glove compartment of her car, along with expired insurance cards and a bunch of outdated road maps. She hoped she'd come upon it years later when she was cool and successful and Blake really, really didn't matter.

She dropped the dress back to the bed, rolling her eyes. It probably didn't even fit. Maybe she should just stay home—she really wasn't up for this. But then she remembered the talk she and the other girls had had at Ava's yesterday. They were off the hook for Granger's murder. It looked like they weren't suspects in Nolan's case anymore, either. It was like she'd been given a whole new life, right? She might as well make the most of it.

And as for that talk about the list, the idea that someone else had overheard who they'd wanted dead and was acting on it? Well, that was crazy.

Okay, she decided—she was going. But she definitely wasn't wearing that peony dress. She walked over to the closet, pushed aside some hangers, and selected a dark teal bouclé-knit shift dress she'd bought in New York when they'd toured Juilliard last year. Her mother had objected—it was kind of short—but maybe that was a good thing. She picked out a pair of boots and a lot of beaded necklaces. Much better.

A few minutes later, she dabbed her lips with a bit of gloss, popped an orange Tic Tac in her mouth, and headed for the door. "Bye!" she called over her shoulder to her parents, who were sitting in the study, listening to a Wagner opera with their eyes closed.

Thirty minutes later, Mac handed her keys over to the valet outside a tiny Brazilian restaurant called Michaela in downtown Seattle. She took a deep breath and stepped inside. A bossa nova remix thumped through the speakers, and Edison bulbs in metal cages hung everywhere, shedding a flattering amber light on the scene. Bartenders were mixing up virgin mojitos behind the bar, and platters full of fried plantains and chicken-cheese *coxinha* were making the rounds. A long table outside the space held name stickers for all of the attendees. There, folded in half, was Mac's name. A thrill went through her as she picked it up. She'd done it—she was going to Juilliard. Her skin tingled with excitement and pride.

"Well, well, well. You came after all."

Mac blinked in the dim light and saw Claire's sneering, pixie-like face looming just inches away. She'd already pasted her sticker on her left boob: *Hello, My Name Is Claire Coldwell.*

Mac swallowed hard, shoving her glasses up her nose. "Uh, I have to . . ." she fumbled, just wanting to get away.

Claire stood in the arch, not letting her pass. She was six inches shorter than Mac, her teeny body always something Mac envied, but she suddenly seemed taller. "Blake dumped me, you know," she hissed. "All because of you."

Mac stared at her chunky heels, thinking about what Blake had told her the other day. So it was true. Whatever. Blake breaking up with Claire meant nothing.

"I'm sorry to hear that," Mac said. And then: "Excuse me." Because, really, what else did she have to say? They weren't friends anymore. They weren't anything.

She elbowed past her ex-friend and stepped up to a group of kids—any kids—just for something to do. They were several nervous, twitchy boys in jackets and ties, and one girl in stiletto ankle booties and a black lace dress that Mac instantly adored.

"Hi, I'm Mackenzie." She held out her hand to a skinny, effeminate boy with delicate-looking hands and long eyelashes.

The boy gestured to his name badge. "Hello, my name is Lucien," he said ironically. "I play the flute."

"Great to meet you!" Mac smiled.

The others went around the circle saying their names and instruments. Then they started talking about New York City. "Has anyone ever been there?" a girl named Rhiannon asked with wonder in her voice.

Lucien nodded. "My parents took me for my birthday last year. It's amazing," he gushed. "I can't wait to go back."

"And it's really expensive, right?" a boy named Dexter who played the piano said. "I heard, like, a pack of gum costs five bucks."

"Yeah, but the energy makes up for it," Mac piped up. She'd been to New York—for an orchestra camp with Claire, actually. She shoved aside the memories of them running around Times Square in matching I-Heart-NY T-shirts, eating bags of candy at Dylan's Candy Bar, sneaking onto the stage at Carnegie Hall to see what it felt like, and being chased away by the security guard. "Although you have to ignore the rumors. Not everyone there is a mugger or a pickpocket. And alligators do *not* live in the sewers."

Dexter snorted and rolled his eyes. "Yeah, but huge rats live in the subways."

"True." Mac grimaced. "And *they* are pretty gross."

Everyone made disgusted noises. Mac could feel Claire's gaze burning into her, but she refused to turn around. She was going to have fun tonight, damn it. And that meant not dragging the past into the present.

A tall, blond boy with broad shoulders and a dimple sauntered over. Mac checked his blazer, but he wasn't wearing a name tag. "This looks like the fun group," he said enthusiastically.

Lucien took a sip of his drink. "We were just talking about subway rats. Standard getting-to-know-you conversation."

The new boy's eyes immediately locked on Mac. "Subway rats? Ick."

Mac giggled and resisted the nerdy urge to shove her glasses up her nose. "You afraid?"

The boy grinned. "Of rats? Nah. I grew up on a farm. But I *have* heard the rodent population in New York City is supersmart. Like, they can do tricks. Fetch, roll over. Speak several languages."

"Argue with cab drivers?" Mac chimed in.

The guy grinned. "Haggle with the guys who sell fake Gucci bags on Canal Street."

"Get past the red ropes at clubs," Mac joked, enjoying herself.

The guy held out his hand. "I'm Oliver. I play piano."

His palms were velvety soft, but with slight calluses at the fingertips. His touch sent a head-to-toe charge through Mac. "Mackenzie. Cello. Nice to meet you."

"Nice to meet you, too, Mackenzie Cello." He held her gaze steadily. "I'm always impressed by the way you cellists fling that thing all over the place like it's nothing. You make it look so easy."

"We learn that first," Mac teased. "Cello Flinging 101. Before we even play a note." She couldn't believe the words were flying out of her mouth so effortlessly. She'd never been able to flirt this way with Blake. Maybe because she'd always put so much pressure on herself around Blake.

"Aha. So now I know. I always wondered." He had a nice laugh, Mac thought—full and open, warm. But then, annoyingly, she felt a sad little pull in her chest. *He's not Blake*, a tiny voice said in her ear.

She flinched. *So what?* she thought fiercely. Blake had hurt her. *No*, she corrected—Blake had *screwed her over*.

She struggled to refocus on Oliver. He was telling some story about another cellist he knew from his school, a tiny Japanese girl whose instrument was nearly as big as her but who completely dominated the instrument. "And how about you piano guys?" she asked when he finished. "It must take a lot of training to learn to move a piano."

"Do I look like the kind of guy who would actually move his own piano? There are people who do that for me." His green eyes twinkled. "That's why I chose it in the first place—so I could have my minions do all the heavy lifting."

Mac tried to keep a straight face. "I see. Does Juilliard know? That you're such a prima donna, I mean."

Oliver leaned toward her. "No. And let's keep that between us, shall we?"

Mac placed her hands on her hips, mock stern. "What's in it for me?"

"Well that remains to be seen, Mackenzie Cello. Doesn't it?"

"I think so," she murmured. Oliver smelled clean—like lemons and something salty, reminding her of the sea. It was a totally different smell than Blake's sugary scent. *And that's a good thing,* she reminded herself.

Someone tapped her on the shoulder, and Mac spun around to find herself face-to-face with a middle-aged woman in a brown tweed skirt suit. "Hello, I'm Olga Frank, admissions officer for the Northwest!" the woman bleated, smiling with all her teeth. "Mackenzie Wright! I've been looking for you!"

Mackenzie took the woman's extended hand. "It's so nice to meet you. Thank you for everything."

Olga waved her hand. "Oh, don't thank me, dear. You earned your spot. Now come with me, there are some other strings I want you to meet." She pulled Mac by the hand toward a clump of kids at the back of the restaurant. Mac looked back at Oliver over her shoulder, giving him an apologetic smile. He winked in response, and she stifled a giggle. Flirting was *fun*.

Fifteen long minutes and endless small talk with two violinists, one viola player, and one harpist later, Mac made her way back through the crowd. She wanted to find Oliver again. Finally, Mac spotted him on the far side of the bar, talking to someone she couldn't see.

Mac looked at the bartender and gestured to the punch bowl. "Can I have two of those?" The bartender complied, smiling as he handed over the cups. Drinks in hand, Mac headed toward Oliver. But as she rounded the corner, she realized who he was talking to.

Claire.

Her old friend was shaking her short, bouncy curls and laughing lightly at something he'd just said. She casually touched his arm as she began to talk. Oliver didn't pull away.

Mac seethed. Claire was in full flirt mode—and it wasn't a coincidence she'd chosen Oliver to flirt with. Mac was willing to bet Claire had seen him with Mac earlier.

Mac stood a few feet from Claire and Oliver, unsure

what to do. She was trying to think of something clever to say to break up their tête-à-tête when Claire looked up and caught her eye. Then she placed her hand on Oliver's elbow possessively and mouthed, *Taken*.

Fierce anger blazed through Mac. Suddenly she knew what she had to do. She wasn't going to meekly back down, the way she had when Claire had gone for Blake. This time she was going to fight back.

With a confident flip of her hair, she licked her lips to give them some shine and headed right for Oliver. *He's mine*, she thought.

This time, she was going to get the guy. No matter what.

CHAPTER EIGHT

THAT SAME EVENING, CAITLIN AND JEREMY were walking up Beacon Heights's main drag. They'd just come out of the movie theater, and they were licking ice-cream cones and looking in the shop windows. The sun had set, all the lights in the shops were on, and the street had a festive atmosphere—music was bumping in the bars, a street guitarist was doing a kick-ass rendition of "Come Together," and clusters of kids were gathered at each corner, laughing and gossiping. Caitlin held her cone in one hand and Jeremy's hand in the other, fully aware of how public they were. But hey—they had to go public sometime. And it just felt . . . *good*. Right. She was with Jeremy Friday, not Josh Friday, and she was totally proud of that.

A dribble of vanilla ice cream slid down Jeremy's chin, and Caitlin reached over to wipe it with her thumb. He grabbed her hand and popped her thumb into his mouth, licking the ice cream from it. Caitlin's body vibrated with the sensation of his tongue on her fingertip. She leaned forward and pulled him toward her, kissing him firmly.

"Mmmmm. Mint chip," he murmured into her lips.

"My fave," she sighed back.

Jeremy looked down at her lovingly. "I know. It always has been. Except for your brief dalliance with caramel swirl in middle school."

Caitlin laughed, but inside, she felt a rush of appreciation. She'd known Jeremy for almost her entire life—they did joint Martell-Lewis–Friday family dinners and even family trips, and then later, while she was dating Josh she spent so much time at his house. She hadn't realized that during all that time, Jeremy had been paying attention to her in a way that Josh never did. He remembered how she'd hated her geometry teacher two years before, and how the first thing she'd had to eat after she'd gotten her braces off was Laffy Taffy, and that her favorite way to rile Taylor up had been to pretend to pull a quarter out from behind his ear, mostly because their uncle Sidney did that and they both hated it. Caitlin could guarantee that Josh remembered *none* of that stuff. But listening to Jeremy reference all those details? It made Caitlin feel so loved. So . . . noticed.

Jeremy pulled her down onto a bench outside the

stationery store. She scooted as close to him as she possibly could, enjoying the warmth of his body as the cool evening breeze brushed her cheeks. "So what did you think of the movie?"

Caitlin wrinkled up her nose, and he tapped it lightly with his fingertip. "I loved it. You?"

"Loved it. But I don't totally get—"

"—how he was able to switch the formulas and then lure the thing with the tentacles out from under the bench?" she interrupted.

"Exactly. It's like you read my mind." He smiled.

Caitlin nuzzled into Jeremy's peacoat, the navy wool scratching against her cheek. Josh would never have gone to see a Japanese anime with her. He would have dismissed it with a laugh as "too freaking nerdy."

Jeremy wrapped an arm around her shoulders and pulled her closer. "I wish we could go to one of our houses instead of this cold, hard park bench."

She sighed. "I know. But maybe we'll get to do that soon. My moms might come around, you never know."

Jeremy raised an eyebrow. "Things are better?"

"Marginally, anyway. Since we got cleared of the charges for Granger's murder, they've stopped trailing me." She rolled her eyes.

"Hey!" Jeremy grinned. "That's awesome. And how about the stuff with me?"

"They'll come around to you, too," Caitlin said in a soft voice.

At least, she *hoped* her moms would. But when she'd told them she was going out with Jeremy tonight, their fakey-fake smiles had dimmed a little.

Suddenly, her phone buzzed in her pocket. She slipped a hand in to grab it and answered without looking at the number.

"Congrats, co-captain!" a familiar voice bellowed into her ear. It took Caitlin a moment to realize it was her soccer coach, Leah.

"Wait, what?" she said into the phone. She could feel Jeremy staring at her questioningly, so she smiled at him and mouthed *Coach Leah.*

"You and Ursula were elected co-captains!" Leah's voice was permanently set to booming. "I tallied the votes from today's practice, and you two were the clear winners!"

Caitlin blinked. "Really?" She couldn't stop a wide, stupid grin from spreading across her face. She thought after everything, her chances would be shot. And despite the fact that Alex had been arrested, she'd still worried that the Granger association would be a mark against her. Not that anyone had made it clear they even *knew* about the Granger association, but still.

And yet . . . she was captain anyway. Her grin grew wider. Not even the fact that she had Ursula Winters as co-captain could bring her down. Caitlin and Ursula had known each other for years, playing on traveling soccer teams and bunking together at soccer camps, but they'd always been rivals instead of friends. It seemed like Ursula was always trying her hardest to contradict Caitlin. If Caitlin said something funny, Ursula refused to laugh. If Caitlin suggested the team wear matching headbands for spirit day, Ursula said that was a stupid idea and they should do rubber bracelets instead. Caitlin didn't know what she'd done to make the girl hate her so much.

Her mind briefly flashed to the conversation they'd had in Ava's bedroom—the one about the list they'd made in film studies, and how Ursula had been in that class, too. But she quickly whisked the thought away.

"That's right!" Leah trilled. "Congratulations, Captain! I know you'll do a great job."

Before hanging up, Leah said a few more details about how she'd need to start leading drills and helping plan spirit activities. Caitlin hit the END button and pressed the phone between her palms. Then she took a deep breath and looked at Jeremy. "I'm captain!" she exclaimed, wrapping her arms around him.

Jeremy was stiff for a moment. "Captain!" he said slowly. "Of . . . what, the soccer team?"

"*Duh!* Yeah!" Caitlin released him from her grip and hopped off the bench, dancing a jig in front of him.

Jeremy looked at her cockeyed. "So this is a good thing?"

"Of course it is!" Caitlin stopped, realizing something was wrong. "What is it? You seem . . . I don't know. Pissed."

Jeremy looked alarmed. "Of course not! I just . . . I thought you were conflicted about soccer. That's all."

Caitlin sat back down. "It doesn't mean I want to stop playing." She reached for his hand. "There's a game in a few weeks where the captains walk onto the field with their Homecoming dates. Will you do that with me? Please?"

"Homecoming?" Jeremy tugged at his collar. "Oh, god. Dances are *so* not my thing."

"Come on. It'll be fun!" She gripped her phone, realizing she had a million people to call. Her moms, Vanessa the Viking, Josh . . .

Josh. Of course she couldn't call Josh—not with Jeremy sitting right there. And probably not ever. It kind of sucked. Josh would appreciate the captain thing in absolutely the right way. He wouldn't ask her if she still felt conflicted. He wouldn't bring up how he hated Homecoming.

Jeremy put his hands around her waist and gave her a squeeze. "Okay, well if you're happy, *I'm* happy." Then he stood. "We should get going. Come on, I'll drop you off."

He led her toward the parking lot, and Caitlin trailed behind him, her happy feeling the teensiest bit dulled. It wasn't that she *missed* Josh or anything. She certainly didn't want him back. She just wished Jeremy's reaction had been . . . different. More enthusiastic. More under-standing, the way he was about everything else.

"So," Jeremy said, squeezing her hand and bringing her mind back to the moment. "Let's do something Saturday night."

"Really?" Caitlin's eyes lit up.

Jeremy nodded. "I'll plan all the details. You just show up. Okay?"

"Okay," she said, getting on the moped behind him and grinning stupidly. He was going to take her out to celebrate, wasn't he? Maybe to that new BBQ place they wanted to try. Or that Asian fusion place with the spicy food Josh was afraid of.

Suddenly, Caitlin felt a rush of euphoria. Jeremy *was* reacting in the right way. She was silly to have ever doubted him.

CHAPTER NINE

THURSDAY MORNING, AVA SLIPPED ON a charcoal DVF wrap dress that hit her mid-calf. She pulled on thick dark tights and knee-high boots, topped it all with a black blazer, then grabbed her widest pair of sunglasses and headed downstairs to meet her father. She could have listed a thousand places she'd rather be going than Lucas Granger's memorial service, but Ava didn't have a choice.

"*Jigar*," her father greeted her, using the Farsi pet name he had always called her. Her mom used to try to call Ava that, too, but her terrible pronunciation always made her father laugh, so she gave up and called her "Muffin" instead.

Ava adjusted the belt around her waist and smiled at him. "You ready?"

"Yes, my dear." Mr. Jalali reached for the doorknob but hesitated. He looked at Ava as if he wanted to ask her something, but then he shook his head and started out the door. "What is it?" Ava called after him, running to the Mercedes and sliding in the passenger seat.

Mr. Jalali started the car, then gave her a long, heartfelt look. "I just hate that we're going to a funeral." He tugged at his collar. "They're still hard, after all this time."

Ava swallowed. He was talking about her mom. It wasn't the only funeral she'd been to—there were others, most recently Nolan's—but her mother's had been, of course, the most devastating. She thought back to that horrible day when she and her father sat in the church—her mother's will had dictated it be a multidenominational service, with both Christian and Muslim traditions—listening to the pastor speak, staring at the big photograph of her mom that they'd picked out together to sit atop her casket. Ava had held her father's hand tightly through the whole service. In her other hand she was clutching the Beanie Baby dog her mother had given her a few days before the car crash. It had been her last gift to Ava, and suddenly it had seemed like the most important thing in the world.

Ava looked over at her father now, wanting to say so much to him. She missed him so badly; it felt like there was a huge distance between them now, a gap she wanted to bridge. It was sweet of him to come with her to this, she realized. He didn't have to be there with her. She breathed in, about to say all this, when a crash sounded through the open window. Leslie burst onto the porch, cell phone pressed firmly to her ear.

"No, no, *no*," Leslie growled into the phone. "I told you I don't want any tulips. Tulips look *cheap*. Do you not understand the ambience I'm trying to create here? This is an important party for my mother. Perhaps I need to find a different floral designer. Because it's not too late, and I'm sure there are—" Leslie was quiet for a millisecond. "Good. That's what I thought."

Ava held back a giggle when Leslie stepped backward and almost toppled over the doorjamb, her free hand flailing wildly in the air. She must have felt Ava's eyes on her, because she spun around and glared. Then her gaze turned to Mr. Jalali. "Firouz? How long is this thing going to take again?"

Ava's father shrugged. "A few hours, maybe?"

Leslie looked pained. "I really need you to help me out with the floral design," she whined, then rolled her eyes. "Whatever." She went back into the house, slamming the door.

Mr. Jalali set his jaw and backed out of the space. Ava stared at the minipurse between her hands, the moment between them now broken. After a minute, her father cleared his throat. "Leslie is trying very hard, you know."

Ava gawked at him crazily. "In what way?"

"She wants to bond with you," Mr. Jalali tried.

Ava snorted. The *last* thing Leslie wanted was to bond.

"She respects you very much," Mr. Jalali added. "She's very impressed by how well you're doing in school, how high you scored on the ACTs."

Ava stared at him. More likely, Leslie thought Ava had slept with one of the ACT proctors so he'd slip her some answers. Why was it so impossible to comprehend that she got good grades all on her own? And even weirder, why did her dad think Leslie was Ava's champion? Was he really that blind? What *else* about Leslie did he not see?

All of the horrible things Leslie had said to her danced on the tip of her tongue, ready to spill out. Her father didn't seem to realize who the woman he'd married truly was.

But strangely, Ava couldn't tell him. It seemed petty, like tattling. She wanted her dad to see things for himself.

And truthfully, the conversation she'd had with her friends the other day was still getting to her. She'd told perfect strangers she wanted Leslie dead. She *didn't* want that, of course—gone would be nice, but dead? It bothered her, too, that the list was missing. *Could* someone have found it? Could that someone have it out for them, picking off their enemies one by one, in some crazy attempt to frame them? But who? And why?

No, it was crazy—not even worth thinking about.

Sighing, she slumped down in her seat and looked out the window at the gray, drizzly day, which perfectly matched her mood.

Before long, they'd pulled up to the church. They followed the procession into the old stone building, Ava's father's hand pressed firmly against her back. When they walked inside, Ava sucked in a breath. Every pew was filled end to end with her teachers, classmates, and friends. She spied Caitlin at the front, then Mac a few rows back. She looked around for Julie—she was surely around somewhere—but didn't see her in the throng of bodies. Then, a quick movement in the outer aisle a few rows ahead caught her eye. She saw the flash of a man in a dark suit stepping quickly behind a pillar, then reemerging on the other side. It was a detective, speaking into his cell phone, his eyes flitting across Ava's row before finally resting on her. She flinched. Had he moved to get into a better position to see her? But why? Now that Alex was in jail for Granger's murder, they weren't suspects anymore. Right?

Alex. Ava swallowed hard. *Don't think about it,* she told herself.

Her attention turned to a girl in a black blouse who sat hunched over, sobbing loudly into a tissue. Behind Ava, another girl in navy wept so hard she gasped for air. Ava looked around the church and saw several more of her classmates who seemed inconsolable. *God, get over it, people,* a voice rang in her head. *He was just a teacher. And a perv at that.*

Then she realized who was crying. There was Jenny

Thiel—whose Texas belt buckle had been prominently featured under her bare boobs in a series of sexts with Granger—gazing sadly at a photo montage of their dead teacher through the years, tears streaming down her puffy cheeks. And there was Polly Kramer, whose henna-tattooed hands had been on full display in a lurid series of pictures, rocking back and forth, the light from the stained glass window casting her face in a scarlet shadow. Justine Williams, Mimi Colt . . . they were all here. Every single girl who'd figured prominently on Granger's iPhone. And all of them were sobbing like the world had ended.

They really loved him, Ava realized with a start.

Ava hadn't thought it could be more disgusting than a high school teacher messing around with several of his students, in his classroom, and getting them to send him naked pictures. But it was worse—*way* worse. Lucas Granger had convinced these girls that he *loved* them. He had manipulated them, lied to them, all so he could fulfill his own perverted desires. She could just imagine him whispering *I love you* to a dozen girls, and she could see the excitement and nervousness on their faces as they bought it. She still couldn't understand why the cops had seemed totally unconcerned when she'd told them about Granger's affairs with his students. Had they even investigated what she said? She'd told them that Granger had hit on her, but it was almost as if they didn't believe her.

Disgusted, she stumbled toward a seat in one of the back pews, her father sliding in next to her. Sean Dillon sat to her left and gave her a quick nod as she settled in. Ava stared at the altar, where an old priest stood from a chair and patted at his robes before approaching the dais. Out of the corner of her eye, she could see Sean turn to whoever was sitting on his other side—probably his girlfriend, Marisol Sweeney—and whisper something, before they both broke out in hushed giggles. She tried to ignore them. But she had a feeling she knew what it was about.

The priest adjusted the microphone, placed his hands firmly on either side of the pulpit, and contemplated the crowd. In the brief pause before he spoke, Ava heard a stage whisper from the pew behind her. She didn't recognize the voice, but she heard the words, which were definitely meant for her ears: "Alex Cohen never seemed right to me."

And then came the response: "Totally. He was always just a little off, right?"

"It doesn't surprise me that he beat someone up at his old school," came the booming whisper behind her. "He always looked like he was about to go apeshit." The other person let out a snicker in response.

Ava's father shifted his weight and turned his head ever so slightly. Clearly he heard them, too. He reached over and gave Ava's hand a reassuring pat.

Ava blinked back tears. She felt suddenly self-conscious,

hyperaware of what felt like a thousand eyes on her. Of course everyone was staring. She was Ava Jalali, the ex-girlfriend of Granger's accused killer.

Ava felt a pull in her stomach, thinking of all the things she'd learned about Alex recently. Since that first kid went on the news, multiple students from Alex's old school had now come forward, confirming that Alex beat his ex-girlfriend's new boyfriend into a bloody pulp. The only person who didn't talk, actually, was Cleo, the ex-girlfriend, and Brett, the dude he'd messed up.

Alex had never told her about any of it. Ava hadn't even known he'd *had* a girlfriend at his old school—let alone that he'd been so jealous of her new boyfriend he took a fist to his face.

But even knowing this, Ava still couldn't imagine Alex killing Granger. Was that crazy? Was it insane to want to believe that he was innocent? She was still angry he'd called the cops on her that night—but she couldn't stop loving him. She hadn't given up on him. Not yet.

The priest cleared his throat, bringing Ava back to the present. "Life's saddest event has brought us together today," he began in a soothing voice. A woman in the front row let out another sob. "We have come to mourn the loss of a child of God—a young man who took it upon himself to fulfill a pure and precious calling. Lucas Granger. A teacher. A guide. A leader. A man who touched the lives of everyone around him. Like another great man who died too young." He paused for effect, letting his words settle over the packed room. "That's right. Jesus was a teacher, too."

A chorus of sniffles and stifled cries echoed around the room. Ava felt a metallic tang in her mouth and fought her gag reflex. Lucas Granger may have been many things, but Christlike certainly wasn't one of them.

CHAPTER TEN

THURSDAY AFTERNOON, PARKER PICKED AT the nubby upholstery of a chair in Elliot Fielder's waiting room. Her feet bounced and tapped nervously on the floor. She still couldn't believe she was here—how desperate was she that the only person she could turn to was the therapist who'd pretty much stalked her?

On Tuesday, after Fielder had told her about her dad, he'd begged to come pick her up. But Parker had changed her mind: She didn't want to talk to him right then. And so she'd caught a bus back into Beacon, bummed around for a few hours, and met up with Julie, resolving never to talk to Fielder again.

But she was still struggling to process everything about her dad's death. She couldn't believe he was *gone*. Really, truly gone. Somehow, she'd expected to feel a different reaction. Joy, maybe, even euphoria. Instead, all she felt was numb—followed by the most pounding headache she'd ever suffered through. And even more annoyingly, she'd started reliving all sorts of awful memories of her dad—his abusive Greatest Hits, if you will. She needed a way to kick him out of her head once and for all.

Which was why she'd ended up back here.

Her phone chirped from the pocket of her hoodie, and Parker jumped. Her skin was clammy with cold sweat. She fumbled for her phone with jittery fingers. "Hello?"

"Where are you?" Julie's voice was worried and tense.

"I'm fine," Parker insisted. She tried to sound steady.

"Why weren't you at the service?"

"What service?"

Julie exhaled. "For Granger."

"*You* were there?" Parker was in no shape for a funeral. But she couldn't believe *Julie* had shown her face. It wasn't like Julie was out making social rounds after the mass email about her hoarder mom.

"Yeah," Julie answered. "I mean, I hid out, basically, but I went. And you should have been there, too. It doesn't look good that you've just skipped."

"Who cares?" Parker said. They weren't even suspects anymore.

"*I cared!*" Julie snapped. "I wanted you there! Parker, we really need to stick together. After everything that's happened—"

Fielder's receptionist appeared in the doorway with an exceedingly sweet look on her face. "Parker Duvall? He's ready for you."

Parker covered the mouthpiece with her hand and nodded at the woman. She didn't want Julie to know she was at Fielder's office. Julie would kill her.

"Sorry, I have to go," Parker whispered into the phone.

"But—" Julie began. "Where *are* you?"

"I'll see you later, okay?"

Parker tapped off the call and slipped the phone back into her pocket. She rose and followed the receptionist into Fielder's large, airy office. Her heart skipped a beat at the sight of him, sitting at his desk, jotting notes on a pad. His lean runner's frame was totally relaxed as he worked. He seemed so harmless and innocent. Not like a stalker at all.

She wanted so badly to trust him again. But how could she get over what he'd done—or how angry he'd been when he'd caught her at his computer?

Fielder's head snapped up, and a smile crossed his face. "Parker! It's so great to see you." He ran a hand through his tousled hair. "I'm just so relieved—so happy—that you're here." He gestured at the chair across from his. "Please, sit."

Parker hesitated. Maybe this was a bad idea. She fought the urge to bolt past him, past the lady out front, through the office door and into the street.

Fielder held her gaze, as if he understood what she was

thinking. "It's okay, Parker," he said gently. "It's safe here. I'm not going to hurt you. I'm just here to listen."

Parker sat down, but she leaned forward in the chair, ready to leap up at any moment. She stuffed her hands in her hoodie pockets and waited for him to speak.

"I owe you an apology," Fielder began. "And I'm truly sorry for scaring you. For following you."

Parker nodded. "You should be."

"I wasn't stalking you. It's just that—you said you had memory gaps. I was just—God, this sounds crazy when I say it out loud—I was just trying to fill in the blanks for you. With pictures."

Parker squinted. "Uh, that sounds like stalking to me."

Fielder pressed his palms over his eyes. "I know. But I'm telling you the truth. I wasn't trying to do anything . . . inappropriate." He paused for a moment, as if deciding whether to continue, then took a breath. "Look, Parker, I have a confession to make. Technically, I shouldn't tell you this as your therapist, but my mother had a lot of . . . problems when I was growing up." He stopped again, swallowed. "She was an amazing, brilliant woman, but she had a lot of memory gaps, too. Like yours. I wasn't able to help her, and then . . . then it was too late."

He shut his eyes for a moment, and when he opened them, they were filled with tears that threatened to spill over onto his cheeks. Parker was astonished. "You remind me of her," he said quietly. "The strong and amazing parts of her. And I guess I just want to do for you what I wasn't able to do for her. But I crossed the line, and I realize that. I'm sorry. So, so sorry."

Parker's chest throbbed, and she realized she was holding her breath. She exhaled sharply. No one besides Julie ever talked to her like this anymore. She had felt invisible for so long. But she mattered to Fielder—that was clear. And that felt good.

"What was she like?" she asked quietly. "Your mom, I mean."

Fielder seemed surprised. He squinted, as if he were seeing his mother again in his memory. "She was sweet, loving. Really fun. She had her issues," he chuckled. "But she was a great mom. She could make even the most boring things, like homework and grocery shopping, into a game. And she was so, so smart. The smartest person I've ever known." He smiled wistfully.

"Then what would happen? How would she just . . . lose time?"

His face darkened. "She would go out for an errand, and then we wouldn't hear from her for a day or so. Sometimes more." He stared at his lap. "I would hold my breath, wondering each time if this would be the time she didn't come back. But eventually, she would walk in the front door. She could never tell us where she'd been, because she couldn't remember—and she seemed frustrated by the questions. So eventually my dad and I stopped asking. We were just happy she came back at all."

Parker hugged a throw pillow from the couch. That sounded a lot like her experience. "Did she ever get help?"

"No. Things were different back then. And she was so strong—she never complained or told us how scared she was. When I got a little older, I tried to talk to my dad and our doctor about it, but we didn't know what to do. And then, one day, she didn't come home."

They were silent as Parker absorbed his words. "Did you ever find her?" He nodded. "Where?" she pressed, suddenly desperate to know.

Fielder flinched. "It doesn't matter. The point is . . ." He trailed off. "I'm sorry, Parker. This has nothing to do with you. We should be discussing *your* problems right now."

"No, I'm glad you told me." Parker leaned forward, staring into Fielder's eyes.

Fielder shook his head. "You know what? I'm glad I told you, too." He coughed awkwardly. "So maybe this means you'll start coming back for more regular sessions?"

His steady gaze sent a jolt through her, and she looked away quickly. The glint in his eye felt familiar, but she had trouble putting her finger on what it meant. Then, it hit her: It was the way guys used to look at her when she walked through a party. His face had that lit-up, hopeful look even the school's hottest football players got when she agreed to go on a date with them. *Attraction.*

It was something she used to feel so routinely that she'd always taken it for granted. But then she thought of how terrible her face looked, how damaged and broken she was. There was nothing about New Parker he could be attracted to. She was disgusting.

And yet . . . could he have somehow seen the old Parker, nestled deep inside? Because she knew that somewhere, deep down, that Parker was still in there. And maybe, with help, New Parker could let her out.

She took a breath, meeting his gaze once more. "Yes," she decided. "I'll come back."

CHAPTER ELEVEN

A FEW HOURS LATER, JULIE let Carson take her hand as they walked across the parking lot downtown. She couldn't believe they were doing this, right out here in front of . . . well, everyone. And more than that, she still couldn't believe he *wanted* to.

People passed them on either side. Julie didn't recognize anyone from school yet, but she knew they would be here—it was Thursday night, prime hanging-out-downtown time. Then a familiar girl slipped around the corner. She had a navy Marc by Marc Jacobs satchel that Julie recognized, because Julie had the same one.

Ashley? Julie's heart started to bang in her chest, and her palms felt clammy. She pulled her hand away.

"What is it?" Carson turned to look at her.

Julie flinched. "Nothing. Sorry. I just thought I saw someone over there."

Carson eyed her for a moment, then shrugged and gestured to an American Apparel store. "Want to go inside?"

"No!" Julie said it a little more forcefully than was normal. But everyone at Beacon High shopped at American Apparel. Surely someone she knew was in there.

Carson was looking at her even more strangely now. She swallowed hard and tried to regain her composure. "American Apparel is so *mainstream*," she said in a flip voice. "I have a secret place I like around the corner. It's so hip that the workers look down on the customers. If you don't have cool facial hair or tattoos or, like, read the right indie blogs, they'll roll their eyes."

Carson raised an eyebrow. "Are you sure *I'm* cool enough to go?"

She smiled in spite of her nerves. "You, Carson Wells, are the coolest of the cool."

"Even without creative facial hair?"

"Please *don't* get creative facial hair," Julie giggled.

Then Carson leaned down and brushed his lips against hers. Julie peeked around to see if anyone was watching, but all the passersby were minding their own business. *Of course they are*, she told herself. She needed to just relax. She could do that, right?

They walked to the corner and turned toward the smaller streets just off the main drag. Julie's favorite boutique, Tara's Consignment, was ahead. It was where she bought most of her clothes; designer cast-offs at a fraction of the price, all she could afford on her lifeguard salary. As she took in the *Gone with the Wind* display in the windows—the owner was obsessed with the movie—she thought back to the last time she'd been shopping at Tara's. She'd bought Parker a studded bracelet. Not that Parker had even worn it.

Parker. Things still felt off between them. They hadn't really talked about what happened to Parker's dad—or the coincidence of him dying not long after Julie had named him in class. Even though Julie still wasn't sure anyone overheard them, she had to admit it was a strange coincidence. She wished she knew what had happened to the notes Granger had taken on the yellow legal pad, documenting what they'd said. She'd sworn she'd taken the pad, but when she'd riffled through her things, it wasn't there.

On top of that, Parker was disappearing more and more often lately, and it seemed like she couldn't remember where she'd been. And whenever Julie asked, Parker got weird and cagey, like she was hiding something.

"*Julie.*" Carson's voice pierced her thoughts. They were standing in front of Tara's now. A few kids with Technicolor-dyed hair who Julie didn't recognize edged past them to go inside.

"Sorry," she said brightly, smiling. "What did you say?"

Carson placed his hands on his hips. "Are you *sure* everything's okay?"

Julie sighed. This was exactly why she'd never had a

boyfriend—she knew she'd never be able to hide her feelings. She wanted to be totally transparent for Carson, she really did. But it wasn't easy.

"I was just thinking about my friend," she admitted. "Parker—I don't know if you've met her yet. She's kind of a loner. I'm worried about her is all. There was a death in her family recently, and I think it's messing with her head."

He wrapped his arms around her shoulders and pulled her in close. "You're such a good person, Julie," he said, running a hand through her hair. "So caring. So selfless. And you're so beautiful. You know that, right?"

Julie felt her skin flush. "Thanks . . ."

Carson pulled her back toward him and kissed her firmly. Julie kissed him back, losing herself in the kiss. Finally, her head buzzing, she pulled away and led him into the store. She bobbed and weaved a little as she walked, practically drunk from the kiss.

"This place is amazing," Carson exclaimed as they walked inside, his accent floating over the racks of tweedy coats, fedoras, and last-year's Barney's best sellers. A guy at the counter gave them a withering glare. Julie nudged Carson to look up. The sales guy was covered in black tattoos, had a curly mustache and a weird, pointy beard, and was reading a manga comic.

"*Nailed it*," Carson whispered, and they both burst into laughter.

Then Carson took a right down a long aisle of Halloween costumes—and not cheesy ones either, but period pieces: full-out, Southern belle hoop skirts, lacy, dramatic *Brides of Dracula* getups, Sherlock Holmes blazers and trousers, vibrant jockey silks, and realistic-looking Civil War uniforms. Julie followed, amazed that Halloween was so close—how was the year moving so quickly? Carson wandered over to a tall rack of full-length gowns and held out a deep plum dress with a high-low hem to Julie. She stepped closer and ran her hands across the strapless bodice, letting her fingers caress the smooth silk overlay. It was red carpet worthy. The stitching was spectacular, and the cut was exquisite—the gown was delicate but structured, obviously the work of a master designer.

"Try it on," Carson said. "It'll look incredible on you."

"Okay," Julie giggled, stopping in front of a round display teeming with men's suits. "But only if you try this one on." She held out a royal blue three-piece suit of plush velvet. "And this." She plucked a bowler hat from atop the rack, stood up on her tiptoes, and plopped it onto his head.

"Deal." He grinned at her and headed for one of the two curtained stalls.

Julie slipped into the other one and dragged the thick curtain across, pinching it at the corners to block out any prying eyes. She kicked off her skinny jeans and boatneck cashmere T-shirt, both of which were bought at this very store a few months ago. The thought of Carson—no more than a foot away, on the other side of the flimsy wall separating their two dressing rooms—made her shiver. She could hear the *whoosh* of his jeans dropping to the floor, and the rustle of his sweater as he lifted it over his head. He was practically naked, and so close. Julie quickly stepped into the dress and reached behind her for the zipper, but she couldn't pull it up.

She stepped out of the fitting room and stood outside Carson's curtain, waiting for him to come out. "Ahem," she said, clearing her throat with mock impatience. "I'm the girl here, and I'm ready way faster than you are."

Carson grunted behind the curtain. "If I'm not mistaken, your outfit consists of exactly one piece, while mine has many, many more." Julie heard the metallic *phhhhttt* of a zipper and then the curtain rings scraped loudly as he flung the fabric aside. She burst out laughing at the sight of his six-foot-two-inch frame draped in head-to-toe blue velvet. His rich skin and sea-glass eyes practically glowed against the color and texture of the suit. She hadn't thought it was possible, but a comical outfit only made Carson *more* handsome.

"Are you laughing at me?" An exaggerated expression of shock was on his face. "Personally, I think I look awesome."

Julie struggled to keep a straight face. "It's perfect. Absolutely perfect."

But Carson wasn't listening to her response. He'd noticed her dress—or, more accurately, her body in the dress. He sucked in his breath. "Wow."

Julie looked down at the gown, which she was holding closed with one hand. "Oh, right. A little help here?" She gestured to the zipper on the back.

"With pleasure." Carson stepped toward her, his crisp suit making a loud crinkling noise as he walked. He spun her around and zipped up her dress. Then Julie looked in the mirror. It fit her to perfection, snug where it was supposed to be snug, the bodice giving her movie-star cleavage.

She turned around again to face him. He was gazing at her with a hungry look on his face. Julie liked the feeling of his eyes on her, but she suddenly became aware of a salesgirl's attention turning toward them. "Um, you forgot your hat," Julie whispered to Carson.

"Oh, of course," he whispered back. He turned and grabbed it from the dressing room and put it on. He looked delicious. "Why are we whispering?"

Julie glanced out the front window of the store to the empty street. "Paparazzi."

"Right." He nodded knowingly. "They'll definitely want a picture of you in that dress."

"Um, I think they're going to be equally excited to see you in that suit. Because you look—"

But then Carson cut her off, grabbing her by the hand

and pulling her into his dressing room. In one motion, he yanked the curtain closed, spun her around, and pressed her against the mirror. Their lips met. Julie felt his body against hers and ran her hands down his back, the velvet crunching under her fingers.

"Are you guys finding everything okay?"

It was the sales guy from the front counter, and it sounded like he was right outside. Julie and Carson tore apart, exchanging wide-eyed, guilty looks.

"Yep," Carson called out, helping Julie adjust the gown and straightening his jacket and vest. Julie turned her back to him and gestured for him to unzip her. She slipped through the curtain into the other dressing room and quickly threw on her clothes, carefully hanging the gown back on its hanger, using the delicate white ribbons stitched inside.

The sales guy was glaring at them, hand on one hip when they emerged. "You're not supposed to share a dressing room, you know."

"Sorry!" Julie chirped.

"We were trying to save the environment," Carson said, which didn't even make any sense. Julie covered her mouth, sure she was going to erupt into laughter.

They dashed for the door and doubled over as soon as they crossed the threshold. Julie's sides hurt, she was laughing so hard. Carson grabbed her by the hand and gave it a squeeze. "You, Julie Redding, are a red carpet knockout. Not to mention really fun in a dressing room."

Julie felt her cheeks redden. "Right back at ya."

"Coffee?"

"Café Mud is right around the corner. It's my favorite."

"Lead the way."

They walked hand in hand and found a table on the patio under an outdoor heater. Julie ordered her usual skim latte, while Carson asked for a cappuccino with extra whip. A young couple with a chubby puppy on a leash sat at the table just next to them. Other couples and groups of friends filled the rest of the tables, and there were sounds of chatter and laughter in the air. Julie felt an unfamiliar sensation in her chest. After a moment, she realized what it was: happiness. For the first time, she truly understood what her friends had said at Ava's house the other day: They were free. They could live their lives. They needed to make the most of that.

Carson reached for her hand across the table. But then a sudden, sharp peal of nasty laughter rang out from across the street. Julie's head spun around toward its source. Clustered together in front of an ATM were three girls from school. They were looking right at her, and they were talking in quiet voices and cracking one another up.

Julie clenched her hands into fists. She peered around for Ashley, certain she was lurking there, but she was nowhere in sight. Cringing, Julie slumped down in her aluminum chair. Maybe if she disappeared for long enough they would leave.

"Hey. It's okay," Carson said, leaning forward. He reached for her hand, but Julie kept both of hers in her lap.

"Ha," she said, letting out a grim laugh.

"No one is even talking about it at school, you know."

Julie couldn't believe how naive that was. "Please. We both know that the moment I come back to school, people are going to be all over me." She stared at the lattice pattern in the table. "I've already been through this, remember?"

"I know. In California. But did you have me back then?"

Julie's lips twitched into a smile. "Well, no."

"Those girls over there?" Carson gestured to them. "They have secrets, too. I guarantee it. They're not perfect."

Julie snorted. "That's where you're wrong. We're in Beacon Heights. Everyone is *actually* perfect here."

Carson shook his head. "Their lives are just as screwed up as yours, mine. Everyone's. Trust me."

"How is *your* life screwed up?" Julie wanted to change the subject.

Carson reached for her hand again, and this time she let him take it. "That's the thing. It's not anymore . . . because of you."

Julie looked away, a lump in her throat. "You don't have to do this," she blurted. "You don't have to sacrifice yourself for me. You're new in town—and cute, and nice. You deserve a chance at being friends with everyone. Not just the freak."

Now Carson looked angry. "Stop saying stuff like that! I've made my choice, Julie. I've never cared about what people think. Now, what will it take for you to come back to school?"

Julie's lip wobbled. "I'm not coming back."

"Do you really think things are *that* bad?"

Julie turned away. "How can you ask that? I'm the laughingstock of the school."

"Have your friends dropped you? Has anyone sent you disparaging texts?"

Julie rolled her tongue over her teeth. She'd received a few emails from Nyssa and Natalie, but she'd deleted them without opening them, fearing the worst from even two of her closest friends.

"What if I walk you to and from every class? And I'll kick anyone's ass who even *looks* at you funny. How's that?"

Julie laughed uncertainly, but she started to wonder. Maybe the sight of tall, buff, alarmingly hot Carson by her side would stave off the rest of the kids at school. She didn't hate the idea of having such a handsome bodyguard.

"Will you come back, for me?" Carson begged.

Julie took a deep breath. "Okay. I'll try it for a *day*."

Carson smiled sweetly. "Good."

"But if anything happens—anything at all—I'm bolting. Got it?"

"Nothing will happen, Julie. People aren't as bad as you'd think. You'd be surprised." He grinned. "Besides, a girl as hot as you shouldn't waste your life hiding in your bedroom. Take it from the guy who looks good in even a crushed-velvet blue suit. I know it all."

Julie smiled at that, feeling a little bit lighter. Carson clearly believed what he was saying. She just hoped he was right.

CHAPTER TWELVE

FRIDAY NIGHT, MAC PULLED INTO the parking lot of Umami, a trendy Thai restaurant in downtown Seattle. She popped her Ford Escape into park and sat quietly in the driver's seat for a moment, watching people stream in and out of the low-slung building festooned with fairy lights. The place was packed, and Mac could smell their famous spicy wings even from here.

She was running late—she and a bunch of the Juilliard kids, including Oliver, had all made plans to get dinner tonight, too excited to wait until the next welcome event to meet up again. She flipped down the mirror and checked her makeup one last time. She'd tried to pull off a smoky eyeliner look and liked the way it made her eyes really pop under her glasses. Just as she was about to open the door and head out, a snippet of news on the radio caught her attention.

"Police are still questioning the suspect they have in custody for the murder of Beacon Heights High School teacher Lucas Granger," a commentator said. "Some believe Granger's death was also connected to that of Beacon student Nolan Hotchkiss."

Mac raised her eyebrows. *Interesting.* Were they saying that Alex was responsible for *both* deaths? Not that she really knew Alex that well, but he didn't seem the type to poison anyone with cyanide. Then again, it felt like she didn't really know *anyone's* true nature these days.

Just hearing Granger's and Nolan's names gave her stomach pains, and she took a few more deep breaths to recover. Everything still felt so up in the air. She just wished someone would confess already to the Nolan thing. Alex . . . a stranger . . . who*ever*. The police might not have her and the other girls behind bars, but she couldn't shake the feeling that she wasn't safe yet.

With a resigned sigh, Mac shut off the engine, threw her leather bucket bag over her shoulder, and ducked out. As she crossed the asphalt, she hummed a few measures of a tune that had been running through her head that she couldn't quite place. A few measures in, she realized what it was: a song for Blake's band that he'd written himself.

She stopped in her tracks. Why the hell had *that* popped into her head? It annoyed her to no end. She needed to stop thinking about Blake for good. Especially now that she might be starting something with Oliver.

Her stomach fluttered giddily. The other day at the Juilliard cocktail party, Mac had rustled up an A game she didn't even know she had. As everyone started leaving, she'd sauntered up to Oliver and asked for his iPhone. "Here," she'd said, typing in her number and handing back his phone with a confident wink. "Now you can call me." Oliver had blinked at her. "Okay," he'd said, grinning. When Mac looked up again, Claire was gaping at them. *Ha*.

And guess what? Oliver had texted her yesterday, and they'd spent the entire afternoon exchanging texts about music, the things they wanted to do first in New York City (Lincoln Center for her, jazz clubs downtown for him), what TV shows they watched. Mac had been tempted to ask Oliver what he thought about Claire, but she knew that would make her sound jealous.

She pushed through the front door and into the lively restaurant, where palm fronds hung low over laughing diners and waitresses delivered sweating glasses of Thai iced tea and coconut drinks. She spotted a long banquet table against the back wall where the group, most of whom she recognized, was chatting excitedly. They looked a lot like her, in chunky knit sweaters, thick black or tortoiseshell glasses, ironic little-girl hair clips on the girls, ratty Mostly Mozart and Interlochen T-shirts on the guys. Mac spied

Oliver leaning back in his chair at the far left end of the table, his hands folded behind the back of his blond head, revealing sculpted biceps and tan forearms. He was even more handsome than she remembered.

Oliver turned and caught her eye, stopping his conversation mid-sentence to smile at her. He held her gaze as she walked over.

"Hey," Mac said, standing by his chair.

"Hey, yourself." Oliver grinned. "I was afraid you weren't coming."

"Nah, just fashionably late," she teased.

She tore her eyes from his and glanced around the table, waving at the group. A chorus of *Heys* and *Hellos* rang out. As Mac took off her coat and threw it over the chair next to Oliver, she felt a firm hand on her shoulder. She turned around and gasped.

"That's *my* seat." Claire shot her an ice-cold smile. She waved a dismissive hand toward the far end of the table, by the bathroom doors. "Try down there. I thought I saw an empty one."

Mac gritted her teeth. She looked over at Oliver, who had gotten distracted by his phone. The worst thing to do, she decided, was to act like this bothered her. Oliver had been texting with *her*, after all.

She tossed her hair over her shoulder. "Oh, sure. That's cool." Then she turned and headed for the other end, where the birdlike Lucien and the surprisingly supermodelesque Rachel slid over to make room. Oliver looked up from his text and made a pouty face, but Mac just smiled at him. There was no way she was getting into a fight with Claire in front of him, but she also felt defeated. Clearly, Claire had won Round One.

"I'm so glad you came out!" Rachel trilled, then pressed something square and cold into Mac's hands—a flask. Mac looked up to meet Rachel's gaze, but Rachel just grinned conspiratorially. Mac took an experimental sip, bitter whiskey slipping down her throat. Lucien nodded approvingly at her across the table. *Interesting*, Mac thought. These Juilliard kids were wilder than she expected.

Mac took another pull of whiskey and was about to pass the flask down, but Rachel caught her arm. "No, keep it between us," she whispered. "You're cool, but some of these other kids are totally straight-edge prudes." She rolled her eyes.

"Got it," Mac said quietly, handing her back the flask. Rachel passed it to Lucien, who took a covert swig— apparently he was one of the cool kids, too. It felt good to be included in a secret circle. Especially one that excluded Claire.

A loud trill of laughter sounded from the other end of the table, where Claire was flirting with Oliver. She was in top form, her eyelashes batting a mile a minute, giggling and tossing her hair. Oliver was laughing at her jokes, but Mac noticed that he pulled away when she put her hand on his thigh. *Ha*, she thought. At least he was fending off her advances for the time being. But would he forever?

The flask had come back to her, and she grabbed it and took another swig. The whiskey began to warm her stomach and relax her mind. When Lucien began to tell a story about his singular and disastrous foray into musical theater, she laughed loudly and raucously. She felt Oliver watching her from the other end of the table—with jealousy, maybe. Like he wanted to have the same kind of fun she was having. *Well then, come down here*, Mac thought. *Ditch boring Claire. I'm way more fun.*

But then, when Claire rose from her chair, beaded clutch in hand, and headed for the bathroom, Mac saw her opportunity. "Be back in a sec. I just need to say hi to someone," she said to Lucien and Rachel. With a determined stride, she walked to the other end of the table, sat down in Claire's still-warm seat, and pushed Claire's drink—a Thai coffee, *boring!*—away. She flashed Oliver her biggest, broadest, sexiest smile. "Hey there! Long time no see."

Oliver smiled back. "And here I thought you were ignoring me."

"Oh, no." Mac leaned forward. "Just making the rounds, you know."

Oliver nodded toward Rachel and Lucien. "What's going on down there in the winds section? You guys seem to be having fun."

Mac's eyes darted back and forth. "Rachel brought in some whiskey," she whispered. "She's got it in a flask."

Oliver's eyebrows shot up. "Lucky. Can you make sure it gets to my end?"

"Only if you're good," Mac said, enjoying that she was suddenly the gatekeeper. Then she placed her hand on Oliver's forearm. His skin was hot and smooth under her palm. "So," she said, "I want to hear more about growing up on a farm. Was it amazing?"

Oliver looked at her appraisingly. "You seem to be the only person who thinks so. Whenever I tell anyone else, they're like, *hayseed!*"

She waved her hand. "Please. Farms rock. I used to want to live on one when I was younger. Did you have goats?"

He flashed her a crooked smile. "Pygmy goats, yeah. We sometimes let them come in the house."

Mac's eyes widened. "That's adorable!"

Oliver nodded. "We had llamas, too—used them for their wool."

"Do you still have them?"

"Yup. Maisie and Delores. My two girls."

Mac smiled shyly. "I'd love to meet them sometime. I've never pet a llama before."

"I think that could be arranged," Oliver said, his eyes twinkling.

"Uh, *hello?*"

Mac looked up. Claire stood over her, nostrils flaring, hands on hips. "You're in my seat," she hissed. *"Again."*

"Oh, sorry. I thought you had left," Mac said sweetly.

"Pull up a chair, Claire," Oliver said, gesturing to a chair at an empty table nearby. "Have you two met? Claire, this is Mackenzie. Mackenzie, this is . . ."

"We've met," Claire said sharply.

Oliver smiled obliviously. "Oh, right. You're both from Beacon! Well, cool, then."

There was no malice in his eyes. No sense that he was two-timing them. But still, Mac didn't want Claire sitting here and ruining her sweet little down-on-the-farm moment with Oliver. Then, suddenly, she realized how she could make Claire leave for good.

Without thinking too hard about it—otherwise she'd totally lose her nerve—Mac reached up, put her hands on Oliver's face, and pulled him down toward her. She kissed him, lightly at first, then with intensity. He seemed surprised, but quickly responded by tangling one hand in her hair and pulling her closer. "Whoa," she heard him murmur.

They kissed for a few moments. Mac could feel everyone else at the table watching them, then heard some whispers. *She's drunk,* someone said. *That's hot,* someone else mumbled. But Mac didn't care. When she opened her eyes, Claire was halfway across the restaurant. She barreled through the front door and was soon on the pavement.

Poor baby, Mac thought with satisfaction. *Couldn't stand the heat, so you got out of the kitchen.*

And then, right on the heels of that, she felt the tiniest pang. She was acting crazy. She didn't kiss boys in public. She didn't act rudely to people—even if they were ex-friends. Who was she turning into?

Oliver pulled back and looked at Mac meaningfully. "I had no idea talking about llamas got you so hot."

Mac blushed, trying her hardest to snap back to the present. "What can I say? Llamas are sexy."

"Do you want to get out of here?"

His question startled Mac, and she instantly realized what an idiot she was. Of course he wanted to get out of here—she'd just kissed him passionately in the middle of a restaurant. She cleared her throat. "Um, okay." The last thing she wanted was for him to think she was a prude. "Let's go."

Oliver grabbed Mac by the hand, tossed some cash onto the table, and waved good-bye. Mac heard more whispers, and Lucien yelled out a *whoo!* but she didn't turn.

He led her toward a dark blue Prius on the far edge of the parking lot, then opened the door and held her hand while she climbed inside. The car smelled like Winterfresh gum, and there were a bunch of Rachmaninoff CDs littered on the floor. Mac stared blankly at the little disco ball hanging from the rearview mirror, its tiny mirrored panes sparkling in the overhead streetlight.

Oliver walked around to the driver's side and slid into his seat. "Where to?" Mac asked once he closed the door. But just as the words escaped her mouth, Oliver leaned across the seats and pulled her close again, kissing her deeply. He was an excellent kisser, brushing her lips with his and holding her face in both hands.

"How about right here?" he breathed into her ear.

Mac tried to shift her body so the curve of the seat wasn't digging into her thigh, but she only ended up banging her knee on the gear shift. Struggling to maneuver himself in the tight space, Oliver leaned sideways and landed on the car horn, which blasted across the quiet parking lot. They giggled and fell back in their respective seats until they caught their breath.

Oliver pressed a lever and scooted his seat as far back as it would go, then reclined the backrest until it was touching the rear seat. With a chuckle, he grabbed Mac's wrist and pulled her over onto his lap, facing him. "Better?" He kissed her neck.

"Um, okay," Mac murmured, taking off her glasses and placing them on the dashboard. She let him leave a trail of soft caresses on her neck, up her jawline, across her cheek. It felt good, there was no denying it. But suddenly, Mac felt sort of . . . separate. She didn't feel the kind of emotion she was expecting. In fact, she kind of felt nothing.

Only, *why*? What was wrong with her? Maybe she was just a freak.

She tried to kiss him some more, but the more their lips met, the antsier she became. Finally, Mac pulled back and laid her hands in her lap. "Oliver, I'm sorry, but . . ." She trailed off, grabbing for her glasses again.

"Oh." Oliver shifted backward. "Hey. I'm sorry. Are you okay?"

She pretended to rub her glasses clean. "Uh, yeah. I just should probably get going."

Oliver stared at her for a beat. He didn't seem angry exactly, just confused. "Did I read this wrong?"

"No!" She shook her head. "You are amazing. It's just that I . . ." She *what*? She didn't even know. "I have to go." She straightened the straps of her bra and grabbed her purse, which had fallen onto the floor. "I'll call you, okay?"

And then she was out the door and halfway to her own car. To her horror, tears were streaming down her face and mixing with the raindrops that had started to fall. What was wrong with her? Was it because she'd made Claire leave? Was it because she'd dragged an innocent guy into her stupid little game? Was it because she felt as heartless as Claire?

When she reached her own car, she plunged her hand into the glove compartment, desperate for a Kleenex. Only, her fingers brushed against something else. It was a white envelope—the card Blake had left with her gummy-worm cupcake.

She climbed into her car, locked the door, and tore it open. On the front of the card was a picture of a giraffe wearing sunglasses, which, despite her tears, made Mac smile. She was a sucker for dorky cards featuring dressed-up animals, and Blake knew it. When she opened it, Blake's crabbed handwriting covered the page.

Dear Macks, it said. *You probably hate me forever. And I understand—if I were you, I'd hate me forever, too. I made a really stupid decision. I never should have listened to Claire. I should have known she was being devious and deceptive from the start. I should have been honest with you, and a stronger person, and because I wasn't, I've probably lost you for good. The only thing I have left is our awesome memories together. You left a tube of ChapStick at my house last time you were here, and this probably makes me a weirdo, but I carry it around in my guitar case, sort of like a good-luck memento.*

I miss you. I love you. I would do anything to get you back. Just name it.

Blake

Tears streamed down Mac's cheeks. And all at once, she knew—*this* was why she felt so empty kissing Oliver. He was a good guy, and he probably would make a good boyfriend . . . but he wasn't the person she wanted, the person she couldn't allow herself to have.

He wasn't Blake.

CHAPTER THIRTEEN

SATURDAY EVENING AT SIX, CAITLIN pulled on a dark gray dress that showed off her soccer-toned legs, slipped into her favorite red ballet flats, and did a full 360 in front of her mirror so that her short black hair fluttered. She wasn't the type to dress up, but tonight called for it. She looked perfect. She hoped she was dressed appropriately for wherever they were going, but Jeremy wasn't saying a word—which, Caitlin had to admit, was part of the fun.

Caitlin loved surprises, which Jeremy just seemed to know; she couldn't remember ever telling him. She also couldn't remember Josh ever surprising her with anything, except for the soccer-turf necklace he'd given her right before they broke up. And it had been such an awkward surprise: He'd given it to her right in front of their families, and it had come in this velvet ring box, so it had looked like he was proposing.

Caitlin quickly touched up her lip gloss and was about to head downstairs when her cell phone chirped in her cross-body purse. It was probably Jeremy, calling to tease her with a clue about tonight's date. He'd done so all day, though he'd only said things like "you'll scream when I tell you" . . . which could mean anything. Did he mean *scream* literally—like it would be scary but also romantic? Maybe he planned a candlelit whale-watching cruise on the Pacific—Caitlin had a love-hate relationship with whales. Or maybe he wanted to do a horror-movie marathon under the stars—she'd huddle next to him all night. "Hey," she giggled into the phone, without looking at the caller ID.

"Where are you?"

"Ursula?" Why was Ursula Winters calling her?

"Uh, we're waiting for you," came Ursula's clipped reply. Then she snorted. "Oh my god, you totally forgot. *She forgot*," Caitlin heard her call into the background, followed by a series of groans.

"Forgot what?" Caitlin asked.

Ursula sighed, as if she'd been expecting this. "The new recruit initiation is tonight, Caitlin. It's *always* the Saturday after tryouts. Didn't Coach Leah tell you on the phone?"

Caitlin flushed hot, then cold, panicking. *Had* Coach Leah mentioned it? She'd been so excited she hadn't really listened to the coach's spiel. But Caitlin had been a member of the team for almost four years. She knew the drill.

She stared at her reflection in the mirror, ready to tell Ursula she had plans. But the words died in her mouth. This was the most important bonding event for the soccer team, and she'd be a shitty captain if she didn't go. She had no choice—she *had* to be there. She would just have to reschedule with Jeremy. He would understand.

She told Ursula she'd be there in twenty, then immediately dialed Jeremy's number. He answered on the first ring. "I'm on my way now, Miss Impatient." There was laughter in his voice. "You getting excited to see what awaits you tonight?"

"Actually, I have really bad news," Caitlin blurted. She had already stripped off her dress, thrown on jeans and a tee, and was heading to the front door. "Soccer initiations are tonight—I totally spaced. But I promise I'll make it up to you, okay? Tell you what—*I'll* cook dinner for *you* tomorrow night. Anything you want. Even chicken tikka masala." Caitlin made a mean chicken tikka masala—her moms had taught her—and Jeremy had been complaining that he hadn't gotten to try it yet.

But there was silence on the line. Caitlin swung into her car and looked at her phone, wondering if they'd been cut off. The timer was still going. "Jeremy?" she asked tentatively. "You there?"

"You're kidding, right?" His voice was small and kind of cold.

She jammed the key in the ignition. "I'm really, really sorry. It's this thing we do every year with the new players. A welcome tradition. I forgot, and since I'm captain, it's my responsibility to run it. I really have to be there."

"And you're telling me *now*?"

Caitlin paused, her hands on the wheel. Where was Mr. Understanding? "I said I was sorry," she repeated, feeling a pull in her stomach. "And I promise to make it up to you. We can reschedule our dinner, can't we?"

Jeremy let out an astonished laugh. "I wasn't just taking you to dinner. I was taking you to see One Direction."

"Oh my god!" Caitlin cried, her hand flying to her mouth. One Direction was her dirty little secret. She was a Niall girl—she kept a little picture of the Irishman taped inside her iPad cover, just for fun. Josh used to roll his eyes every time he saw it. He would rather have died—or never played soccer again—than see One Direction with her. This was just further proof that Jeremy was the best boyfriend ever.

Which officially made her the worst girlfriend ever.

She squeezed her eyes shut. "Oh, Jeremy. I'm sorry. I didn't know."

"Yeah. I had gotten us front-row seats. But it's . . . whatever."

138

He sounded so crushed. And suddenly, Caitlin was, too. She racked her brain for a way to make this work. "Wait—hang on. Let me see if I can—"

"Forget it." Jeremy cut her off. "Enjoy your night of *hazing.*"

Before Caitlin could respond, Jeremy was gone. He had hung up on her.

Her mouth hung open. She quickly hit REDIAL, but he didn't answer. "Jeremy, call me back!" she bleated at his voice mail, then she immediately called again. Still no answer. She couldn't believe it. Was he *angry* at her?

Her phone buzzed, and she pounced on it, eager to take Jeremy's call. But it was Ursula again. Caitlin waited a beat, considering her options. If Jeremy had picked up, she would have told him she'd go. The initiation mattered—but not as much as front-row seats. But it annoyed her, too, that he hadn't even listened to reason. He'd just hung up on her.

So she picked up the call. "Can you pick up some Silly String on your way over?" Ursula whined. "Since you've clearly done nothing *else* to help?"

"Sure," Caitlin said, wilting. "I'll be there soon."

Caitlin couldn't think of anything she was less in the mood for than initiations, but she made the short drive to Beacon High's multimillion-dollar, brand-new athletic facility anyway. She pulled into one of the team captain parking spots—for the first time ever—and checked herself in the mirror. Her eyes were puffy, but there was nothing she could do about that now.

She tried Jeremy again. Still nothing. "I can probably be out of here by nine," she said in her sixth voice mail of the hour. "Just say the word, and I'll be there. Thank you *so much* for those tickets. It's just . . . well, it's amazing."

Then she dashed into the gym with Silly String in hand. At the sight of her, the whole team, newbies included, jumped up and began tossing rolls of toilet paper to one another. Ursula was emptying out the last Costco-size package, throwing rolls over heads to the players in the back. "Roll out!" Ursula instructed, drill-sergeant style. "And . . . decorate!"

"Follow me!" Caitlin said, remembering how initiation went. The first order of business was to toilet-paper a bunch of trees by the soccer field. The captain—or co-captains, in this case—always sprinted as fast as she could to get there, the other girls following behind. The slowest girls had to climb the highest trees and throw the most toilet paper.

She grabbed two rolls and headed for the double doors that led outside. She was at the front of the pack, racing across the field at top speed. She could hear the other girls huffing behind her as they unspooled their toilet paper and began to drape it across the sheds and fences. It felt weird to run, strange to do something so active and silly when Jeremy was so angry at her. But it wasn't like she had a choice. She was captain. That meant something.

She steered the group off the field, down the hill, and onto the main walk on campus. When everyone else caught up, she singled out some of the slowest runners and pointed to their trees. The new players hurled the small white spools up into the branches, caught them when they fell, then threw them again. Then Ursula, who'd caught up, too, started a call and response chant: "*Hey newbies!*"

"*Hey what?*" they responded.

"*Hey newbies!*"

"*Hey what?*"

Caitlin yelled at the top of her lungs as well, giggling at the old rhyme. For a moment, she even forgot about Jeremy. But then it all came thundering back. She reached into her pocket for her phone. He still hadn't called.

The girls stopped on the quad to catch their breaths. Then, a rumble of footsteps and male voices bounced off the school buildings. The boys' soccer team rounded the corner, running in formation. Josh was in point position at the front. Caitlin gazed at him for a moment. He met her eyes and cocked his head a little. That's when Caitlin realized. If anyone could tell she was upset, it would be him. She turned away, embarrassed.

"Okay, let's hit the locker room next for the Kool-Aid treatment," Caitlin told the team, trying to sound chipper. She faced the new girls. "Babies," she called out in a thunderous voice. "Get in formation. It's time to put on your diapers for your Kool-Aid bath!"

The girls groaned and laughed. Caitlin marched after them, but then she felt someone touch her shoulder. She whirled around. Josh was standing behind her.

"Hey." His tone was cool, but he was studying her face carefully.

"Hey," she replied awkwardly. She kept her face turned away from him, hoping he wouldn't get a good glimpse of her puffy eyes.

"You all right?"

Caitlin was surprised by the real concern in his voice. She swallowed hard. "Sure," she said stiffly. "I'm perfect."

Josh crossed his arms over his chest and kept his eyes on her. "Come on. What's up?"

Caitlin felt a welling of emotion in her chest. Why was Josh being so nice to her when she had hurt him so badly? She shrugged. "Just dumb stuff. Nothing major."

"Is it Jeremy?" he said quietly. He waited patiently, staring at her.

Caitlin's hands flew to her face and she covered her eyes for a second. "Yes. It's Jeremy. He's . . . he's mad at me. I forgot about the team thing, and he had gotten us tickets to a concert, and he was going to surprise me. And now he's really, really pissed. I feel terrible."

She peeked at him, expecting him to roll his eyes and say she got what she deserved, but instead, Josh just shrugged. "Is he mad you bailed on him, or mad you're doing a soccer thing?"

Caitlin frowned. "I don't know." But Josh had a point. If she'd had to cancel on Jeremy because of something else—a family commitment, or something with school— would he have hung up on her? It was like soccer was his trigger.

Josh sighed. "The thing about Jeremy is he sees things in black and white. You're either this person"—Josh jerked his thumb in the direction of their teams—"or you're that person. You can't be both."

Caitlin's mouth hung open. It was actually true. And it surprised her how he'd put it: not in a disparaging way, but simply matter-of-fact. Jeremy was Jeremy.

"You're the captain," Josh went on. "You had to do this for the team. If he cares about you, he'll understand."

He held her gaze for another moment, then turned away and called "Move it on out!" to his team. "We need to paper the tops of those trees, where the *girls* couldn't reach."

The boys laughed and high-fived one another, and the girls good-naturedly booed and catcalled. "Caitlin, let's go," Ursula called out from across the field. "Locker rooms, now."

"One sec," Caitlin called back, her eyes still on Josh. She wanted to thank Josh for what he'd just told her—and how nice he'd been, especially given the circumstances. He had moved past the math building and was climbing a massive tree, a roll of toilet paper jammed into his shorts pocket. She wandered over there and watched as he unrolled the streamer of paper to decorate the branches. The paper was so light that it got picked up by a slight breeze and blew back toward him.

Then he looked down and saw her. "Oh," he said. "What's up?"

"I just wanted to say that—" Caitlin started. She swallowed hard. "You're really . . ."

"What's that?" Josh tilted toward her to hear her better. Their eyes met. Josh gave her the old smile he used to save only for her. Caitlin's heart did a flip.

But suddenly, she heard a sharp crack of wood.

"Shit," Josh yelped, the branch beneath him snapping. His hands flailed to grab another branch, but his fingers closed on a clump of leaves instead. They tore away in his hand, and all at once he was falling hard out of the tree and onto the grass below. He landed with a sickening thud just a few feet from where Caitlin stood.

Caitlin screamed and raced to his side, her heart beating

like a drum. His eyes were closed. He looked hurt. This was *her* fault. "Josh?" she cried, her voice tinged with tears. "Are you okay?"

Slowly, his eyes fluttered open. "I—I'm fine," he said weakly. He sat up and looked at her, a dazed look on his face. "I think it's my ankle."

"Can you walk?"

He thought about this, then shook his head. "I don't think so," he whispered.

A bunch of other kids had rushed over by now, too. Shaken, Caitlin pulled out her cell and dialed 911. Adrenaline coursed through her as the operator picked up and said an ambulance would be there soon.

Soon enough, an ambulance roared up, and two burly EMTs loaded Josh into the back. Caitlin's nerves were jumping everywhere—ambulances would always remind her of Taylor, no matter how long she lived. She watched as Josh peered at her from the gurney. He was grinding his teeth and squeezing his eyes shut to fight the pain. She broke free of the crowd and put one foot on the bumper. "Josh, do you want me to come with you?"

Josh met her gaze, but then the EMT stepped in the way. "Are you family?"

She shook her head.

"A girlfriend?"

Caitlin drew back. It wasn't her job to ride with Josh to

the hospital. Not anymore. She froze, the finality of the end of their relationship suddenly very real. "No," she said quietly. "I'm not."

The EMT closed the door with a loud clang. Its lights flashing, the ambulance let out one loud *whoop* of the siren, turned out of the driveway, and sped up the main road.

CHAPTER FOURTEEN

THE FOLLOWING MONDAY MORNING, JULIE sat in her car, idling in the parking lot of Beacon High. Kids were gathering in clumps to recap their weekends. School buses huffed at the curbs, doors were slamming, and a group of girls stood by the art wing with a large banner bearing Lucas Granger's face. The first bell blared, indicating that there were fifteen more minutes until homeroom began.

She totally wouldn't be ready in fifteen minutes.

Julie buckled her seat belt and put the car back in drive. Then she felt a hand on hers. "Hey. You can do this."

She looked up. Carson had wanted to pick her up this morning, but she'd insisted on picking him up instead, so she could make a quick getaway in the middle of the day if she needed to. "Come on," he said, with a warm smile. "I'll be with you every step of the way."

Julie looked cautiously at the students streaming into the building. "I don't know," she whispered. "I can't face Ashley."

"Yes, you can. If we see her, we'll just turn and go in the other direction, okay? Or even better, we'll *face* her, and tell her what a pathetic bitch she is."

Julie's eyes flicked to the girls holding the Granger banner. She hadn't been back to school since Granger was killed, and she'd assumed that stuff would have started to blow over by now. But it seemed like there were more Granger groupies than ever.

"Come on." Carson opened the car door. With a long sigh, Julie turned off the ignition, grabbed her purse and books, and followed him into school.

It had only been a little over a week since she was last here, but Beacon High felt different—and *looked* different. There was a new fern in the lobby. There were all sorts of Granger posters in the halls. And Julie was different, too. When she'd left, she had still been Perfect Julie Redding, with a constant stream of people following her down the hall. Now she was dirty and shameful, leaving only the stench of cat piss and rotten food in her wake. At least that's how she felt.

They made their way down the hall, Julie walking with her head down, Carson leading her by the elbow. "Julie!" someone called from behind her.

Julie flinched at the sound of her name, certain it was Ashley. But when she turned, her good friend Nyssa Frankel stood waving at her. Natalie Houma was by her side, sporting a totally normal smile.

"Did you study for the chem test?" Nyssa asked in a sing-song. "I'm so screwed. Like, who needs to know how to balance equations?"

"Um, no . . ." Julie stammered, feeling dizzy. "I mean, yes, I studied. A little. But I think it's going to be hard."

"You're coming on Friday, right?" Natalie chimed in. "You got my email, didn't you?"

"Friday?" Julie had no idea what they were talking about. More than that, why were they acting so normal, not even mentioning the fact that she'd been gone a week? Then she remembered that Natalie *had* sent an email. Several, in fact. But Julie hadn't read them.

"My Halloween party," Nyssa explained. "We need to talk costumes at lunch. I'm thinking maybe sexy super-heroes. Or sexy Disney princesses?"

"You can't make *everything* sexy, Nyss," Natalie teased, rolling her eyes at Julie. "Right, Julie?"

"Um . . ." The second bell, which indicated they had only five minutes before homeroom, rang before Julie had a chance to answer. Natalie just shrugged and scampered off with Nyssa, both of them waving Julie good-bye. Julie turned to Carson, an astonished look on her face. "I can't believe it."

Carson grinned. "See?" He leaned down and kissed her softly on the cheek. "I told you you'd be fine. So this means you'll go to Nyssa's Halloween party with me on Friday night? Maybe as a sexy Cinderella?" he teased.

Julie felt herself laugh. "Definitely not as Cinderella," she said, shoving him playfully. She couldn't believe she was even thinking of going to that party. But maybe she could.

They walked to Julie's locker, which to Julie's amazement wasn't covered with evil messages or pictures of cats. Then Carson checked his watch and made a face. "Listen, I hate to do this to you, but I left a book in my locker. I really need it."

Julie blinked at him. Carson's locker was clear on the other side of campus, and her first class was in this building. If she went with him, she'd be late. If he stayed with her, he'd be late. "Um . . ." she said. She glanced around nervously. Her classmates were chatting, slamming locker doors, cramming last second with their noses buried in thick textbooks, sending hurried texts before the second bell. No one was paying any attention to her, and for the first time in a long time, that was a good thing.

It's fine. No one cares. Then Julie spotted Parker down the hall and felt even better. Parker had stayed with her last night, but she'd disappeared sometime this morning— while Julie was in the bathroom, nervously throwing up.

She hadn't expected Parker to actually show up at school.

"Go get it," she told him, tucking her shiny hair behind her ears. With Parker as backup, she would be fine. "I'll be okay."

Carson looked worried. "Are you *sure?*"

Julie nodded, watching as Parker drifted down the hall toward her. "I have to try it sometime, right?"

He kissed her again. The scent of his shampoo—something coconutty and delicious—washed over her. "I'll see you after class, okay? I'll be waiting right here." He headed quickly down the hall.

Julie caught Parker's arm as she passed, and Parker spun around. Her face was in shadow under her hood, but she looked different somehow. It took Julie a moment to place the expression on her friend's face, but when she did, it was a total shock. Parker looked *happy.* "Hey!" Parker exclaimed, patting Julie's shoulder. "You made it!"

"You made it, too," Julie said.

"Yeah, I figured I'd show up." Parker snorted sarcastically, but the corners of her mouth turned up ever so slightly. Before Julie could pester Parker about why she was in such a good mood, Caitlin, Mac, and Ava swept toward them in a group hug.

"Welcome back!" Caitlin crowed.

"Good morning, girl." Ava waved, a stack of bangles clattering together on her slim wrist. "Nice to see you here."

"We missed you," Mac said earnestly, wrapping a hand around Julie's arm and giving it a reassuring squeeze.

"Thanks, guys." Julie was totally overwhelmed by their support.

"So. Lunch. You and us." Caitlin was using her tough soccer captain tone. "No discussion."

"We'll meet you here." Ava nudged a stray strand of hair behind her ear. "Sound good?"

Julie spun the dial of her locker, about to tell them that she had lunch plans with Natalie and Nyssa. But as the final number of the lock fell into place, she sensed that the hallway had gone quiet. She looked over her shoulder for a split second, thinking the hall had cleared out, but it was still full of kids—kids watching *her*. At the same time, she heard a snicker a few feet down the hall.

Her heart began to pound. Maybe she'd spoken too soon, telling Carson she was okay. Her fingers curled on the lever that opened her locker, and there was a sharp *click* as she opened the door. The latch went slack in her hand, and the locker door swung open. There was no time to stop it. Julie felt the *ping . . . ping . . . ping* of something small and pebble-like hitting the tops of her shoes, and then an avalanche of grit and dust gushed out of her locker, covering her up to the ankles and coating the entire front of her dress with a gray film. A familiar scent rose up from the floor, coating the inside of her nostrils.

Kitty litter.

Julie's mouth dropped open, and a puff of scented powder landed on her tongue. She gagged. Ava shrieked, just as Mac leaped backward, horrified, her hands flying to her face, her mouth hanging open in an alarmed O. Parker stood next to them, her hands clenched into fists, her face red with fury. A few final grains of litter fell to the ground; the tinkling sound boomed in the stunned silence.

Then, as if on cue, Julie heard the first titter from a few feet away, then the next, then fully formed guffaws and a chorus of *Holy shit* and *Dude, that was awesome!* A huge crowd had formed. Julie made out the faces of Nyssa and Natalie, who, aside from the film studies girls, seemed like the only people who weren't laughing. Their eyes bulged as they stared at her, looking concerned but helpless.

A cluster of juniors parted as someone pushed through to the front of the crowd. And then there she was: wearing a Julie-esque wrap dress, her hair in Julie-like ringlets, and with a smug, triumphant, hideous grin. Ashley, the girl who haunted Julie's nightmares. A handful of girls surrounded her, wearing the same cruel expression. They all giggled nastily.

"Welcome back, Miss Julie," Ashley crowed. "And here. I thought you might want this." She sauntered up to Julie and placed something on her head. Julie swatted at it, her fingers touching plastic. It was a *litter box*. Kids howled with laughter, and she heard the telltale snap of iPhones taking photos.

Julie teared up, wishing she had something to say, some way to shut them all up. But instead all she could do was knock the litter box to the ground, wade out of the Tidy Cats sea, and push through the nearest door to the parking lot.

She ran a few steps, more grains of kitty litter spilling off her clothes. She could tell kids were watching her from the windows, laughing. Once she was far enough away, she let out a wrenching sob. How could she have been so stupid? She had known in her gut that she should never have come back to school today. But she'd let Carson—sweet, clueless Carson—convince her.

Suddenly, something horrible struck her: What if Carson was *in* on this? He'd been the one to convince her to come back, after all, and he'd abandoned her at her locker.

But before she could think that through, Julie felt someone grip her firmly on the upper arm. "Goddammit—" she barked, shaking off the hand and spinning around, ready to fight whoever had come out here to torment her more. But she was face-to-face with Parker, who looked as angry and vengeful as Julie felt. Parker grabbed Julie and hugged her hard, as though she was holding onto Julie against a storm.

"I can't believe that bitch did this to you," Parker snarled. "She's going *down*."

"It's so horrible," Julie said, the tears falling freely now. Parker was the only one she ever let see her cry. "All that kitty litter . . . all those kids laughing . . ."

Parker pulled Julie closer as her shoulders racked with sobs. "I'll do anything for you, Julie," she whispered into Julie's ear. "You just say the word, and she'll pay."

Julie considered it for a moment, then pulled back. Parker's face was wild, and for a moment, Julie was suddenly afraid of her. "No," she said, placing an arm on Parker's shoulder. "We're better than that."

"I know." Parker took a deep breath. "But I *wish* we could," she whispered. "I wish, just once, people would get what's coming to them."

CHAPTER FIFTEEN

THAT AFTERNOON, MAC, AVA, AND Caitlin stood shoulder to shoulder on the cracked, weedy sidewalk in front of Julie's house. Clearly they weren't the first ones who had visited since Ashley sent out Julie's address in her email blast: *Hoarder* was spray-painted across the cracked driveway, and *Get Out of Town, Dirty White Trash* had been scrawled across the garage door. Skinny, mangy cats wove in and out of the random holiday decorations in the front yard as though they were big scratching posts. Several junked vehicles stood on blocks in the side yard. The grass hadn't been cut in ages; it was full of dandelions, and probably ticks.

This wasn't a place Mac ever wanted to visit. But Julie's Subaru was in the driveway—she was home. And they needed to make sure she was okay.

Mac felt terrible for Julie. Before she'd gotten to know her in film studies, she'd always admired her from afar—Julie was this glowing, friendly, beautiful girl who always wore the perfect clothes and said the perfect thing. It was amazing that the entire time she'd been hanging on by such a thread and concealing such an enormous secret. But Mac understood why she had. This was Beacon, after all, home to kids whose parents were cutthroat CEOs, Nobel laureates, and heirs to Fortune 500 companies. There was no room for imperfection in Beacon, and certainly not for hoarding.

Mac's phone beeped, and she looked at the screen. *What are you up to?* Oliver had texted.

Her heart sank. She wanted to like Oliver, she really did. And he'd been so nice after the make-out fail outside the Thai place, texting her casually, sending funny emoji texts. But every time she saw his name on her phone, she just felt . . . nothing. Shouldn't she be more excited if she actually liked him? Why, instead, did Blake's face always pop into her mind? She kept thinking of that card he'd written. The ChapStick he kept in his guitar case for a good-luck charm.

"Well, let's go," she said to the others, dropping her phone in her pocket without replying. She started up the walkway, eyeing a shifty-looking cat who had stopped, paw in the air, on the brown grass before slinking into a dirt-caked, deflated kiddie pool. The other girls followed behind her, and she pressed the rusty doorbell, which let out a metallic scraping sound. A shadow passed behind the curtain in the front window, but no one appeared. After a moment, Mac pushed the bell again. Still nothing.

"She has to be in there," Ava whispered. "Her car's here."

They all started when the curtain flew open, yanked back by an unseen hand. Julie's swollen, puffy-eyed face appeared in the window. She looked like she'd been crying since she left school that morning. It was as if a light had gone off in her, and now she was dulled, broken. Without a word, Julie disappeared from the window. For a second, Mac was afraid she had retreated back into her house, but then the door groaned open.

A damp, foul smell escaped the house and washed over the porch. Julie stood in the doorway wearing her bathrobe, its crisp whiteness practically glowing against the backdrop of junk, trash, and health hazards that loomed behind her. Her shoulders slumped, and her hands hung limply by her sides.

No one spoke for a moment, until Ava broke the awkward silence. "We came to take you for a mani-pedi!" she chirped, too perkily.

Julie fixed her eyes on the floor, where a small tribe of cats had gathered near her slippered feet. "Uh, no offense, but no one's looking at my nails."

Mac reached out a consoling hand to Julie's arm. "Danishes at that awesome new bakery in town, then. The evening batch comes out of the oven right around now."

Julie shook her head sadly. "Thank you. But I'm not leaving. *Ever.*" Her shoulders heaved up and down. "Sorry, guys. I'm just going to go back to sleep."

"Are you sure?" Caitlin asked quietly. Julie nodded. "Well . . . call us, okay?" Caitlin added. "For anything. Even if it's super late at night."

There was nothing else to do but retreat down the path to their cars. Ava and Caitlin had come together—Ava had offered to give Caitlin a ride since she lived close. They called out good-bye to Mac and drove off. But Mac hesitated. Slamming her car door, she turned back to Julie, who was still standing on the porch, staring blankly out at the street.

"I know how it feels," she said, then winced. That wasn't exactly true. "I mean, I've been teased, too. Humiliated."

Julie blinked. "Yeah?" she said, in a small voice.

Mac took a step back toward the house. "By Nolan Hotchkiss. It's why I . . . you know. Went along with every-thing." She glanced around, wondering if she should be saying this out loud, outside, but it didn't seem like there was anyone around. The Redding house was probably the type of place most neighbors avoided *walking* past if they could.

Julie cocked her head slightly. Then she glanced over her shoulder into the house. "Do you want to . . . come in?" she asked, a little hesitantly.

"I'd love to," Mac said quickly, worried Julie would change her mind.

The house smelled like mildew, cat pee, and the dead mouse that had festered under the dishwasher at the bagel place Mac worked at last summer. But Mac pretended it didn't bother her. She kept her gaze straight ahead, trying not to gape at the towers of boxes and stacks of ripped, ugly furniture and piles of clothes that reached to the ceiling. Julie edged down the hall, turning sideways at particularly narrow points. "Cat box," she said, pointing to a litter box in Mac's way that was so clumped there was hardly a dry spot left. Then she opened a door at the end of the hall. "Here. This is my room," she said, her cheeks pink with embarrassment.

Mac walked through and gasped. Unlike the rest of the house, Julie's room smelled like perfume and fresh laundry. Two neatly made beds were side-by-side in the corner, and the books on the shelves had straight spines. It was like she'd stepped into a different house. A different *universe*.

"It's so nice in here," Mac blurted.

"Yeah, unlike everywhere else." Julie sat on the bigger of the two beds. "You know, I've never had anyone else in here . . . except for Parker." Her gaze moved to an army-green backpack across the room, then she shrugged.

"So you told Parker about . . ." Mac gestured toward the hall.

A regretful look clouded Julie's face. "Yeah, though not at first. I should have told her sooner. It brought us a lot closer."

She heaved a huge sigh. Mac was about to ask what she was feeling—all the Parker stuff had to have taken its toll on Julie—but then Julie said, "So what did Nolan do to you?"

Mac cleared her throat. "Oh, just pretended he was into me to make some money from his friends."

Julie's eyes widened. "*God.* I'm so sorry."

"Yeah, well." Mac fiddled with her purse, the memory rushing back to her. "I just know what it feels like, is all," she said, peeking at Julie. "To think one thing, to have your life going one way, and then to have the rug snatched out from under you . . . and everyone laughing at your expense."

Julie flopped onto her bed. "The worst was that I went to school today and thought everything would be fine. I'm such an idiot. I *know* Beacon. I know what everyone here is capable of."

"Not everyone," Mac urged. "You have us." She looked away, thinking back to Nolan, how she'd wanted so desperately to think he was really into her. "But I get it," she added. After all, Nolan wasn't even the worst—look what Claire had done, plotting to mess up her Juilliard audition. And they were supposed to be *friends*.

She shifted her weight on the bed, and suddenly her purse tipped over and a bunch of things toppled out. A hairbrush skidded across the floor, followed by Mac's wallet. She dove to collect the stuff, embarrassed to mar Julie's perfect space. Then Julie said, "What's that?"

Mac followed her gaze. The card Blake had given her the other day had fallen out. It splayed open, displaying Blake's heartfelt message inside. Mac quickly snatched it up, but by the look on Julie's face, she'd probably seen some of it.

Her ears burned red. She lowered her eyes, feeling a sudden onslaught of tears. She hadn't told any of the film studies girls about the Blake thing. She hadn't told anyone. It was too confusing, and she was too ashamed of her part in it.

"Want to talk about it?" Julie said softly, a concerned look on her face.

"No!" Mac cried. Then she shook her head. "I mean, god, I don't want to bug you with my problems. I'm here to make sure *you're* okay."

"Please, I *need* a distraction." Julie hitched forward. "What's going on? It's a guy, isn't it?" she said knowingly.

Mac stared at her checkerboard Vans. All at once, it

was like a volcano rumbled inside her, threatening to burst. "It's Blake Strustek," she blurted. "He's been a friend for years, and I've loved him for years, but now it's all ruined."

She spilled out the whole story about Blake—how she'd had a crush on him first but Claire had started dating him; how, according to Blake, Claire had lied and said Mac wasn't into him. How they were in a band together, and lately, something had started between them—behind Claire's back. How she'd never meant to hurt Claire. But when she got to the part about Claire and Blake tricking her in order to sabotage her Juilliard audition, Julie's mouth dropped open.

"That's *not* how best friends treat each other!" she cried.

"Don't I know it," Mac said darkly.

Julie crossed her arms over her chest. "Now it makes sense why you mentioned Claire that day at film studies. I'd always wondered."

Mac winced at the memory of that conversation. As soon as she'd said Claire's name, she'd felt horrible— especially because Claire had been right across the room and could have *heard*. She'd just been so angry at Claire that day, though—she'd seen her and Blake canoodling in the hall, and all of her feelings of betrayal and resentment had rushed to the surface.

"I should have never said that . . . I was just having a bad day," she sighed. "It's not like I actually want her *dead*."

"Of course you don't," Julie said firmly.

"And, I mean, just because I said it doesn't mean it's going to come true," Mac said loudly, thinking of the theory Caitlin had brought up the other day at Ava's.

"Of course not," Julie said. But then she shifted awkwardly. "Still. I hate that those names are even out there, on that notepad. And, I mean, two out of the five people we named are . . . you know." She averted her eyes.

"No one can link that to us," Mac said quickly. She needed to say it out loud, somehow, to undo the jinx. "It's too crazy of a theory. No one would pick off the people we named. It doesn't make any sense. No one hates all of us like that . . . or everyone we named like that."

Mac's phone rang, and she looked at the screen. Her mom was calling. Suddenly, she remembered that she'd made plans to go out to dinner with her parents—more Juilliard celebrations. She stood up, slipping the phone in her pocket. "I have to go," she said sadly, looking at Julie. "Are you going to be okay?"

Julie nodded. "Thank you for staying and talking with me. It helped, really . . . having you here."

Mac nodded and started out of Julie's room, hating that she was leaving Julie inside such a small space. She navigated around the boxes and the cats, and soon enough she was outside again, breathing fresh air. But her chest was still heaving, and she knew why. It was all the talk about the list, and that terrible conversation.

She wondered, suddenly, what Claire was doing right now. Was she at home? Was she safe? *Should* Mac worry about her? It was ironic—the girl she hated, the girl who hated *her*, might be the person who needed her the most right now.

CHAPTER SIXTEEN

AFTER DROPPING CAITLIN OFF, AVA gripped the steering wheel hard, her vision steady. Instead of turning off toward her house, she took a left up a steep road that wasn't regularly traveled. Unless you were going to the Upper Washington Correctional Facility—which Ava was. It was where Alex was being held. Bail was set at twenty-five thousand dollars, and his parents, two teachers, were still trying to raise that kind of money.

There were all kinds of things she should be doing this evening, like studying for a history exam or updating her Lady Macbeth Facebook page—a project for AP English.

But something inside her had cracked today. It was something she couldn't really explain, a trigger she couldn't put her finger on, but all of a sudden she'd realized, she *had* to go see Alex in prison. No matter how many newscasts she watched of kids saying how Alex had violently beaten up that kid at his old school, she needed to hear *him* tell her that. More important, she needed him to tell her that he wasn't guilty, that he hadn't killed Granger.

Her phone buzzed, and she looked down. *Hey, I still have your lip gloss,* Caitlin texted. *Wanna swing back for it?*

Ava had let Caitlin borrow the lip gloss in the car, but there was no way she was going back now—or explaining what she was about to do. *I'll get it at school, no biggie,* she replied. It was weird: She probably *could* tell the girls that she was visiting Alex. But she wanted to keep this to herself, until she figured it out a little more.

When she pulled into the police complex fifteen minutes later, she was still trying to figure out what she was going to say. Rolling back her shoulders, she walked through a door marked VISITORS and wrote her name down on a clipboard.

After a terrifying check-in and pat-down process, during which Ava was pretty sure the female officer gave her an extra squeeze or two while no one was looking, she sat in the visitors' room. The concrete floor was mottled and stained by mysterious substances, and the cold metal tables and chairs were bolted to the floor. The air had a sharp tang to it, as if urine and toxic cleaning fluids had melded together to create a new brand of oxygen. Ava's nose burned. The thought of Alex alone in this place sent a pang through her.

A heavy metal door creaked open at the back of the room, and Ava reflexively jumped to her feet. A linebacker-sized guard lumbered through first, then stepped to the side, revealing a pale, exhausted, and handcuffed Alex. Ava's heart leaped into her throat, and she choked back a sob.

Alex raised his head and looked up at her. His gaze was so intense, so desperate, and so sad. He seemed heartbroken. Ava resisted the urge to run over and wrap her arms around him.

"Alex—" she started.

"I'm sorry," he said at the same time. "Ava, I'm so sorry. I never meant for any of this to happen. I didn't mean to get you in trouble. I know you didn't do this—any of it." He held his breath, trying to stem the tide of emotion. Ava suspected he was trying hard not to cry. Alex was the emotional one in their relationship: God, he'd cried during *Toy Story 3*. That memory made *her* want to cry, suddenly, but she held it together.

"You didn't do it, right?" she whispered.

Alex shook his head fiercely. "Of course not. I would never—Ava, I could never *kill* someone. You know me better than that."

Ava nodded. "I know. I just needed to hear you say it." She plopped down into the hard seat. "But why did you go over there? Why did you *text* Granger? And what happened at your old school?"

Alex sat across from her and leaned over the table toward her before continuing. "Well, I'll start with the easiest one. I texted Granger, *Don't touch my girlfriend again or I'll kill you* because you told me he'd hit on you, and then the police didn't even *believe* you." He lowered his eyes. "I'm sorry. It was stupid. I just . . . felt so, helpless, you know?"

Yeah, Ava thought. *I do know.*

"I'm sorry I never told you about what happened at my old school," he went on. "I couldn't, really. But I beat up that guy because he *raped* my ex-girlfriend."

Ava gasped.

"She came to me right after it happened," he went on, "and she begged me not to tell anyone. Her parents were crazy, and they would have flipped out if they found out she wasn't . . . anyway. I didn't tell anyone. But I couldn't just let it go, either. I wasn't going to tell anyone her secret, but that asshole deserved to *pay* for what he'd done. I mean, I *saw* the bruises on her." He shook his head and closed his eyes at the memory.

Ava exhaled slowly. She wanted so badly to believe him, and she could definitely identify with how he wanted to take matters into his own hands with the guy who'd hurt his ex—she and the others had done that with Nolan, after all. But she realized she was still really angry, too. "Okay. But why did you tell the cops you saw me that night?"

"Because I *did* see you." Alex looked away. "And you weren't exactly . . . clothed. I was pissed."

Ava glared at him. "So you assumed the worst, without asking me?"

He held up his palms. "No, I didn't call them until later. I'll explain. But Ava . . . what *were* you doing there?"

Ava exhaled and steeled herself. "It wasn't how it looked," she began, her voice quavering.

"So explain to me what it *was*."

Her heart was pounding hard. She needed to come clean, she realized. It was the only way they could ever rebuild the trust they'd once had. But could she do that? She looked at him. "Alright," she said quietly. "I'm going to tell you. But you're not going to like it."

Alex nodded, but a nervous look washed across his face. "Okay."

"You remember what Nolan did to me sophomore year? The rumors he started about me sleeping with teachers to get higher grades?" she said, and Alex nodded again. "Well, I wasn't the only victim of his bullying, not by a long shot. Some of the other girls and I got to talking in film studies, that day we watched *And Then There Were None*."

Ava gained confidence as she spoke, emboldened by the sense of sheer relief she felt just saying the words out loud.

She told Alex about the prank they'd played on Nolan, and how someone had used that opportunity to kill him. About how they suddenly looked guilty—really, really guilty—in Nolan's death. She told Alex how Granger had hit on her when she went to his house for help with her paper. Alex grimaced and shut his eyes for that part.

Then she told him about the pictures and texts she'd found on Granger's phone—and how Nolan had been blackmailing him. "Wow," Alex said, a little shocked. "Those two deserved each other."

"Totally," Ava said. She explained how they'd gone to Granger's house to dig around for evidence they could use against him, but he'd come home before they could get out. Finally, her cheeks burning, Ava described how, in an effort to save her friends, she sacrificed her last shred of dignity and fooled Granger into thinking she wanted to sleep with him. When she sent him to take a shower, they had all slipped out—though Ava had raced into the backyard and dug up the flash drive with proof of Nolan's blackmailing, which Granger had buried. Then she had run to join the others in the car. Which was exactly when Alex saw her sprinting across the lawn, her dress still half-unbuttoned.

"I feel sick just telling you all this," Ava said, her voice catching. "I hate myself for putting this whole thing in motion in the first place."

Alex shook his head. "I wish you'd told me about the

prank, but I get why you did it. Nolan was really shitty to you. And Ava." He looked her in the eye. "None of the rest of this is your fault."

Ava's lips parted. "Thanks," she whispered. It was amazing how calmly Alex was taking all this. She'd expected much worse.

"So, all of you were in there," Alex said. "And *all* of you left?"

"Yes," Ava nodded. "Why?"

"Well," Alex said slowly. "I saw you leave. But then I saw someone run *back* across the lawn to Granger's afterward." He looked apologetic. "I thought it was you again."

Ava frowned. "I went right home. And took a long, hot shower."

Alex ran a hand through his curly hair and shot her a sheepish look. "*That's* why my prints were on Granger's door. I ran over there when I thought you went back in." He shifted on the metal bench. Ava noticed for the first time how his orange prison shirt hung loosely off him. "I wanted to catch you, but the door was locked. Then I heard a scream—I thought it was *you* screaming, and I was so scared. I thought maybe he'd"—Alex choked up, then regained control of his voice—"I was afraid he'd done something. To you. *That's* when I called the police. I told them I'd seen you go inside and that there were screams. But when the cops showed up, Granger was dead, and whoever was *really* in there was gone."

Ava stared at him, her heart pounding hard. "And you didn't see who it was?"

"Nope." Alex looked frustrated. "She slipped out without me seeing."

"You're sure it was a girl, though?"

"Definitely. She had on a hood, or maybe a hat. But she was built like a girl, I'm sure of it. I—I thought maybe you had gotten a sweatshirt and gone back in."

Ava ran her hand across her forehead, trying to process what he'd told her. "Didn't you tell the police this?"

He stared at the table. "Of course I did. But they don't believe me. They think I made up the other girl to cover myself for the murder."

"But what about the prints on the kitchen knife? Yours aren't there, right?"

He shrugged. "Apparently there are *no* prints on the knife. Whoever did it was wearing gloves."

"Oh my god," Ava whispered. She leaned back, feeling sick. Things were even more messed up than before. She had no idea how to feel.

Alex leaned forward and took both of Ava's hands in his. The guard cleared his throat pointedly, and Alex sat back again. "I'm so sorry, Ava. I should have trusted you. I shouldn't have kept any of this from you."

"I shouldn't have kept any secrets from *you*, either." Ava studied his deep brown eyes, smooth skin, and perfect features for a moment. She had missed him so much, it was physically painful. "And I forgive you," she whispered.

Alex gave her a bittersweet smile. "I forgive *you*," he whispered back. "And for now, that's all that matters."

They held each other's gaze for a long moment. There were so many things Ava wished she could undo, but for right now, she was just happy to have Alex back. But she didn't *really* have him back: He was still in prison. And until she figured out who had really killed Granger, there he'd stay.

CHAPTER SEVENTEEN

JULIE SAT ATOP THE LIFEGUARD stand, twirling her whistle. She was at the Beacon Rec Center, where she worked, watching a pool full of kids below. Suddenly, a little girl in a pink tankini looked up at her and pointed. "Cat lady!" she cried.

Julie flinched. How did that little girl know about her?

"Cat lady!" a boy joined in, climbing out of the pool and standing at the bottom of the lifeguard chair. "Dirty, dirty cat lady!"

All at once, the whole pool was in an uproar. Everyone was laughing, from all of the kids to the people swimming laps to the other lifeguards patrolling the space. When Julie looked down at herself, she wasn't wearing her Juicy tee and Adidas shorts but a nightgown seemingly made of cat hair. And what was she *doing* here, anyway? Hadn't she vowed not to leave the house ever again, even begging off sick from work? And when she looked across the pool, a girl stood there, her mouth open in a loud, mean laugh. It was Ashley. She was rounding up the kids, pointing at Julie. "There's the cat lady!" Ashley taunted. "Go get her!"

"No!" Julie screamed. She looked around for Parker, whom she understood, inherently, must be close by. "Parker, *help!*"

Just as the kids ran for Julie, she woke up, shooting up straight in her car. She looked around. It was Tuesday, late afternoon.

Her phone, which was somehow clutched in her hand, was ringing. She stared at it, still disoriented. The dream felt way too real. She hated when that happened.

The phone bleated again. It was a local number, one that Julie had seen before but couldn't place. "Hello?" she mumbled into the phone, her head still fuzzy.

"Ms. Redding?" a stern voice intoned.

She blinked hard. The voice was familiar, but her brain was too muddled to know why. "Yes?"

"This is Detective Peters. I understand you were not in school today."

"That's right," Julie replied cautiously, growing more awake and wary. Since when did homicide detectives care about truancy?

"Ms. Redding, I'm going to need you to come down to

the station. Your friends are on their way as well. I can send a patrol car over for you if you need me to. I'm assuming you're at home?"

"Uh, thanks. I mean, no, that won't be necessary." She rubbed her eyes with her free hand. "What's this about?" she repeated.

"I'll explain everything when you get here. Which I suggest you do quickly." He paused. "And Julie . . ." His voice had suddenly shifted from professional and firm to dark and threatening.

"Yes?" she asked nervously.

"Don't even think about not coming." He hung up before she could reply.

Thirty-five minutes later, Julie stumbled into the police station in sweatpants, a bulky hoodie, and running shoes. Her hair was twisted into a loose bun piled on top of her head. She had no makeup on, and she couldn't have cared less. What did it matter anyway? All anyone saw when they looked at her was cat hair, like in that dream.

Detective Peters stood in the lobby, scratching his pointy chin, a serious look on his face. He had deep bags under his eyes and fast-food crumbs on his shirt. He looked haggard, like he'd been pulling all-nighters ever since Nolan died.

The other girls huddled together nearby, looking as confused and worried as Julie felt. Julie was relieved to see

Parker there, her hoodie pulled down over her face. She seemed less upset than she had been in the school parking lot the day before, after Ashley had pranked Julie, but Julie could tell from the way she shifted from one foot to the other and clenched her jaw that she was tense. Julie met her friend's eye, and Parker looked back. Julie wondered where Parker had spent last night—she hadn't ever shown up at Julie's. In fact, Julie hadn't spoken to her since the kitty-litter prank outside school. Parker had turned her phone off again. It was beginning to get pretty frustrating.

Then Julie cast her eyes around at the others. *What's going on?* she mouthed, raising her eyebrows. Caitlin shrugged. Mac frowned.

"Now that you're all here," Peters said gruffly, "let's go on back."

He led them through the same maze of desks and cubicles they'd passed through the other day, into the same interrogation room with the same one-way mirror. "Have a seat, ladies."

Parker sat closest to the door, and Julie sat down next to her. Peters dropped into a chair at the opposite end of the table. His scalp was visible through his thinning hair as he flipped through a stuffed manila folder on the table. Then he looked up and slowly moved his gaze around their half circle, studying them one by one.

Finally he spoke. "Alex Cohen has been released from custody."

Ava let out a gasp. "That's wonderful! What happened?"

Peters's expression was blank, a perfect poker face. "What you girls should really be worried about is all the evidence that's pointing at *you*."

Parker's head shot up, and Julie put a cool hand on her wrist to calm her. Caitlin and Mac audibly gulped. Ava's face fell. Julie's heart began a steady beat against her ribs, and her head spun a little. She'd been expecting this, though. Hadn't she?

"After forensics finished their investigation, your involvement in the crime seems clearer than ever," the detective went on. "Your prints are all over that house." He paused for a moment, letting his words sink in. "If you killed Hotchkiss, then maybe Granger was on to you. Then you needed to get rid of *him* so he wouldn't talk." He tapped his pen on the table, clicking and unclicking the button on the end. "Now," the detective finished, "does anyone want to tell me the truth, once and for all? If you talk now, things will be much easier for you. I highly suggest you tell us what you know."

Julie didn't dare look at any of the other girls. She could feel Parker practically vibrating with anger and frustration in the seat next to her. *Don't say anything,* she willed to the other girls. Because what *could* they say? Everything they'd done made them look guilty. She was dying to know if the cops had found the note on the yellow legal pad, the one that described how they'd kill Nolan *and* all those other people. She prayed they hadn't.

Peters turned back toward Julie. Their eyes connected for a moment before he looked down to her hand patting Parker's arm. His expression was quizzical for a moment, then he jotted down a quick note in the folder. After another minute of silence, he breathed out. "All right, ladies. We'll do things the hard way."

He rose from his chair, stepped across the room, and motioned at someone outside the door. A middle-aged woman in thick glasses, a terrible pantsuit, and mid-height heeled loafers stepped in briskly, her lips pressed together, and nodded in the girls' direction.

"This is Dr. Rose," Peters said. "She's a psychological profiler, and she's going to speak to each of you one by one. Then we'll see if your stories match." He looked carefully at all of them. "I know you're putting up a unified front, but you don't know everything about one another. And trust is a tricky thing."

Ava frowned. "What are you implying? That one of us did it and isn't telling the others?"

Peters shrugged his shoulders and grinned. "You said it, not me."

He turned to leave the room. Just before he reached

the door, he spun back around and looked straight at Julie. "We'll start with you," he said matter-of-factly, with a nod to Dr. Rose. Then he pulled the door shut firmly behind him.

Julie could feel the other girls' eyes on her, but she said nothing. She clutched Parker's arm and stared at the table.

"Julie Redding, right?" Dr. Rose said crisply, fixing her steady gaze on Julie. Her eyes looked huge behind her glasses, like she was holding a magnifying glass up to her face. "Let's go into my office. The rest of you, I'll call to schedule."

Ava's hand shot up. "Will our parents know about this?"

"Yes, after the interviews we'll have to tell them," Dr. Rose said. "Now, Ms. Redding, with me."

Dr. Rose whirled on her heel and headed out the door. Julie swallowed hard and stood, too. She glanced at Parker, and her friend gave her an encouraging nod. "It'll be okay," she whispered. But then Julie glanced at Ava, Caitlin, and Mac. They looked terrified.

Julie turned to Parker. "Meet me outside after?" she whispered. Parker nodded, and the other girls looked at one another worriedly. Julie wondered if she should ask them to meet her, too, but Dr. Rose cleared her throat impatiently before she could.

Julie followed Dr. Rose down a long hallway and into a small, dimly lit office. The room was practically bare except for a handful of framed degrees clinging to the walls, a metal desk with a faux wood veneer top, and two chairs. Julie inhaled, exhaled. *One . . . two . . . three.* She felt calmer immediately. She even managed to smile at the doctor as they sat down on either side of the large desk.

"Alright," Dr. Rose said. "Let's begin."

Julie looked around the office. "Where's the lie detector?"

"I'm sorry?" Dr. Rose asked.

"Aren't you going to give me a lie detector test or something?" Julie waved her hands in the air as she spoke.

"No, Julie. That's not what I'm going to do." Dr. Rose took off her glasses and placed them on the table between them. She looked nicer, almost friendly. "We're just going to talk."

We're just going to talk. For a moment, Julie thought about telling Dr. Rose that she already had a therapist, until she remembered that Fielder was a huge, freaky jerk. "What do you want to know?"

"Well, for starters, tell me a little bit about your life. Your home life, I mean."

It felt like Julie had a pebble lodged in her throat. Why on earth would the woman want to know *that?* She cycled through a series of lies, but then realized they would probably get her nowhere. Dr. Rose surely knew everything, anyway. And if Julie *did* lie, she would be seen as unreliable—most likely a killer.

"Uh, my mom and I moved here from California a few years ago," Julie started. "My mom is . . . um . . . she has some . . . issues."

Dr. Rose nodded and pulled out a white spiral-bound notepad. "And those have been hard for you, haven't they?"

Julie winced. So Dr. Rose *did* know. But there was something so kind about her voice. So soothing. Suddenly, a dam broke loose in Julie's chest, and she couldn't get the words out fast enough. "She's a hoarder. A serious, like, diagnosable hoarder. Our house is filthy, and I think there must be twenty-six or twenty-seven cats living there. And my mom—she's just . . . really messed up. And she hates me. She makes me feel like I'm the cause."

Dr. Rose nodded, listening closely. "And how does all of that make you feel?"

Julie considered that for a moment. "Ashamed. Embarrassed. I didn't want anyone in Beacon Heights to know, because when people found out in California, they were—" Julie shuddered. "God, they were so cruel. I was just a kid, you know? They called me such mean things, and no one stopped them. Not the teachers, not their parents. It was . . . it was awful."

"And you were afraid that would happen again here, weren't you?"

"Yes. So I tried to prevent it this time."

"How did you do that?"

She took a breath. "I kept my home world and the outside world totally separate—I lived two lives at once. I never invited anyone to my house—ever. Except for Parker, she knew."

"Parker Duvall?"

"Uh-huh." Julie cleared her throat. "I told Parker my secret. And from then on, she was welcome. But no one else was—I couldn't risk anyone else knowing the truth."

Dr. Rose made a note on the pad. "Go on."

Julie tried to peek to see what Rose had written, but the pad was out of view. "So, um, I never dated much, because I couldn't bring anyone over. And it worked, for a long time. No one knows—at least no one knew, until the other day." Her eyes welled up.

Dr. Rose made a few more notes. "What happened the other day?"

Julie let out a sad chuckle. "Ashley Ferguson. That's what happened the other day."

"Who is Ashley?"

"She's this girl at school who, kind of, worshipped me, I guess. She dressed like me, she dyed her hair like mine. She followed me around . . . it was really weird."

"Sounds like she really looked up to you. Isn't that flattering on some level?"

Julie shrugged. "I guess, maybe at first. But it was really too much. I mean, she showed up in the bathroom of a restaurant when I was on a date, stole a lipstick right out of my purse."

Dr. Rose scribbled furiously. Julie was tempted to lean over and see what was important enough to jot down, but she resisted the urge.

"The other day, she sent out an email to the entire school telling them about—" It was still hard to say the words out loud. "About my mom. And my house. And me. So now everyone knows."

"And what is that like for you?"

"It's awful. I can't even go to school. Well, I tried yesterday, but that b—I mean, Ashley filled my locker with cat litter. She's like the new Nolan." As soon as she said his name, Julie regretted it.

Sure enough, Dr. Rose's eyebrows shot straight up. "Nolan Hotchkiss?"

Julie swallowed hard, her heart rate picking up. *One . . . two . . . three . . .* "Yes."

"Are you saying Nolan did things to you, just like Ashley?"

Julie looked away, studying the frames on the wall. *Letitia W. Rose, PhD, University of Washington.* "No, he did things to Parker. I hated him for what he did." Julie's voice cracked, and her throat burned with anger. "But I didn't *kill* him."

"Tell me what Nolan did to Parker, Julie."

Julie sighed. She'd repeated this story to the police so many times already, and it never got any easier to tell. "The night her dad . . . attacked her, she was at a party at Nolan's house. She called me, and she was slurring and sounded really messed up. But she also sounded freaked-out, like she was out of control."

"What did she say?"

"She said, 'I think he slipped me some Oxy.'" Julie paused. "She was talking about Nolan—they were really good friends. The thing was, Nolan knew that her dad was . . . nasty. Parker's dad beat her all the time—nothing she ever did was good enough. Drugs were the things that made him the angriest. He threatened to kill her if he ever caught her on them." Julie took a breath. "Parker thought Nolan did it on purpose, like he thought it would be funny if her dad beat her up." She clenched her hands into fists. "I told her I'd come get her and take her home. She was so messed up when I got to Nolan's. She begged me to let her come to my house so her dad wouldn't see her like that, but, well . . . I hadn't told her about my . . . situation. I was afraid to let her come over. Parker and I were best friends, but she was *so* popular. I was afraid she'd drop me if she knew." Tears suddenly spilled down her cheeks as she relived the memory. Parker had begged and begged, and she'd made up a lame excuse about how her mom was throwing a party and didn't want guests. "It'll be fine," she'd told Parker, as she drove Parker home despite Parker's drugged-out protests. *God*, Julie was an asshole.

"So you took her back to her house instead," Dr. Rose finished for her.

Julie nodded. She took a breath and found the strength to finish the story. "That was the night her dad . . ." She faltered and shut her eyes, wishing she could push away the memories that flooded her: of the months Parker had spent in the hospital, stitches crisscrossing her face, neck, and arms; of Parker's broken bones and swollen limbs; of Parker learning to walk again. Julie could have prevented all that if she had just been brave enough.

"She's my best friend, and I let it happen to her." Julie shook her head and pounded her fists into her thighs. "It was because of me," she whispered, her voice filled with rage and self-loathing. "I was so selfish. All I cared about was my reputation."

"You didn't know what would happen, Julie. What Parker's father did to her—that is on him. Not you."

"That's nice of you to say," Julie said. "But is it really true? It's amazing that Parker forgave me. She should hate me." She felt her face crumple. These were things she'd never said out loud—not to another therapist, and not to Parker. *Maybe you shouldn't have forgiven me. I'm worthless, after all. I did this to you. It's my fault.*

The doctor was silent for a moment, but her gaze was

on Julie's face. She looked like she was thinking hard about something. "So you feel Parker has forgiven you, Julie?"

Julie shot her an astonished look. "Well, sure. I mean, why else would she still be my friend? And I'll never let anything bad happen to her again. I would *die* first."

"I understand." Dr. Rose gave Julie a warm smile, like she really did understand. Then she sat back. "So did you or did you not kill Lucas Granger?"

Julie flinched, surprised at the swift turn in the conversation. "Of course not."

"And Nolan? You hated him, but that wasn't you either?"

"No way." Julie picked at a loose thread on her sweatpants. "I'm not capable of murder."

Dr. Rose nodded. "No, I don't think you are. But what about your friends?"

Julie blinked. "What *about* them?"

"Do you think *they* are capable?"

Julie stared, trying to gauge what Dr. Rose was getting at. Did she think one of the others had? Ava? *Parker?* Julie couldn't bear the idea of Parker being questioned. "Of course not," she said hoarsely. "None of them." But the way Dr. Rose was looking at her, she started to wonder. Was there something she and the police knew that Julie didn't? She tried to remember everything about the night Granger died. Just because she hadn't gone back to Granger's house didn't mean the others hadn't. But that was crazy, right? She couldn't start distrusting them now.

"Okay." Dr. Rose stood. "Well, this has been very helpful. I may have further questions for you, so please keep your phone close by." She stood up and opened the door, holding out her arm to let Julie know she was free to go. "Thank you for your time, Julie."

Julie stood up slowly, totally nonplussed. She grabbed her purse and stepped past the doctor. "Bye."

She scurried down the hall and into the lobby, expecting to find Parker waiting for her, but she wasn't there. Frustrated, she stepped into the late afternoon sunlight. Parker was nowhere to be seen. Julie pulled her phone from her pocket and dialed Parker's number. Straight to voice mail. For a brief, paranoid second, Julie was afraid Parker had heard everything she'd said about her to Dr. Rose, including how much Julie blamed herself, and suddenly decided that *she* blamed Julie, too—and took off.

She rubbed her eyes, then headed over to her car. For a moment she sat in the seat, not sure what to do. There was no way she could go home. She didn't want to talk to anyone, either. So she turned the ignition, pulled out of the parking space, and just . . . drove, around little neighborhoods, through downtown Beacon, even by the water. She really, really needed to decompress.

But the drive wasn't proving to be very therapeutic, and

after circumnavigating Beacon, she was still jittery and anxious. When she glanced at the phone lying on the passenger seat, she noticed that the screen was lit up with Instagram alerts—dozens of them. She tapped on the app, and when *@ashleyferg has tagged you in a photo* popped up, her stomach swooped.

Slowly, she tapped on Instagram. It was another photo of Julie's house, but this time, a Department of Health Services van sat out front. So did a vehicle with the words BEACON ANIMAL RESCUE printed on the sides. The shot showed officials and workers standing on the porch or hauling cat carriers out of the house. Julie's mother stood in the yard, her mouth an angry triangle, her hair askew, her face more insane-looking than ever.

Julie gawked. When had this happened? *Today?* Then she looked at the caption.

Julie Redding, queen of the felines no longer! #nofilter.

Julie dropped onto the bench behind her. "Oh my god," she whispered. Ashley had called Animal Control on them. This was going to be a nightmare. Those cats were all her mom cared about . . . and now they were going to be taken away. It meant Mrs. Redding would focus all her attention on Julie. All her wrath.

Just when she thought her life couldn't get any worse. That *bitch*.

For some reason, the word echoed in her mind. She

suddenly heard Parker saying it yesterday: *That bitch is going down*, with that horrible look on her face. She looked again at the Instagram post. Ashley had put it up almost an hour ago. Had Parker seen it yet? *That bitch is going down. I am going to get her.* And even when Julie said they couldn't do that, Parker had said, *I wish we could. I wish, just once, we could.*

Oh, god. Suddenly Julie wondered if she knew exactly where Parker was right then. Was she getting *revenge?*

Julie tapped at her phone, pulling up Ashley's number. No one picked up. She quickly logged on to the Beacon High student site and found Ashley's home address. She ran to her car and sped out of the parking lot, only forcing herself to slow down so she wouldn't get pulled over. She dialed Parker again and again. Still no answer. "Parker, where *are* you?" she cried. "Look, I hope you're not freaking out over that Instagram. Because I'm not. I'm fine. Okay?"

She took a right, then a left, then another left. A steady monologue drummed in her head. *Parker probably isn't with Ashley. That doesn't even make any sense—she's not the same girl as before, the girl who got in people's faces and shook things up. You're being crazy.*

Julie slammed her car door shut and ran up Ashley's driveway. The front door was wide open. As she dashed through it, Julie heard a scream.

Adrenaline pumping through her body, she followed the sound upstairs, down the hall, and into a bedroom. Ashley's room had the exact same bedspread that Julie's had, but in the queen version—Julie didn't even stop to think of how Ashley had figured *that* out. She stepped farther into the room and saw steam billowing from the open bathroom door, where the shower was running full blast. She burst into the bathroom and took in the scene. There was a bottle of Aveda rosemary-mint shampoo—the same brand Julie used—lying on the tile. A toothbrush and a cup lay on the floor, too, as well as what looked to be a broken ceramic cow figurine. Had someone knocked them there? The shower curtain had been torn from the rod, but the shower water was still flowing at full blast. Then, Julie looked *into* the tub. And that was when she saw it.

Ashley.

Julie was pretty sure she screamed. Despite being in the tub, Ashley wore a fuzzy pink bathrobe, and she was soaked. Her wet hair dripped halfway down the drain. Her fingers were pruney. Her eyes were closed. There were scratches on her arms, and a bruise forming on her temple.

Julie's mind went into warp speed. She squatted down next to her and pressed her fingers against Ashley's throat, searching for a pulse . . . but there was nothing. She held a hand in front of Ashley's mouth and nose. No breath—not even the faintest rustle.

"Oh my god, oh my god," Julie said, looking around. Had Ashley slipped? But the more she took in the scene, the more it seemed there had been a struggle—there were fingernail marks in the wallpaper, magazines were strewn all over the floor, and, of course, there was the fact that Ashley was lying *in* the tub instead of on the bathmat.

Had Parker done this?

Don't think like that, she told herself, but all Julie could think of was Parker's determined face the other day. *Just say the word,* she'd said. Only, Julie *hadn't* said the word . . . had she? Her thoughts felt muddled suddenly. All she could think of was that crazy dream she'd had, the one where she'd cried out for Parker's help. She'd been holding her phone when she woke up—had she called Parker while sleeping? Then she thought of Ashley's Instagram again. What if Parker had seen it and just . . . snapped? What if Parker had done this for her—killed for her?

And then, with a flash, Julie was back in film studies that day in class. Parker had smiled at the group and said, *Or Ashley Ferguson. I'd like to see her slip and crack her head open while she's in the shower washing her copycat hair.*

No. It couldn't be.

Julie snapped back into the present. If Parker had done this, then her fingerprints were probably all over the room—and now so were Julie's. She couldn't call the police, because she could never do that to Parker. She knew what she needed to do, and she felt a surge of strength from deep within her that was going to let her do it.

Julie took a few steadying breaths, then got up on her knees and scooted forward. She folded Ashley's heavy arms across her chest and straightened out her legs. Then she looked around the room for the tools she'd need. Julie was going to get rid of all the evidence—every drop, every fingerprint. Even the body.

That was what you did for best friends.

CHAPTER EIGHTEEN

ON WEDNESDAY MORNING, MAC PULLED into the school parking lot and grabbed her phone. She'd been thinking about a certain song the whole drive here—a remix of Rossini and Rihanna, her favorite composer and her favorite guilty pleasure music—and she wanted to watch the YouTube clip again. But when she finally found the email that contained the link, she realized why she might have been thinking about that particular song: Blake had sent it a few weeks before, when they were sort of seeing each other. *Thought you'd like this*, he'd written, punctuating the email with an XO.

"Stop!" she said to herself aloud, slamming her hands onto the steering wheel for good measure. She had made up her mind that she wouldn't give Blake another chance, and she had to stick to that. Why was it so freaking hard?

But maybe there were other reasons she was feeling a little shaky this morning. She'd met with Dr. Rose, the psychological profiler, late yesterday afternoon. Twice Mackenzie had to sit on her hands to keep them from shaking, and three times she'd caught herself humming a Dvořák piece, something she did when she was nervous. Dr. Rose had asked a bunch of benign-sounding questions about Mac's self-esteem, her involvement with Nolan (which she'd totally downplayed), whether she'd liked Granger's film studies class, and why she'd felt the need to follow her friends into his house the night he was killed. Mac couldn't even remember what she'd said, she'd been so nervous.

And then, strangely, Dr. Rose had asked her about the other girls. Ava seemed very tightly wound, the doctor commented—did she seem traumatized about her mother's death? Same with Caitlin—she lost her brother, that sort of thing had to make her angry, right? And Julie had her troubled homelife, and Parker, well . . . "Sounds like you're involved with some friends who have some serious baggage," the doctor had concluded. "And you know, people who have . . . *issues*, well, they can act out in other ways."

Mac had stared at her. "You mean by killing people?" she'd asked.

The doctor just blinked. "Of course not," she said. "Unless that's what *you* think."

Mac didn't know what to think. *Should* she suspect the others? In some ways, it made sense: They'd all been right there for that conversation in film studies. And if one of them killed Nolan, of course she would kill Granger to shut him up—and involve the other girls as unwitting accomplices. Caitlin hated Nolan more than any of the rest of them. Or what about Ava? Nolan had started those awful rumors about her, and Granger had *hit* on her. Maybe she had a secret violent side.

But then Mac shook off the thought. These were her *friends*. They weren't killers. Her only hope was that they could get through the interviews without raising more suspicions and questions about their involvement. The last thing she wanted was for Juilliard to find out she was being questioned or for her parents to worry any more than they had to.

Sighing, she got out of the car and started across the parking lot and looked at the other texts on her phone. There was one from Oliver, a simple *Are you okay?* She winced, not knowing how to respond, and decided not to respond at all.

As she made her way toward her locker, Mac noticed small clusters of kids gathering in the hall. They were whispering to one another, then breaking apart to form new groups and whisper some more. The air was filled with an electric charge. What was going on? Then Mac noticed

Alex Cohen at his locker, his head down. Maybe *that* was the reason for all the murmuring—Alex had been accused of murder and spent this week in prison, and now he was back. Even though Mac believed Alex wasn't guilty and was glad, for Ava's sake, that he'd been cleared, she still felt wary of him. He *had* called the cops on them.

She opened her locker and began sorting through her books. Nyssa Frankel opened her locker a few feet away as she exchanged rapid-fire sentences with Hannah Broughton. "She's just gone," Mac heard her whispering. "That's what her mom told the police."

Mac's ears perked up. *Who* was gone? Julie? Mac knew Nyssa and Julie were friends. What if Julie was overwhelmed from talking to Dr. Rose yesterday and just . . . *took off*?

Hannah placed her hands on her hips. "Do you think she was *kidnapped*? I heard her room was, like, totally spotless. Which was really weird—apparently she's a total slob."

Mac set her mouth in a line. Julie definitely wasn't a slob. . . .

Nyssa shut her locker with a loud click. "Do you think she ran away?"

Hanna shook her head firmly. "If Ashley was running away, wouldn't she have at least taken her phone? You know she can't live without it."

Mac's eyes widened. *Ashley?*

She turned away from the girls, pulled out her phone, and called up the local news site. Sure enough, the top story was *Local Teen Missing from Home*. The story explained how Ashley Ferguson's parents had found her missing when they came home from work. Her car was in the driveway and her phone in her room, charging. They'd waited a few hours, thinking she'd just gone for a run, before finally calling the police around 10 PM.

A creeping sense of horror flooded through Mac until her hair practically stood on end. Ashley had been on the list.

Slamming her locker shut, she turned down the hall and saw Caitlin and Ava talking in a huddle in the corner. Mac broke into their circle. "Okay, what the *hell?*" she whispered.

"I guess you heard?" Ava asked, her gaze darting back and forth.

Mac nodded. As she brought her hand to her face, she realized her fingers were shaking. "We shouldn't talk about this here," she said, looking around the busy hall. "There are so many people—"

"But, you guys," Caitlin interrupted, her voice shrill. "What's going *on?*"

Mac picked at a loose string on her sweatshirt cuff. "We shouldn't assume the worst," she said in a low voice. "It could be completely unrelated, okay? Or Ashley could have run away. I mean, we said she'd . . . *you know* . . . in the shower, right? And that isn't what happened. She's just disappeared."

But as they looked at one another, it seemed clear that wasn't what anyone thought. Caitlin started to shake. "This is our fault," she whispered. "*We* said those names. And now everyone's dying."

"Stop." Ava caught her arm. "We really, *really* can't talk about this here."

"Maybe we should just turn ourselves in," Caitlin said frantically, her voice rising. It was clear she had to talk about this right then—there was no waiting. "Before anyone else is killed. Before anything else happens. What do you think?"

"And what good would that do?" Ava hissed. "You really think whoever's doing this will stop once we're in prison?"

"Maybe!" Caitlin cried, her voice turning a few heads.

"*Shh*," Mac warned her, hoping that the passing students assumed they were talking about an upcoming history exam. She leaned closer to the girls. "Do you hear yourself?" she said to Caitlin. "You want to throw your life away for some stupid *conversation* we had? Like we're the first people ever who talk about people we want dead. Come *on*, Caitlin."

"We're the first people whose people we want dead actually *end up dead!*" Caitlin whispered, the blood pumping at her temples.

"Let's think about this logically," Mac said, her voice low. "Maybe we can figure this out ourselves. We should question some of the girls Granger was fooling around with. I mean, they had motive to kill Granger, right?"

Ava nodded. "Alex said he saw a girl go into Granger's house some time that night, after we left. It could have been one of them."

"That covers Granger," Caitlin agreed. "But what about Ashley? Parker's dad? It doesn't make *sense*."

"Is there someone who *does* make sense?" Ava snapped.

Mac couldn't help it—her eyes darted toward Ava suspiciously. She thought about her own conversation with Dr. Rose. It was hard not to have some hypotheses. She barely knew these girls.

Ava stiffened. "*I* didn't hurt Granger," she said defensively, as if reading Mac's mind. "And I didn't do anything to Ashley."

"Neither did I!" Caitlin said quickly. She looked at Mac with sudden mistrust. "Where were *you* yesterday?"

Mac's mouth dropped open. "Why would *I* hurt Ashley?" she asked, astonished. "I don't even know her!"

Ava shrugged. "Why would any of us? Maybe you knew that Ashley overheard our conversation in film studies. Maybe you had to stop her before she broke the news, the same way she spread that rumor about Julie. You have a lot to lose, Mackenzie. You just got into Juilliard. You need to protect your future, don't you?"

"Are you insane?" Mac cried. It was one thing for her to suspect the others, but how could they suspect *her*? She pointed at Ava. "I could just as easily say the same thing about you. And what about your boyfriend? He's got a history of violence!"

Ava's eyes flashed. "There's more to that story than you know. Alex beat up that guy because he *raped* someone."

"Yeah, but Granger hit on you," Caitlin pointed out, barely hearing Ava's explanation. "You make the most sense to want him dead."

"I'm sorry, have we forgotten that Nolan drove your brother to suicide?" Ava hissed, her lips curling. "You make the most sense for *that*. Got any cyanide on you, Caitlin?"

Caitlin's mouth dropped open. "How dare you!" She was about to lunge at Ava, but Mac caught her arm.

"Just hold on a minute!" Mac felt herself snap into a more rational frame of mind. "Everybody take a breath, okay? It's clear that all the stuff the cops said to us is messing with our heads. But does it actually make sense?" Then she looked around. Ava and Caitlin were frowning. *They didn't do it*, she told herself. She wanted so badly to believe that.

"What about Julie?" Caitlin said softly. "Does anyone know where she is?"

"I tried to call her this morning, when I heard the news about Ashley." Ava's throat bobbed. "She didn't answer. And I'm sure she's not in school after what Ashley did yesterday."

Mac pulled her bottom lip into her mouth. "Maybe we should ask her where *she* was yesterday, after our meeting at the police station. That's about the time Ashley . . . you know."

Ava widened her eyes. "You're not saying—"

"Of course not," Mac interrupted. "Or . . . I don't know. Ashley *was* ruining her life."

"And did you see that Instagram?" Caitlin whispered. "Ashley called Animal Control on Julie's mom. They took away all the cats. It was on the news."

Ava put her hands on her hips. "You two are awfully quick to point fingers."

"So are *you*," Caitlin snapped.

The bell rang, and they all flinched. Ava slung her Chanel bag over her shoulder. "We'll talk later," she said tightly to Caitlin.

"Unless we're in jail," Caitlin mumbled under her breath.

The two of them didn't even look at Mac, which gave her a pang of regret. She'd screwed up. She shouldn't have let on that she was even considering either of them as a suspect—it had only pulled them apart. They needed to stick together right now, not be fighting in the hallways.

She pushed her glasses up her nose and started down the hall, still fuming. As she turned into the orchestra room, she caught sight of Claire lingering by the bulletin board, reading an announcement about rehearsals. A horrible realization stopped her in her tracks as the film studies conversation rushed back into her mind. First Nolan, then Parker's dad, then Ashley . . .

And then . . . Claire?

CHAPTER NINETEEN

THE REST OF THE SCHOOL day was a blur as Caitlin tried—and failed—to focus on classes and soccer practice. In chemistry, she kept watching the door, sure someone was going to burst in and announce that Ashley Ferguson was dead. At soccer, she kept her phone on her—much to Coach Leah's chagrin—waiting for a call that the police wanted to see her again. Or, even worse, a text that said that someone else on their list was dead. She kept one eye on Ursula Winters, too, wondering if Ursula was behind all this. She *was* in their film studies class. Had she heard their conversation that day? Was that why Ursula was snickering as she took a long pull from her Gatorade bottle? Were those scratches on Ursula's arms from a struggle with Ashley Ferguson in her house?

But *why?*

Caitlin avoided her new friends, too, freaked out by the conversation with Ava and Mac that morning. Not that they wanted to talk to her anyway. When Ava saw her at the end of the hall between fourth and fifth periods, she turned and walked in the opposite direction. When she and Mac were next to each other in the cafeteria line, Mac shifted to the salad line to avoid speaking with her. And on top of everything, Jeremy was also avoiding her. Although maybe she was avoiding him, too. They'd had a few stilted conversations after their botched date on Satuday, but Caitlin could tell he was still upset . . . and maybe she was still upset, too. She'd left him message after message the night of the concert, trying to apologize and reason with him. He was seeing this as so black and white.

On top of all that, her appointment with Dr. Rose was this afternoon. She walked into the police station so on edge that she felt like even her eyelids were trembling. She felt guilty—for *everything*. Which didn't even make sense. Just because she'd been part of a conversation where a bunch of girls named people they wouldn't mind seeing dead—and said enemies then *died*—didn't make her a murderer. It wasn't like her words were magic or they were God. But what *was* happening? Who was doing this?

Could it be one of them?

"Sit down, Caitlin," Dr. Rose said, gesturing to a chair across from her. Caitlin sat stiffly, her hands in her lap.

The clock ticked noisily in the corner. Caitlin stared at the spines on the books in the corner. They were all technical psychological journals that would probably put her to sleep.

"So." Dr. Rose tapped her nails on her clipboard. "I heard a girl went missing at school today."

Caitlin's head whipped up. She hadn't expected Dr. Rose to talk about *that*. "Uh, yeah," she said as casually as she could. "Ashley Ferguson."

"Do you know her?"

Caitlin shook her head. "Not really. She was in a few of my classes, that's all."

"Film studies, right?"

A chill went up Caitlin's spine. What did Dr. Rose know? "Uh, yeah," she said vaguely.

"The man who taught that class recently died, didn't he?"

Her heard pounded fast. "Yeah."

Dr. Rose made a note. Caitlin was almost positive it had something to do with the Granger—breaking into his house—film studies—Ashley connection. *God*, this all looked so bad for her. "So did Ashley ever give you any trouble? I heard she was a bit of a bully."

Caitlin shook her head with an honest no. "I barely knew her."

"But she *was* giving someone trouble, wasn't she? Someone you know?"

Caitlin felt a pull in her chest. "Well, maybe," she said in a small voice.

"You can tell me who it is." Dr. Rose leaned forward. "Everything you tell me here is confidential."

It was weird: At school when they were talking, Caitlin had felt like she couldn't trust the other girls anymore, that it was every man for himself at this point. But now, faced with a cop—well, kind of a cop, anyway—she couldn't bring herself to tell on Julie. It felt like a huge betrayal. Julie was nice and sweet. She didn't deserve the way Ashley had treated her, and she couldn't be capable of murder.

"Ashley sent that email to the whole school about Julie's mom being a hoarder, didn't she?" Dr. Rose said smoothly.

Caitlin blinked. So Dr. Rose already knew. "Something like that."

"Then she put kitty litter in Julie's locker, and she posted a picture on Instagram. Is that right?"

Caitlin lowered her eyes. The cops were checking *Instagram* now?

"Did Julie seem upset by what Ashley was doing to her?" Dr. Rose asked.

Something in Caitlin broke loose. "Of course she did," she blurted. "Anyone would be. Ashley was so, *so* mean—and Julie had done nothing to deserve it. Julie's a good person. She would never hurt anybody, not even a bully."

"There was a situation in your life where someone you loved was bullied, right?"

Caitlin froze. "Well, yes," she said in a muffled voice. "My brother, Taylor. Nolan Hotchkiss picked on him. And then he killed himself."

"So you're a little sensitive about bullies, aren't you?"

She shrugged. "I guess."

Dr. Rose wrote something on her notepad. Caitlin wished she could see what it was. Did it say Caitlin had extra motive to hurt Nolan?

"I didn't do anything," she said suddenly.

"I'm not saying you did," Dr. Rose replied pleasantly.

Afterward, in her car, Caitlin almost ran two red lights and crashed into an oncoming school bus, she was so distracted. It was so hard to read what Dr. Rose had thought of her. Did she suspect Caitlin now? Did she suspect Julie? Or was she just good at asking annoying questions?

She drove without knowing where she was going, finding herself at Jeremy's house even though she hadn't called to say she was coming. She stopped at the curb, grabbed her keys, and let herself in—something she'd been doing for years. This was the first time she'd done it for Jeremy, though, not Josh, and that felt a little weird.

She found Jeremy in the den, watching a black-and-white zombie movie that she vaguely remembered Taylor watching once. The memory made her smile a little. "Hey," she said quietly.

Jeremy didn't look up. "Hey."

Caitlin's stomach swooped. She needed him now. *Badly*. She walked over and sat next to him, trying to lean into his side, but his shoulder was stiff. Finally he put a hand on her knee, gave it a squeeze, then took it off again. At least it was something . . . but it wasn't enough.

"How was your day?" she asked, turning to look at him. But he kept his eyes on the screen, where a zombie was tearing into a cow.

"Pretty good."

No question about how *her* day was. No details about the zombie movie they were watching. No comment even about the freaking *weather*—she'd take anything at this point.

"So you're still mad at me?" she finally asked.

Jeremy looked down at the floor for a moment. "I'm trying. I really am. It might just take me a little while longer to get past it."

"Okay." At least he was being honest about his feelings. She took his hand. "Well, will you let me know when you're totally past it so we can make out again?"

Jeremy couldn't help but chuckle. "Okay."

Before Caitlin could say anything else, she heard an awkward clomping and shuffling sound, and Josh appeared in the doorway. His face was red from exertion, and he leaned heavily on his crutches. His left foot and lower leg were completely swallowed up by an enormous cast. Only his toes peeked out. When he saw Caitlin and Jeremy, his face clouded a little. Caitlin felt Jeremy's body tense up next to her on the couch.

Caitlin dropped Jeremy's hand and shifted forward. "That thing's massive," she said, pointing at the cast. She couldn't just pretend Josh wasn't here.

"Yeah." Josh started clomping toward the laundry room.

"How bad is your break?" she asked.

He paused in front of the TV. "Pretty bad. I may not be able to start next year."

Caitlin widened her eyes. "Holy crap. I'm sorry." Once again, she couldn't help but think it had been *her* fault.

Josh just shrugged. "I mean, what can I do? I'll hit physical therapy hard. I'll try my best, but if I can't start, I can't start. The UDub coach has promised I'll still have the scholarship."

Caitlin was stunned by his calm demeanor. She would have guessed Josh would be a hostile mess. If he was in a bad mood, he usually went outside and kicked the ball around for a while. He never seemed as relaxed or happy as he did after a long practice. But here he was, totally sidelined—with even his college career in jeopardy—and he seemed . . . okay.

"Uh, can you move?" Jeremy broke the silence. "I can't see."

Josh looked at his brother for a beat, then shrugged and passed by, making his slow, painful progress across the room again. Caitlin watched him recede, noting that he hadn't said anything nasty to Jeremy about his choice in movies, or made Caitlin feel awkward at all for being here with his brother. When had Josh become so mature? Had breaking up with her done that?

Then she turned and looked at Jeremy, surprised at his nastiness. Jeremy met her gaze for a moment, his eyes narrowed, his features sharp and on alert. He looked like he was about to defend himself . . . or maybe bite her head off. On instinct, Caitlin flashed him a reassuring smile. *I'm with you*, she hoped her look told him as she pushed thoughts of Josh out of her head. *There's no need to be jealous.*

It seemed to defuse the tension. Jeremy's face relaxed into an almost sheepish expression. "Uh, thanks!" he yelled toward Josh, and though it was totally fake, Caitlin appreciated the effort.

"So, where were we?" she asked teasingly, sliding closer to him. "Oh, that's right—we were scheduling our next make-out session."

Jeremy put his arm around her. Still mystified by the confused thoughts she'd had about Josh, Caitlin leaned into Jeremy and felt his body soften as she curled into him, pressing close together, forming a perfect curve.

CHAPTER TWENTY

PARKER SHOT UP STRAIGHT. WHERE was she? She knew she'd been sleeping—and it felt like it had been for a long time. She looked around, taking in the familiar sights. A square room with a makeshift window. A musty smell in the air. Outside, she caught a glimpse of the side of a white stuccoed house far in the distance. Wait a minute. She *knew* that house.

She jumped up, quickly pulling up her hoodie and locating her kicked-off shoes across the space. She was in the woods behind Nolan Hotchkiss's house. Long ago, someone had built a hunting cabin here. No one used it anymore but, for whatever reason, it had never been torn down. Parker and Nolan hung out there a lot when they were friends—they used to call it their clubhouse—and when things were really shitty at home, she sometimes crashed here. She'd brought Julie here a few times, too, though Julie said the place freaked her out.

"Jesus Christ," she said aloud. What had possessed her to come *here*? Was she insane? They were already suspects in Nolan's murder—the last thing she needed to do was get caught skulking around near his property. She'd really lost it.

When she pushed out the door, the woods were quiet. She walked toward his house and through his backyard. Police tape no longer surrounded the property; it was back to looking perfect and pristine, as though no crime had ever happened. Heart pounding, Parker padded across the dewy grass, toward the bus stop a few avenues over. She didn't see anyone on the way, no 6 AM runners or dads walking dogs. Had she honestly gotten away with sleeping here?

But it didn't surprise her, in a way. As usual, it felt like she wasn't even there.

That afternoon, Parker pushed open the heavy door to CoffeeWorks, the hole-in-the-wall coffee shop she'd been frequenting lately. It wasn't Café Mud, the steel-and-reclaimed-wood mother ship of cool where most Beacon High students hung out during free periods. But the dim lighting and strong coffee was exactly what Parker needed right now. Something rattled against her cheeks, and she put up her hands to see what it was. *Julie's earrings.* The silver wire chandeliers with the pretty beads. She'd forgotten she'd borrowed them. She was forgetting more and more every day. In fact, when had she last *spoken* to Julie? She vaguely remembered sitting on a bluff all alone last night, drinking from a six-pack of beer, talking to Julie on the phone. Julie had been in one of her hysterical moods. Julie had started by saying something about how Mac had stopped by and had told Julie all these terrible things about Claire—apparently she'd practically annihilated Mac's chances at Juilliard. Then Julie had moved on to Parker. She'd asked where Parker was and when was she coming back to Julie's. She'd badgered Parker, telling Parker it felt like she was keeping secrets. *You can tell me,* Julie had urged. *You need to tell me.* But Parker had groaned, rolling her eyes. *I'm not keeping* secrets, she'd said. But, in fact, she was keeping one big secret: She had started seeing Fielder again.

As Julie continued to pester her, Parker had felt crowded, and then things had devolved into a fight again . . . and Parker couldn't remember the rest of the call.

Which is probably why she'd woken up where she did that morning.

Parker rubbed her face with her hands, feeling the nubby scars under her palms. She really needed to get it together. She needed to talk more to Elliot—er, Fielder—about focusing. Maybe he could give her more visualization techniques. She shut her eyes and tried to hear his calming voice. It immediately soothed her. The sessions she'd had with him so far must be working.

Then she took stock of the room. The espresso machine whirred and chugged, a barista banged wet grounds into the garbage, and the door opened and closed behind her, sending a cool draft of air washing over her legs.

"Can I help the next customer?" the pierced and tatted gender-neutral cashier called out.

Parker stepped up to the counter and ordered a triple latte. Just as she dumped a few bucks on the counter, she heard a familiar voice behind her.

"So this is where you come instead of school, huh?"

Parker spun around. It was Ava, her long silken hair framing her face, her almond eyes perfectly outlined with plum liner. Her tone was friendly, and she was smiling.

"Hey," Parker said. She shrugged sheepishly, realizing that it was after noon—and she *wasn't* in school. Then again, neither was Ava. "You playing hooky, too?"

"Oh, I just needed some caffeine. I'll probably go back for seventh period." Ava gestured to a table near the window. "Want to sit?"

Parker shrugged. "Okay."

They got their drinks and went to a table in the back, near an old-timey Pac-Man arcade that Parker had always thought was a nice touch. Ava stared into her cappuccino. Parker realized she'd never actually spoken to Ava—or any of the others—without Julie there. She wondered how Ava thought of her. As a Julie hanger-on? A freak, after all that stuff with her dad?

Stop shortchanging yourself, Fielder had told her in their last session. *People don't automatically look at you and see a freak. Smile every once in a while. You'll be surprised who smiles back.* Okay, it was a little Walt Disney–It's-a-Small-World happy, but maybe she should try it.

She smiled carefully at Ava. "How are you holding up?"

And just like that, like Fielder said, Ava gave her a smile in return. "Okay, I guess. But I'm freaked out because of the cops. Aren't you?"

"Yeah, totally." Parker stirred sugar into her latte with a splintering wooden stick. "It's pretty scary." Scary couldn't even begin to describe it.

The police will figure out the real truth, don't worry, Fielder had said to her, when she'd blurted it out to him in a session yesterday—after which he'd gotten her coffee, saying that caffeine might help her headaches. Parker hoped he was right, about the caffeine and the police. She hated that they were suspects again.

"How are you feeling about Ashley?"

Parker cupped her hands around her cup of coffee. "You mean the cat litter and the Instagram? Not great, honestly."

An image of her friend's pained and humiliated face in the hallway the other day flashed through Parker's mind. And Parker couldn't fathom what Julie's homelife must be like right now without those cats as a buffer. Maybe *that* was why she'd stayed away from Julie's the past two days.

Ava frowned. A tiny wrinkle formed between her eyes. "No . . . I mean that Ashley's been missing since Tuesday."

Parker froze, her mind shifting gears. "She's *what?*"

"Her parents can't find her. The police are looking everywhere." Ava's expression was strange. "You haven't heard?"

Parker felt her lips start to tremble. Something prodded at her memory, but she couldn't quite figure out what. "That's terrible," she said, staring off into the distance. On the other hand, it was wonderful Ashley was gone. She wouldn't torment Julie anymore.

"But we shouldn't worry about it, right?" she said. "I mean, that's where you're going with this, aren't you? Just because we rattled off some names doesn't mean we have any control over them dying or going missing or whatever."

"Maybe," Ava said distantly. She started to tear her napkin into tiny shreds.

Parker swallowed hard. Was Ava worried that someone *was* killing off the people on their list?

"Well, at least Alex is cleared," Parker piped up, changing the subject. "Everything cool with you guys?"

Ava stirred her coffee. "Um, yeah," she answered, still distracted. "I think we're going to be okay."

Parker nodded, happy for Ava. "I'm really glad it worked out. If only getting *him* cleared didn't get us back in trouble."

"Yeah." Ava stared at the floor. Then she peeked at Parker. It looked like she wanted to say something, but then she looked down and clamped her mouth shut.

"What?" Parker asked.

Ava's eyes darted back and forth. Once again she seemed to be mustering up courage, but then the light in her eyes dimmed. "Oh, nothing. Hey, I heard Nyssa Frankel is still having a party on Friday, despite everything."

Parker shrugged. "Nyssa never cancels her parties." Back when they were friends, Parker used to say that Nyssa could be in traction from two broken legs and she'd still hold her annual Halloween celebration. "I probably won't go, though."

"Really?" Ava touched her arm. "Maybe we all should. It would make us seem normal, you know?"

"Maybe," Parker said absently, though she doubted it.

A few droplets of coffee dribbled from Ava's cup onto the table. She wiped them up with a napkin, clearing her throat awkwardly. "I love this place. I came here after our meeting with the cops the other day, actually. I was so freaked, I just wanted the biggest frappé I could buy. That was really stressful, don't you think?"

Parker squinted, trying to recall what she'd done after the police station. She'd blown off Julie, she remembered, not waiting to meet up with her after Julie's interview with the psychological profiler. She'd felt bad about that later—she remembered bringing it up to Fielder yesterday. *Julie probably wanted me to stick around and see how it had gone,* she'd said. *But I just . . . couldn't.* Fielder had asked Parker why, and she'd told him she'd felt compelled to bolt. *Because of something that happened?* Fielder had asked, but Parker said she wasn't sure. *Maybe it was because the idea of someone prying into people's psyches scares you,* Fielder pointed out. *You have trust issues. Am I getting somewhere?*

Parker realized suddenly that Dr. Rose hadn't yet contacted her for her own interview. Then again, that was probably good: She already had a psychologist. She didn't need another one.

She looked up and noticed Ava wasn't listening anymore. She had spotted something by the front door and frozen in her seat. "Uh oh," she whispered.

Parker spun around to see a blond, bedazzled, heavily tanned blur barreling straight for Ava. "What the—" She watched in confusion as a middle-aged woman in a gray silk dress grabbed Ava by her arm. After a beat, Parker recognized her from Ava's house the other day. It was Ava's stepmom.

"I knew I'd find you in this shithole!" the woman spat, smelling heavily like booze and perfume.

"Hi, Leslie," Ava said through clenched teeth. She turned toward Parker. "I'm sure you remember my friend—"

Leslie cut her off. "I come all the way down to school to sign you out so you can help me set up for my mother's arrival tonight, and they can't even *find* you, you ungrateful bitch." Leslie yanked Ava to her feet roughly, pelting her with questions. "Do you skip school often? What do you think your father would think about that? And how dare you not be there for me?"

"I'm sorry," Ava said. She pulled away from Leslie and straightened her clothes. "I—I forgot. And didn't think you wanted me involved." Her voice was strong but guarded. Parker recognized the tone—she'd used the same one with her dad plenty of times. It was her *don't wake the bear* voice. Don't say anything to piss him off. Though, inevitably, Parker always had.

Leslie tossed her head. "Oh, I *don't* want you involved. In fact, it would be best if you were absent the entire weekend. Your father agrees."

Ava gasped. She glanced around the coffeehouse. Patrons were staring. "He would never say that," she whispered.

Leslie tittered. "Just ask him. He'll tell you. He wants

you out of our lives completely, Ava dear. And you know what? All those things you're accused of? He thinks you're guilty."

Ava's eyes flashed. "You're a liar."

Leslie rolled her eyes. "Takes one to know one."

Ava's bottom lip trembled. "I should tell him all the things you say to me. How much you drink. I think he deserves to know the real you—don't you?"

Leslie's mouth dropped open. With frightening speed, her talon-like fingers flicked out and wrapped around Ava's wrist again. "How *dare* you."

Ava winced in pain. Parker stared at Leslie's nails. They were digging so deeply into Ava's skin that little flecks of blood began to appear. All at once, Parker was awash in a flood of similar memories about her father. She felt the cuts in Ava's skin as acutely as if they were on her own arm.

Parker shot to her feet. "Hey," she started, reaching toward Ava to pull her back.

But Leslie had released Ava's arm as though nothing were amiss. She turned to Parker, looking at her for the first time. At first, there was a hint of a sweet smile on her face, but then her eyes narrowed, and her look turned dismissive. She turned back to Ava. "You're following me. *Now*."

With that, she spun on her absurdly high heels and marched back to her car. Tears streaming down her face,

Ava grabbed her purse, leaving her coffee on the table, and with one heartbreaking sob, she headed out the front door, too.

"Ava!" Parker followed fast on her heels. "Ava! Wait!"

But Ava jumped into her car and slammed the door before Parker could get to her. She revved her engine, backed roughly out of her parking space, and was gone.

Parker stood alone in the parking lot. *Poor Ava.* Why hadn't anyone stood up for her? Why hadn't she, just now? A crashing barrage of memories flooded Parker's mind: of her father hitting her, her mother standing by watching. Of the sound of her father's voice when she came home high on Oxy . . . *that* night. Of her mother saying "Oh, Parker, how could you?" as if it were all Parker's fault. Her stomach roiled, and her head continued to spin. Her hands trembled, and her breath came in ragged bursts as she tried, desperately, to get herself under control.

Just as her heart rate began to slow, Parker's phone let out a chipper sound in her pocket. She pulled it out, her grip steadier. *Fielder*, the screen read. Parker stared at it for a moment as the phone continued to vibrate in her hand, then she pressed IGNORE. She wanted to see him—she knew he really cared about her, that right now he might be the *only* person who really cared about her—but she didn't want to talk to him until she got her thoughts straight.

Leaning back on the bench, Parker closed her eyes and

took deep, calming breaths. She smelled the tang of rain on the asphalt, felt the cool air brushing against her skin. *Ava, you're not alone. I'm here for you,* she said silently, sending her thoughts out to Ava on the breeze.

CHAPTER TWENTY-ONE

TEARS LEAKED FROM THE CORNERS of Ava's eyes faster than she could wipe them with her sleeve. She blinked to clear her vision and voice-dialed Alex on her car's Bluetooth. When he picked up, her composure fell apart again. "She's so awful!" she sobbed. "I can't take it anymore!"

"Whoa . . . slow down," Alex said. "Where are you? Are you okay?"

Ava took a few deep, slow breaths, steadying her voice. "I'm fine. It's just—Leslie. She just *attacked* me in public, and now I have to go home and see her again, and this whole weekend is going to be full of family time and it's going to be so terrible." She couldn't imagine what Leslie's mother was going to be like—if she had even a tenth of Leslie's attitude, she'd be unbearable.

Alex groaned. "I'm sorry. She's so freakin' evil."

"Look, I'm sorry to ask you this, but can you meet me at my house? I need a buffer. And I don't feel like I can rely on my dad right now." She winced, thinking of what Leslie had said about him not wanting her around. It wasn't true, was it? He didn't think she was guilty, did he?

"Of course," Alex said. "I'm at work. Be there in fifteen."

"Wait, you're at work?" Ava asked, sniffing. "You shouldn't come over, then." Alex's boss at the ice cream shop had given him his job back as soon as the charges were dropped, but she knew it would take longer for people's trust in Alex to be totally restored. This was not the time for him to be pushing it.

"Are you sure?" Alex asked. "Why don't you go to my house instead? I can bring over double-double caramel fudge later," he offered.

Ava sighed, slowing at a stoplight. "I wish," she said, imagining the scene, hanging out and eating ice cream and being *normal*. "But I should probably face this."

"I'll be there as soon as I can, okay? I'm out of here in . . ." She heard him pull the phone away from his cheek so he could check the time. ". . . ninety minutes. I'll come straight to you. Okay?"

"Okay." Ava was flooded with relief and gratitude. "I love you."

"I love you, too. It's going to be okay. I promise."

They clicked off the call just as Ava pulled into her

driveway. Her heart sank at the sight of Leslie's car, parked at a crazy angle, its front tires on the lawn. How could Ava face her? Then again, what was her alternative?

Just as she put her foot on the bottom step, she heard Leslie's voice in the kitchen, rising and falling in an emphatic tirade. She couldn't make out the words, but she could hear the tone—angry. Ava knew Leslie was telling her father about her, and sure enough, a moment later, she heard her father's low murmur in response. His voice sounded soothing. Maybe he was agreeing with everything she said.

Horrified and definitely not ready to face the music, Ava ran upstairs to her room and slammed her bedroom door. She fell forward onto her bed, misery washing over her. A knock on her door made her jump. To her relief, her father's head peeked inside, not Leslie's.

"Ava?" He sounded unsure.

Ava turned away, facing the wall. "What?" she asked woodenly.

He took a few steps into the room. "We were hoping you could come downstairs and help set up for the party."

Ava said nothing. It was just about the last thing she wanted to do.

"You know I expect you to put on a good face this weekend," her father said. "It would mean a lot to me and Leslie."

"Uh-huh," Ava answered, without intonation.

Then he cleared his throat. "Leslie told me you were mouthing off to her," he added softly. "Is that true?"

Mouthing off. So what was Leslie doing to her? Ava looked down at the rug. As she moved, her father gasped. "Ava," he pleaded, reaching for her arm, where there were still deep red marks where Leslie's nails had dug into Ava's skin. "Where did you get those marks?"

Ava looked at her father, then quickly turned away. She wanted desperately to tell him the truth. But even if she did tell him, Leslie would make up something to get herself off the hook and figure out a way to punish Ava for it later. What was the point?

"It was an accident," she muttered. "Just some dumb thing at school."

Ava's father just looked at her, his eyes wide and sad. "You've become so different," he said. "So . . . *withdrawn.* It's like I don't know you anymore. Leslie is worried about you."

Ava stared at him. Leslie had him so *convinced,* and she was freaking sick of it. Something inside her cracked, like a dam breaking. "I'm not different!" she burst out. "*You're* the one who's changed! You're the one who doesn't spend time with me anymore, or give me the benefit of the doubt, and it's like you've just *forgotten* Mom, and—"

A loud, sickening *thump* cut through Ava's words. Ava and her father jumped off the bed and ran to look out the window—where the sound had come from. Ava gazed out across the yard but saw nothing amiss. Then she looked straight down, and screamed.

Leslie lay limp and still on the grass. Her body had fallen at an awkward angle, her knees pointing one way, her torso the other. Her neck was twisted in a sickeningly unnatural direction.

Ava made a small gurgling sound at the back of her throat. Mr. Jalali pushed around her at the window. When he saw his wife, his face paled. "Dear god," he whispered. His knees buckled, and he clutched the windowsill to keep himself upright. Ava pulled him to his feet, and together they raced downstairs and outside.

The ground was wet with early evening dew. Leslie was in the same crooked position, but up close her face looked lined and haggard, and a thin dribble of chardonnay bubbled at the corner of her mouth. "Oh my dear," Mr. Jalali said, dropping to his knees and throwing himself against her chest. "Oh my sweet, sweet dear."

"Dad, don't touch her!" Ava screamed. "You could hurt her!"

Mr. Jalali backed up, his eyes full of fear. Ava knelt down and put her ear to Leslie's mouth, listening for breath. She heard a faint inhale, then a wheezing exhale. "Call 911," she said shakily. Then she looked up at the house. Above them, the doors of the master bedroom balcony were wide open, as if they'd been flung outward. Had Leslie stepped out for some air? Lost her balance, toppled over?

Ava looked back down at Leslie, who had turned a ghostly shade of gray. Her heart began to pound as she remembered her words about Leslie from that day in film studies. *Maybe she could fall off her balcony after she finishes her nightly bottle of chardonnay.*

Someone had done this.

And then something else gripped her: That same someone might still be in the house right now.

Ava jumped back up and faced the front door. Something moved at the corner of her eye, and she turned. Was that a shadow, creeping toward the backyard? Stumbling forward, Ava rounded the rose bushes at the corner of the house and burst onto the patio, which was half-decorated with elegant tables, place settings, flowers, and candles in elegant silver candlesticks, all for the party. But there was no one there.

Everything was still. Ava sucked in deep, gasping mouthfuls of air, terror and confusion and horror coursing through her. She wanted to tell herself that it *was* an accident—that she hadn't seen anything at all back here.

But she knew, deep down, that this wasn't an accident.

CHAPTER TWENTY-TWO

JULIE SAT ON A SWING in the playground a few blocks from her house. It was attached to a church, but only a few kids ever visited, so she always had the place to herself. She came here when she was feeling especially stressed, or when it felt like the walls in her house were closing in on her—which was, admittedly, quite often. Just sitting and swinging usually calmed her down, especially with the backdrop of the orange-and-purple sunset glittering through the clouds. But not tonight. Maybe not ever again. She felt scattered and horrible. She couldn't stand to be at home—with all the cats gone, her mom had done nothing but wail loudly about how it was all Julie's fault—but she couldn't go anywhere, either. Apparently, Social Services had been notified that there was a minor living in the cat-riddled house, and someone was supposed to come out and interview Julie soon, but that didn't make her feel better, either. So what—they'd send her to *foster care*? That hardly seemed like an improvement.

It felt like the whole *world* was closing in on her. She pulled out her phone and tried Parker one more time, but there was still no answer. Where *was* she? And what had she *done*?

Julie tried to go back to that horrible day on Tuesday, but she just couldn't. All kinds of horrible scenarios of what Parker might have done to Ashley siphoned through her thoughts like water. It was easier to try and block it out as best she could . . . at least until she got hold of Parker and asked her the truth. Then again, did she actually want to know the truth? She was undoubtedly an accessory in her friend's crime—if Parker had even done it. And if she hadn't, well, Julie still was an accessory to someone.

She squeezed her eyes shut as she remembered Ashley's slack limbs and blue lips; the way her head bobbed and fell forward as Julie dragged her heavy body through the woods; the mud that covered Julie's feet after she weighed down the body and rolled Ashley into the river behind her house; the disgusting *thunk* of Ashley hitting the water. And then there was the deep abyss of thoughts that kept rearing their heads, scaring Julie even more: What about all the other awful things that had happened? Nolan, Granger, Parker's father? Parker had hated all of them—could she have been the one behind all those murders? Julie had kept such poor tabs on her friend lately; whole *days* had gone by when she didn't know where Parker was. She had meant to be a better friend, to keep watch on Parker, but her personal life had spun out of control, and she hadn't been able to keep track of both of them.

But she hadn't thought Parker was off doing . . . *this.* Julie shut her eyes, terrified to even think it.

"Julie?"

She looked up sharply, then gasped. Carson stood at the edge of the playground, his arms at his sides. He was staring at her not unkindly, though he looked worried.

She jumped off the swing and grabbed her jacket off the nearby bench. "I have to go," she said abruptly, not meeting his eye.

"Wait!" He followed after her. "I want to talk to you."

Just a few days ago, the sound of his voice had made her heart skip a beat. Now she felt . . . nothing. "I can't see you anymore," she said bluntly.

Carson looked like he'd been slapped. "I don't understand," he said. "What did I do?"

Julie lowered her eyes. At first she'd thought Carson had baited her into going back to school as a favor to Ashley. A crazy thought, but she just didn't know who Ashley had under her thumb. But in one of the many messages Carson had left for Julie over the past few days, he'd somehow sensed she was worried about this and told her it absolutely wasn't true.

She believed him now, but it didn't matter. She couldn't be with him anymore. Carson may have been willing to understand that her mother was a hoarder, but there was no way he'd understand that she was now an accessory to murder. If he found out what she'd witnessed, what she'd *done*, well. He'd want nothing to do with her.

And Julie couldn't afford to be close to anyone except for Parker. She needed to protect her friend at all costs. She'd ruined Parker's life once; she wasn't doing it again. It was just easier this way.

She turned and faced him. "I just have a lot of stuff going on right now. I have to get my head straight. I'm sorry."

"Is it the cats stuff? Animal control? How are you holding up?"

Julie wanted to laugh. She *wished* her life was that simple. "It's not that," she said. "It's . . . complicated."

"I'm here to listen, though," Carson insisted, his voice gentle. "Who else do you have to talk to?"

"I'm fine." Julie shoved her hands in her pockets and walked on. "I have Parker."

Carson followed her. "Actually, Julie, we need to talk about Parker."

Julie whipped around, the blood draining from her face.

What did Carson know? What was he suggesting? "No, we don't," she whispered, and then she started to run.

She careened down the block, her jacket flapping in her hands. The streetlights had come on, and she could barely see, but she didn't want to stop running until she got to her property. At one point, she peeked over her shoulder, relieved that Carson wasn't following her. *We need to talk about Parker.* She should have known better than to ever get involved with Carson. Now he was trying to interfere with her and Parker. She wasn't going to let anyone come between them.

Just as she reached her curb, her phone buzzed again. It was a text from Ava, who'd been trying to reach her a lot lately. *Leslie pushed off balcony,* the text said. *In a coma.*

Julie's stomach swooped, and her knees felt wobbly. *Another person off the list.* This couldn't be happening. Then her heart stopped.

Could this be Parker's work, too?

She frantically dialed Parker for the millionth time. No answer. Spinning off her porch, she fled to her car and threw herself into the driver's seat. She had to go to Ava's now.

Police cars and ambulances swarmed Ava's picturesque suburban street, their lights casting an eerie-colored glow over the manicured lawns. Julie parked far away from Ava's house and cut behind the neighboring houses, across the backyards, drawn forward though she wasn't sure what she was looking for. She reached the thicket of trees on a slight rise above Ava's backyard and looked around, suddenly having a premonition. Parker was here somewhere.

She plunged into the woods. Only a hundred yards in, a familiar figure sat huddled at the base of a towering tree, rocking from side to side. Julie gasped. Parker's hoodie was pulled over her head, and her face was covered in dirt. Her eyes rolled upward. Just the sight of her brought Julie to her knees.

"Parker," Julie whispered as she squatted down. She pushed the hoodie back from Parker's face, but Parker didn't look at her. Julie put a hand on her arm. "Parker?" she whispered.

Parker continued to rock and mutter to herself, as if Julie wasn't even there. Julie leaned closer, panic rising in her chest. "*Parker!*" she cried, gripping Parker by the shoulders.

Parker stopped her movement and went quiet. She looked straight into Julie's eyes, her gaze suddenly lucid. "Julie," she whispered. "Oh my god, Julie." She sounded terrified.

Julie pulled her in and held her tightly. "It's okay, Parker. It's okay. I'm here."

Parker's face screwed up and she let out a loud sob. "I think I've done something awful. I think I've done a *lot* of something awful."

CHAPTER TWENTY-THREE

PARKER HEARD JULIE'S FAMILIAR, COMFORTING voice as if from a million miles away. Then she heard her name again, this time a little louder, a little closer. Parker concentrated on bringing herself to Julie's voice, and finally, she snapped back into place. She felt the damp soil beneath her and heard the rustling leaves on the trees swaying high above their heads. She was in the woods. Behind Ava's house.

Ava's house. Everything else rushed back, too.

Sensory memories flooded through her: her biceps flexing as she pushed Leslie, hard; Leslie's fingernails piercing Parker's skin as she clutched desperately, fighting to regain her balance; the sensation of relief when Leslie released her grip and fell, her mouth forming a frightened and silent oval, over the balcony railing before landing with a resonant *thud* at the bottom. Parker had done it, but it was as if her body had gone through the motions on autopilot or something. She didn't remember *deciding* to do any of that.

And then more memories bombarded her, too. Ashley Ferguson stood in her bathroom, getting ready to take a shower. She spun around as Parker came up from behind her, her arms raised to defend herself, her face twisted in fear but not exactly surprise. Parker felt her wrists strain as she shoved Ashley back, hard, against the tile in the shower. Then she felt the sweep of her leg and the contact of her shin on Ashley's calves as she kicked her feet out from under her. The floor vibrated as Ashley's head cracked against the tile.

And what about the feel of the cool grass against her ankles as she darted back into Granger's house after the others had left? She felt the weight of the knife handle in her hand, and she recalled the look of surprise on his face as she slipped into his room, where he stood in a towel. "What are *you* doing here?" he'd spat.

Then, a flash, and she was sitting in a booth at a diner on the outskirts of town, slipping a thick wad of cash to a grizzled older guy with a hat pulled down low over his face. She'd found him on craigslist. "Please take care of it," she'd said, and he nodded. And then her father had died in the prison yard.

Finally, her thoughts returned to the start of it all—that

party at Nolan's house. . . . She felt the slippery plastic cup in her hand as Julie passed it to her, and she felt her fingers shake as she fumbled for the vial of cyanide in her pocket. She'd shielded her hands and pretended to spit in the cup, as the others had, instead dropping the powder into the warm beer. Then she'd handed the cup to Ava, who took it to Nolan.

She'd done it. She'd done *all* of it. All those memory gaps—her brain was somehow keeping her protected from the truth. And it explained why she'd been steering clear of Julie lately: She couldn't bear to tell her the truth, but she also couldn't hide something like this from Julie for long. Julie knew her better than she knew herself.

A bright flash of a thought entered her mind: She hadn't told anyone *else*, had she? No. Not Fielder. She wouldn't have done that. No matter how many times he bought her coffee, no matter how safe and appreciated he made her feel, she would never have told him that. Because he would have asked *why*—and he would have made Parker answer. Then again, wasn't the answer obvious? Nolan deserved it. So did Ashley. Even Granger. But Leslie? Instantly, the woman's angry face when she confronted Ava in the coffee shop popped into Parker's mind. Leslie had *hit* Ava. Parker sure as hell knew what *that* felt like.

The world spun violently, and she dug her hands into the dirt to steady herself. "I think I've done something awful," she repeated, glancing fearfully at Julie. "I think I've done a *lot* of something awful."

"Parker? *Parker!*" Julie cried. "What do you mean?" Her eyes widened. "You did it, didn't you? All of them? You're just . . . going down the list?"

Parker's head began to throb and fill with explosive noise, but still the answer rang out clearly: "They all deserved it."

Julie made a noise somewhere between a gasp and a sob. "Oh, Parker." She sounded heartbroken. "No, they *didn't.*"

"They did," Parker insisted. She felt so, so sure. "All of them did."

Julie looked crushed, but there was something determined in her face, too. She placed her hands on Parker's shoulders, her expression stern. "You have to promise me something, okay? You *cannot* do this again. From now on, we're going absolutely everywhere together. I'm not letting you out of my sight. I'll go to school with you and go to your classes instead of mine. You stay at my place every night. Where you go, I go."

Parker nodded. She felt too shaky and dizzy to speak.

"The only person left on that list is Claire Coldwell," Julie went on. "We can still save her, Parker. She doesn't deserve anything bad to happen to her."

Parker's eyes narrowed. "What are you *talking* about?" she sputtered. "*You* told me about what Claire did to Mackenzie.

How she'd, like, stolen her boyfriend and basically sabotaged her future—and how Mackenzie had shown up at your house in tears. Claire's a horrible person. As horrible as the rest."

Julie shook her head. "No, she's not, Parker. She's a bitch, sure—but she doesn't deserve to be hurt."

Parker crossed her arms over her chest. "I need to stand up for my friends."

Julie placed her hand over Parker's. "You don't have to do it like this. It has to stop, Parker. Can you stop?"

Parker peered at her friend. Julie seemed really, really upset. Suddenly, the weight of what she'd done crushed down on her. She shut her eyes. Of course Julie was right: Parker was a monster. She'd interpreted a ridiculous conversation in film class literally. But none of them really wanted those people dead.

She gulped, all at once finding it hard to breathe. "I don't know who I am anymore," she said hoarsely.

"It's okay." Julie petted Parker's arm. "I'm going to help you. I promise. But for now, we have to get you out of here. Keep you safe."

Parker swallowed hard, a metallic taste in her mouth. "You want to help me?"

Julie nodded. "Of course. I'm the one who hid Ashley's body for you—I've been helping all along."

Parker blinked. *Ashley's body.* Had she really just left Ashley dead on the floor? "You knew I was there?"

"I guessed you'd been there," Julie explained. "I cleaned everything up, wiped down all the fingerprints. They'll never know it was you." Then she looked toward Ava's property. "But as for this, let's hope you didn't leave prints. And for Granger and Nolan and your dad . . . well, I'll do the best I can."

Overwhelmed, Parker let out a heartrending sob and collapsed into Julie's arms. "I don't know what I'd do without you," she cried through tears. "I'll do anything you say."

"Good," Julie said. She helped Parker up, and they walked through the woods to Julie's car. But only a few paces in, Parker could already feel herself wavering. Something else inside her, some deep dark part of her, had taken over when she'd done all those awful things.

How did she know that something wouldn't take over again?

CHAPTER TWENTY-FOUR

MAC COULD BARELY MAKE OUT what Ava was saying through her hysterical sobs. She pressed the phone to her ear, trying to discern a few clear words. Finally she pieced together a sentence, but she almost wished she hadn't.

"Someone pushed my stepmother off her balcony!"

"Jesus," Mac gasped. "Just breathe, Ava. Breathe." She took her own advice, inhaling and exhaling slowly. "Is she . . . did she . . ."

"She's alive. She's in a coma."

Mac shut her eyes. "Oh, thank god, Ava."

"What's happening, Mac?" Ava sniffled into the phone. "What are we going to do?"

Mac stood up and shut her bedroom door. Her parents were downstairs fixing dinner, but her sister had spent a lot of time lurking around her room the last few days. Mac wasn't sure if Sierra was being supportive or suspicious, but either way, she didn't want her hearing any part of this conversation.

What *were* they going to do? It was clear now that this wasn't a coincidence. The killer was going down their list like it was the telephone tree parents used when school was canceled. And it was, in some way, their fault. If they hadn't said those names, none of this would have happened.

She sat back down on her bed and gripped her phone hard. "We need to stay calm and stick together, okay?"

"Yeah." Ava gulped. "The scariest part is that the killer was *in* my house the same time I was."

Mac shuddered. It was a horrible thought. She tried to imagine the killer downstairs in her own house, right that second. Her limbs went cold with fear.

"I could have seen her—maybe I could have stopped her—if only I'd known to look." Ava began crying heavily again.

Mac cocked her head at Ava's words. "I'm still not sold on the fact that the killer is a girl."

"Alex *said* he saw a girl going into Granger's," Ava said. "And . . . I don't know. It just feels right."

There was an awkward silence. Then Mac realized something. At least there was one upshot: There was no way Ava was the killer, and Ava had to know that Mac wasn't, either—otherwise she wouldn't have called her. Maybe they could start trusting each other again.

"Have you heard from the others?" Mac asked.

Ava cleared her throat. "I texted Julie but haven't heard from her yet. I'm going to try Caitlin next."

Mac shut her eyes, trying to imagine one of the others sneaking into Ava's house and pushing a random woman off a balcony. They weren't capable of that, were they? It had to be someone else.

They clicked off the call, and Mac tossed her cell onto her bed and paced the room anxiously. Her cello beckoned, but she couldn't imagine playing. Then, her phone chirped from under the folds of the comforter. She fumbled around for it. Blake had sent her a Snapchat of a pink sprinkles cupcake, her favorite flavor. And he'd drawn little glasses and a mustache on the cupcake. The sight of it somehow cheered her up.

Mac grimaced. No, no, *no.* But before she even knew what she was doing, she dialed Blake's number. It rang once . . . twice. . . .

What are you thinking? She quickly pulled the phone away and hit END before he could answer, stabbed at her phone to make sure she'd really hung up, and then turned it off so that Blake couldn't call her back. *Why would you talk to Blake ever again, after how he treated you?* a voice in her head scolded her.

But the card he'd written was tucked into her underwear drawer, under a Miracle Bra she'd always been too chicken to wear. She and Claire had bought them together, giggling in a Victoria's Secret back dressing room.

Claire. Mac felt a pull in her stomach. Claire was the only person on their list who hadn't yet been attacked. First Nolan. Then Parker's father. Then Ashley, and now Leslie.

Mac thought back to what she'd said in film studies that day. *Maybe a hit and run, something totally accidental.* She hadn't *meant* that—she'd just wanted to participate in the conversation. And for god's sake, it was all just talk! But now, if anything happened to Claire, Mac would blame herself forever.

Her heart began to rattle in her chest. What if the killer—whoever it was—planned to finish off the list, tonight?

Mac tried to think. She had to stop this. She had to protect her ex-friend. There was only one thing to do. She grabbed a sweatshirt and ran for her car, shouting out a quick "Be right back" to her parents as she raced past them.

Five minutes later, she pulled into Claire's driveway. Blessedly, Claire's car was parked in the garage, and there were lights glowing in her upstairs bedroom window. Mac exhaled, took a moment to compose herself, and glanced up and down the street. The only other cars were parked in the semicircular driveways. No one idled at the curb or had even turned onto the block. Okay. That was better. But she still needed to see with her own eyes that Claire was safe.

She hustled to the front door and rang the bell. High-heeled footsteps click-clacked across the tile entryway. Warm light and Beethoven on the Sonos sound system washed over Mac as Mrs. Coldwell swung the door open wide. The house smelled like homemade pasta and freshly baked bread.

"Mackenzie! What a pleasure to see you." Mrs. Coldwell's broad smile was so sincere, it sent a pang straight through Mac's heart. She had always loved Claire's parents, who were gentler and more relaxed than her own.

"Who is it, Mom?"

Mrs. Coldwell spun around and beamed at her daughter. "Look who's come to visit!"

Claire stood with her toes curled around the top stair. She was wearing a frayed MELLO CELLO tee and pajama pants, and her hair was in a headband. Her face took on a pinched expression when she saw Mac. "What do *you* want?" she asked sourly.

Mac blinked hard. She hadn't actually thought about what she'd say if she found her ex–best friend in one piece. She was just so relieved to see her standing there that she didn't care how ridiculous it must have seemed that she'd shown up on her doorstep as if nothing had happened between them. "I . . . uh . . . I just wanted to come say hi," she blurted.

"Well, isn't that nice?" Mrs. Coldwell asked in a sing-song. "Can I get you some hot cocoa, Mackenzie? A homemade chocolate chip cookie?"

"That's okay," Mac said. Mrs. Coldwell smiled for another beat, then murmured something about leaving the girls alone. She slipped into the back of the house.

Mac shifted awkwardly in the foyer, staring at the pictures on the console table. There was still a picture of her and Claire from a few years ago on the stage at the Seattle Symphony Hall. They were smiling so lovingly at each other, arms around each other's waists.

Then she looked up at Claire. "What are you up to tonight?"

Claire glared. Her tone was acidic, her expression withering. "Why do *you* care?"

"So you're not leaving the house?"

Claire just stared. "Does it look like I'm leaving the house?" She placed her hands on her hips. "What do you *want*, Mackenzie? To rub it in that you're seeing Oliver?" She rolled her eyes. "He seems lame, if you ask me. I never wanted him anyway."

Mac pulled her bottom lip into her mouth, wanting to retort that it had definitely seemed otherwise at Umami.

But it didn't matter. Nothing mattered except keeping Claire safe.

"Uh, I'm not dating Oliver," Mac blurted. "We're just friends. That's what I came to tell you, actually." The words rushed out fast, though they weren't a lie. She hadn't heard from Oliver in days: It seemed like he'd gotten the picture. "He's yours if you want him."

Claire made a face. "I don't want your sloppy seconds." Then she slammed the door in Mac's face.

Still, Mac didn't feel bad. Problem solved, after all. She practically bounced along the driveway, filled with relief. Claire was safe—for tonight, at least.

She pressed the button on her keychain and her Escape beeped, flashing its lights. Just as she pulled the door handle and ducked inside, she spotted a car gliding slowly, shark-like, down the street toward her, its lights off. Mac slumped down in the driver's seat and peeked out the window as the car made its way past Claire's house. With a gasp, she recognized the make and model—an older Subaru Outback. And she flinched when she saw the lone figure sitting stone-faced behind the steering wheel.

Was that . . . *Julie?*

CHAPTER TWENTY-FIVE

"CAITLIN? ARE YOU EVEN LISTENING to me?"

The sound of Jeremy's voice through the Bluetooth snapped Caitlin back into reality. Her mind had been wandering—and so had her car, apparently. It was Thursday night, and she'd been driving around aimlessly for at least an hour, something she often did when she just needed some quiet time to sort out her thoughts. Squinting through her windshield, she realized that she had steered out of her own neighborhood and all the way to the outskirts of Beacon Heights.

"Sorry, I'm here." She scrambled to catch up to what Jeremy had been saying over the phone. Something about a sci-fi movie marathon at a little art house in Seattle the following weekend. "That sounds great. And—oh. The whole team is bugging me to go to Nyssa's Halloween party tomorrow. You'll come, right?"

"A Halloween party?" Jeremy sounded circumspect.

"I'm not really in the mood, either, but maybe it will be fun," Caitlin said. "We'll dress up, have some beers . . ."

Jeremy snorted sarcastically. "Since when do you know me as someone who likes to dress up and drink beer?"

Something inside Caitlin twisted—she'd really hoped Jeremy would just say yes without complaint. "I'm planning on going as a UDub cheerleader, if that helps," she said enticingly, trying to keep the mood light. "It involves a super-short mini . . ."

He sighed. "Okay, okay. I'll go, but only for you." She heard him swallow. "Are you okay? You've been kind of . . . strange, lately. Not really yourself."

"Yes! I'm fine. Just really tired." She yawned as if to emphasize the point. "I haven't been sleeping well. It's making it hard to think straight."

"So then nothing's going on?"

Jeremy sounded more resigned than irritated. Caitlin hated keeping stuff from him, building up the stacks of lies between them. Even little things: Though her parents had been informed, she'd kept it from Jeremy that a psychological profiler had questioned her. She could have explained it easily to him, but she'd decided not to. And then there was everything worse: What if he knew about Granger? And how would he see her if he knew she'd sat in a circle of girls and named people they wanted dead—and now those *very people* were getting murdered right and left?

"Is it the stuff with Ava's stepmom?" Jeremy guessed.

Caitlin took a breath. "Yeah," she admitted. The story had been all over school. "I just feel so bad for Ava," she said.

Jeremy sniffed. "I thought you told me Ava hated her stepmom."

Oops. Caitlin had told him that. "Well, hate is a strong word," she said quickly. Then she looked out the window. "You know what? I think I'm lost."

"Where are you?"

"On the edge of town. At least I *think* I am."

"What're you doing all the way out there?" His voice was sharp.

Caitlin braked as a pickup truck pulled out in front of her. "I don't know," she said absently. "I just sort of . . . ended up here."

"Maybe we shouldn't talk on the phone while you're driving. And maybe you shouldn't be driving when you're so tired."

"Yeah," she sighed. "I'll call you when I'm home. And hey—"

"Yeah?"

"I'm excited about that movie marathon. Really."

Jeremy clucked his tongue. "Well, I'm not excited about

the party, but hey. At least it's an excuse to see you in a cheerleader skirt."

Caitlin tapped the button on her steering wheel to disconnect the call, and the car went silent. There was another secret she was keeping from Jeremy, too: She and Josh had exchanged a few texts in the past several days. Nothing serious, mostly just a random *hi* or *how are you feeling*, but still. Josh was her ex. Jeremy wouldn't be happy about that.

Caitlin knew she should just cut Josh loose, but she felt so bad that she'd been the cause of his injury. It was nice to talk to him, too. He was so much calmer these days with his injury. It was as if the pressure to play soccer had been a noose around his neck, cutting off the circulation to his brain—sort of like it had been for her. Maybe they had more in common than she thought.

So did that mean she *hadn't* picked the right boy? *Of course not*, she told herself. *You said it yourself—you're just tired.*

The news, which she had on very low in the background, caught her attention, and she turned it up. *Officials are still trying to nail down a suspect in the Nolan Hotchkiss murder case*, a reporter said in a droning voice. *Hotchkiss was killed several weeks ago from cyanide poisoning at a party that took place at his family's residence in Beacon Heights. Detectives speculate that his death and the death of Lucas Granger, a*

Beacon Heights teacher, might be connected, though they don't have evidence to prove that yet. In other Beacon Heights news, seventeen-year-old Ashley Ferguson, who disappeared from her home two days ago, still has not been found.

Caitlin shuddered. It was a wonder the news hadn't mentioned Parker's dad and Ava's mom in that little synopsis, too. Was it only a matter of time until detectives figured out they were all linked?

She took a turn at a stop sign, then slowed. All at once, this neighborhood was familiar—especially the junked-up, falling-down house at the end of the street. Caitlin drummed her fingers on the steering wheel, surprised at herself. She'd driven all the way to Julie's house without realizing it.

She ran her tongue over her teeth and pressed gently on the gas. No one had seen Julie in days; she hadn't been answering calls or texts, either. It was definitely worrying. Was she hiding out because of the Ashley stuff? She knew Ashley was missing, right? What about Leslie's death? How had her interview with Dr. Rose gone? It was like Julie had dropped off the face of the earth.

Caitlin pulled up to the curb in front of Julie's dilapidated house, hopped out of her car, and wended her way around the old appliances and piles of trash blocking the walkway. As she neared the porch, a gruff, unfamiliar voice called out from the shadows.

"What are you doing here?"

Caitlin jumped, then searched the darkness. She could just make out the outline of a person hunched over in the shadows near the front door. She stepped closer to the house and peered at the small, defeated-looking figure whose face was obscured by a bulky hood.

"Um. Hi?" she asked tentatively.

"I *said*, what are you doing here?"

The head lifted, and Caitlin gasped. It was *Julie*. A shrunken, shriveled, pale version of her, anyway. This person had the same features, the same colored hair framing her face, but her eyes were flat and lifeless, her complexion ashen, her demeanor stiff. She seemed like . . . a *zombie*.

Caitlin knelt down to her cautiously. "A-are you okay?"

"Fine." Julie looked away from Caitlin, studying a stack of faded, wet newspapers that looked glued to the corner of the porch. Next to them was a row of dried brown plants— dead stalks, really—in cracked ceramic pots that looked like they'd been sitting there since the seventies. "But seriously. What are you *doing* here?"

Caitlin was alarmed by the coldness and distance in Julie's voice, and a prickle of unease skittered across her skin. She looked around the porch, unsure where to rest her eyes. "I . . . I, uh, just wanted to check on you. We haven't heard from you. That's all."

Julie's gaze flickered to Caitlin for a split second.

"Thanks for the concern. But I'm never going to school again."

She sounded so certain and determined. Also so robotic. Caitlin took a breath, wondering if she should even press the issue further. But she did. "Look, I know it must be really hard to think about coming back, but it's okay. We'll be there for you—we'll protect you. Plus, I don't know if you even know this, but Ashley isn't . . . well, she's not at school right now. She's missing."

"I heard," Julie said.

"Oh," Caitlin said, surprised. "Well, okay then. But don't you think it's scary? Considering . . . you know. Our list."

Julie turned and stared at her, her eyes still lifeless. It sent a shiver up Caitlin's spine. "*All* of this is scary," she whispered. And then she shut her eyes and crumpled back to the porch. "I'm really tired," she mumbled.

Caitlin nodded and stood. "Okay. I'll let you get some rest, then."

Julie lurched to her feet awkwardly. "Maybe." She shuffled to the front door, her face angled downward.

"Will we see you tomorrow?" Caitlin blurted out, cringing at her overly chipper tone.

But Julie didn't respond. She opened the front door, wobbled through it, and closed it behind her with a wheezing clatter.

Caitlin stood on the front porch for a moment longer,

too astonished to move right away. It was like she'd been talking to a completely different girl right then. Someone she didn't know.

She knew she should leave that instant, but something made her remain in place, listening. Through the door, she heard Julie's muffled voice. Julie sounded mildly agitated. When she was done speaking, there was silence—whoever Julie was talking to was speaking too quietly for Caitlin to hear. Julie's voice murmured again, then more silence. Was it her mother, perhaps?

The curtain flickered, and Caitlin jumped away, suddenly feeling like she was eavesdropping. She turned and started to head down the stairs but crashed into a rusted metal pot and scraped her shin, hard. "Ow—crap!" She leaned down to rub her leg, and when she did, she caught a glimpse of something tucked into the far corner of the porch, behind the newspapers and potted plants. It was a plastic tub, slick with droplets of rainwater collected on the lid. A red biohazard symbol—Caitlin recognized it from chemistry class—was emblazoned on the front. She moved closer and read the label: FERTILIZER. And below that: *For agricultural use only. Contains Potassium Cyanide.*

Confusion and fear radiated in waves through Caitlin's body. It took her brain a moment to catch up. She stared at the bucket, reading the words over and over.

That's what killed Nolan.

CHAPTER TWENTY-SIX

FRIDAY AFTERNOON, JULIE SAT AT her desk, staring blankly at her computer, while Parker sat on the bed behind her, leafing through *Us Weekly*. It was midday and still so weird to be home while everyone else she knew was at school. But whatever. She was never going again. No one could make her.

Julie logged on to Facebook. She wasn't even sure why— it wasn't like she was going to just start messaging people or posting like nothing had happened. She could just imagine the post: *Sorry I haven't updated in a few days! Been too busy recovering from public humiliation, avoiding the cops, and covering up for my best friend—the serial murderer. Good times!*

She had barely finished typing in her password when dozens of notifications popped up. One after the other, they delivered the happy banalities of normal life—the life she and Parker would never have again. She read the messages about Nyssa's Halloween party. *Who's ready to start the party early? See you at my place in 3 hours! Only the costumed need apply!* Nyssa had written. A bunch of people had replied with enthusiastic *likes*.

Julie had forgotten it was her old friend's Halloween party tonight. For a brief moment, she was transported to parties of years past—such happier times. Like the one two years ago: She'd dressed up as a Vegas showgirl, with a plume on top of her head and a sparkly dress that showed off her toned body. People had taken tons of pictures of her for Facebook, and she'd been unofficially voted best outfit of the night. She'd danced all night with her friends—including Parker. Parker hadn't been at last year's, though—her attack had happened only weeks before. Julie vaguely remembered going, but not really having that great of a time—she'd still been so shaken.

She felt Parker's hand brush against her shoulder and turned. Her best friend was leaning over Julie, reading the post. "Looks like everyone's going," Parker murmured, pointing to a list of comments under the invite.

Julie stared at the post, too. Her gaze focused on a particular name: There, halfway down the page, Claire Coldwell had written *Count me in!* She whipped around and stared at Parker, her heart beating hard. Had Parker seen Claire's name? Was that a whisper of a determined smile on her face? Julie remembered how adamantly Parker had said that Claire deserved justice, too.

"We're not going," she said emphatically.

Parker gave Julie a crazy look, then held up her hands in a *back off* gesture. "Since when do *I* want to go to a party?"

Julie swallowed hard. "Okay," she said slowly. "Just making sure."

Then she shut her eyes. This Parker thing was getting to her at the best of times and putting her in full-on, hyperventilating, major-insomnia-panic mode in the worst. Just two days ago, she thought there was nothing she wouldn't do for her friend, and she'd sworn that she would protect her at any cost. But now Julie wasn't so sure. Parker had *killed* people, with her own hands. Just knowing that made Julie feel so guilty and responsible. Keeping this secret— even for Parker—was wrong.

On the other hand, how could she turn in her best friend? The only person who had been there for her through everything? Julie wished there was someone she could go to for guidance. She had even considered talking to Fielder about it, despite his questionable behavior toward Parker, but eventually she'd decided it was just too risky. She couldn't trust him, and if anything happened to Parker, she'd never forgive herself.

"Sorry," Julie said, casting Parker a smile. "I'm just tired and stressed. Don't mind me."

"Hey, I totally understand," Parker said. "But don't you think that being cooped up in here is probably not helping?"

Julie stiffened. "We have to stay here . . . at least until we figure out what comes next."

"How long is *that* going to be?"

"I don't know!" Julie knew she needed to make a plan—maybe an escape route for her and Parker to leave the city. She had to get out of here before the police figured it out—or before Leslie woke up and remembered that Parker had pushed her. But she just felt so *stuck*. And exhausted: She couldn't even put forth the effort to take the first step.

A faint chime sounded through the closed bedroom door. Julie and Parker exchanged a look, their eyes wide.

"Was that the doorbell?" Parker whispered.

"Yeah." Panic bloomed in Julie's gut. They weren't expecting anyone, and she was pretty sure Caitlin and the others had gotten the hint that she just wanted to be left alone. The bell rang again.

"*Julie—aren't you going to get the door?*" Mrs. Redding screeched from somewhere down the hall.

She needed to answer it, but she really didn't want to leave Parker alone. Finally, she cast Parker a warning look. "Stay here," Julie hissed at Parker. "I really mean it."

"I promise." Parker sat back down on the bed and pulled her knees into her chest.

Julie worked her way carefully down the hall, side-stepping boxes. She opened the door to find Detectives McMinnamin and Peters, looking awkward in their suits and ties, standing amidst the wreckage of Julie's house. Their faces were dead serious. Julie was relieved she'd told Parker to sit tight in her room.

"Hello, Ms. Redding," Detective McMinnamin said brusquely. "Mind if we ask you a few questions?"

"Uh, sure." Julie kept her voice neutral, but her mind was racing. Should she step outside and talk to them on the porch? Or would they find that weird and think she was hiding something inside? But if they came in and saw just how awful her house was, wouldn't that make her even more of a suspect in their eyes?

"Why don't you come inside," she said evenly, as if she invited people into her house on a routine basis.

She pushed open the stubborn front door, nudged aside a heap of old blankets with her foot, and led them into the living room. The detectives studied the room with a detached observation. They looked unfazed, their professional poker faces intact.

Julie threaded a narrow path through the crammed space, over to the couch she had honestly forgotten was in the house. She grabbed a moldering stack of magazines and placed it atop a column of boxes nearby. She moved a tall tower of board games—Parcheesi, The Game of Life,

Battleship, Trivial Pursuit—games Julie never remembered playing even when she was little. Even after all that, she'd barely cleared enough space for the two men to sit down. At least there was one positive thing in all this: The cats were all gone, Animal Control having removed them a few days before. The place still smelled like cat pee, but at least there weren't a dozen creatures rubbing up against the officers' legs.

"Please, have a seat." Julie gestured at the couch.

"Thanks." McMinnamin plopped down with a heavy sigh, pulling a small notebook out of his back pocket.

"I'll stand, thanks," Peters said in his deep baritone.

Julie pushed aside a basket teeming with pouches and pots of cosmetics samples and tiny bottles of hotel shampoos, then perched on the edge of the coffee table, trying to look as natural as possible. The room was silent for a moment. Julie listened carefully for any noises from her room down the hall. So far, Parker had been silent as a mouse.

McMinnamin cleared his throat. "So, Julie, we're actually surprised you're home tonight. We hear there's a big Halloween party."

Julie blinked. How on earth did the cops know that? Did they keep tabs on all the Beacon parties . . . or just recent ones, in light of what happened to Nolan? "Uh, I'm not really up for partying these days," she muttered.

McMinnamin nodded, as though this were completely understandable. "We'd like to ask you some questions about one of your classmates, Ashley Ferguson. You probably know that Ashley has been missing from her home for a couple of days now. Yes?"

"Uh-huh," Julie recited.

McMinnamin stared at her with his rheumy blue eyes. "Her family is very worried about her, and we're just following up on every lead. We heard you and Ashley had some problems."

Julie shrugged. "Ashley found out about"—she gestured at the room, the house, the yard around her—"all this. My mom's hoarding. And she exposed it to the entire school in an email."

McMinnamin and Peters blinked and waited for her to continue.

"But I was trying my best not to let it get to me." She looked back up at the detectives, locking eyes with McMinnamin. "High school can be brutal sometimes."

McMinnamin pursed his lips, as if deep in thought, then clicked the top of his pen a few times. "Where were you on Tuesday afternoon, after you left Dr. Rose's office at the police station?"

Julie pretended to think about where she'd been, though she'd been rehearsing her lie for days. "I was with Parker." McMinnamin's eyebrows rose slightly, and he looked over at Peters. Peters nodded. "We were out shopping. All after-noon," Julie said confidently.

The officers stared at her, their eyes narrowing. "Parker who?" McMinnamin finally asked.

Julie resisted the urge to roll her eyes. "Uh, Parker Duvall? My best friend?"

McMinnamin glanced down at his notepad. He scribbled a few notes, then exchanged a silent look with his partner. "Right. Parker Duvall," Peters said. "Got it."

Julie was seized with a sudden fear that she'd said the wrong thing. *Are they going to want to question Parker now?* She wasn't sure Parker could handle it. Maybe she shouldn't have mentioned Parker at all. Maybe she should have said she was with Carson. He would have covered for her.

McMinnamin's voice brought Julie out of her reverie. "Okay. Thanks for your time, Julie." He stood.

"If you think of anything else," Peters added, "will you let us know?"

"Of course," Julie assured them.

McMinnamin shook her hand. Peters tapped two fingers to his forehead as a good-bye. She led the men to the door, trying to seem as if she had all the time in the world. She shut the door behind them and leaned against it, relief washing over her. That hadn't been that bad at all. Except for the part where she'd basically steered them right toward Parker. But they hadn't asked where Parker was or anything—or given any indication that they wanted to speak with her. And by the time they *did* come back, having realized that Parker usually camped out at Julie's house, Parker and Julie would be long gone.

First, though, she needed to make one call. It had become painfully clear to Julie that she couldn't handle this alone. She needed help—and there was only one person she could think of to call, despite her many, *many* reservations. Julie picked her way along the hallway back to the living room couch and sat down. She didn't want Parker to hear her do this. She slipped her cell phone from her pocket and tapped F-I-E into the contact search window. Elliot Fielder's name popped up instantly, and she dialed his number.

"Parker?" He sounded anxious. "Is that you?"

Parker? Julie was confused. Why would he be expecting *Parker* to call? She hung up the phone reflexively and pushed back through the hall and into her room, ready to ask questions.

That was the problem, though: The room was empty. Julie looked around, her heart lurching into her throat. "Parker? Parker?"

Her gaze focused on her computer screen. Facebook was still open, but the page had changed—now Mac's page was up. Julie stepped closer. A picture was highlighted. It was of Mac and a blond boy Julie didn't recognize, sitting in a dark car, their heads tilted close. It was clear they were making out. A caption was beneath it: *Once a slut, always a slut.* Claire Coldwell had written it.

Julie sat back. "Shit," she whispered. She didn't know what this situation was, but she knew one thing for sure: Parker had been looking at it. And maybe, for her, it was the last straw, just like Ashley's Instagram had been.

She jumped from the bed and zigzagged as fast as she could through the labyrinth of waste lining the hallway, back to the front door again. She flung open the front door. The yard was still, the street quiet.

Parker was gone.

CHAPTER TWENTY-SEVEN

AVA STARED AT HERSELF IN the bathroom mirror at Beacon Memorial Hospital. Her eyes were red, her nose was chapped and flaking, and she looked wiped out. She patted the puffy bags under her eyes, pulled her hair up into a messy ponytail, and tossed a bunch of crumpled tissues into the metal trash can. When she walked out of the bathroom, she passed a police officer going in the opposite direction. She cringed, but the officer didn't even look at her. *Maybe he should,* she thought with a start.

Leslie was still in a coma, making little progress, but at least she wasn't getting worse. Ava's father had spent every moment by her side, and Ava had spent a good deal of time at the hospital, too. No matter how much she hated Leslie, she wanted to be here for her dad.

The police had investigated Leslie's fall and determined

that it was an accident—her blood alcohol level had been extremely high, and she'd already been agitated. They assumed she'd drunkenly slipped off the balcony in her sky-high heels. Still, Ava felt nervous about the whole thing. Thank god she had an airtight alibi, since she'd been with her father when it happened. But she couldn't help thinking about that yellow legal pad from Granger's house. Where *was* that thing? What if someone found it?

In some ways, Ava longed for Leslie to wake up. At least then she might be able to tell them who had pushed her.

She slumped back to the waiting room and found her father sitting in one of the uncomfortable couches, a cup of what was probably cold coffee in his hands. Leslie's mother, Aurora Shields, who had made her appearance just hours after Leslie's accident—an incredibly awkward situation, as they'd put her up in their house but had absolutely no idea what to do with the woman, who complained about everything from the uncomfortable sheets to the lack of soy milk in the fridge—sat stiffly across from him, her hands folded in her lap. Mrs. Shields eyed Ava coldly when she walked back in. Ava wondered what Leslie had told her mother about her. Probably nothing good.

She gave Mrs. Shields a polite smile, walked over to her father, and leaned her head on his shoulder. He looked up and wrapped her in a tight hug. As he held her, Ava cast her eyes on the paperwork he'd been reading. "McAllister

Cemetery" curled across the top page in a dignified and serious script.

Ava frowned. "You have to think positive, Dad. She's not . . . you know. *Yet*." She eyed Mrs. Shields, who was clearly paying attention.

Mr. Jalali nodded, then folded the papers on his lap. "I'm just trying to cover all the bases, *jigar*. And anyway, Aurora and I thought it would be a good idea just to see what our options are." He eyed Mrs. Shields, too. That's when Ava realized it had probably been all Leslie's mom's idea. *Jesus*. Leslie was in a coma for mere days and her mother was already buying up a burial plot. Perhaps that was why Leslie was such a shitty mother—she'd had a terrible role model.

Ava let out a small whimper, briefly thinking about her own mother and her regrets about Leslie. Mr. Jalali looked at her sympathetically, his eyes wet with tears. "This must be so hard for you, dear. It's bringing back memories for me, too."

Ava cringed. It *did* bring back memories: She and her father had kept vigil at this very hospital after her mother's accident, though not nearly for as long. Mrs. Jalali's death had been sudden, and it had only been a brief wait in the ER before the doctors told them they couldn't save her. But the smell of hospitals still turned Ava's stomach, as did the dreary art on the walls, and the pale, drawn faces of all the family members waiting to hear whether their loved ones were going to recover or die. For some reason, when she heard the news about her mom, Ava hadn't started crying. Instead she'd walked numbly to the vending machines and stared at the snacks lined up in neat rows behind the glass. She'd fed quarters into the thing and selected Bugles, her mom's favorite snack, as if buying them would bring her back.

Ava knew that if Leslie died, she wouldn't be hit with the same grief—it would be guilt instead. But she did recognize how hard this probably was for her father. However bizarre it seemed to her, Leslie had been the second love of his life—and Ava had taken that away. She stroked his arm, feeling the need to comfort him. "We have each other. We always have. It'll be okay."

"You're such a good girl," Mr. Jalali whispered, which gave Ava a guilty pang. Then he looked at her. "Don't you have a Halloween party tonight?"

Ava shook her head. "I'm not leaving you alone." Especially with Mrs. Shields.

"Oh, Ava." He sighed. "You should go, have some fun. I know how much you love costume parties. Is Alex going?"

Ava shook her head. "He has to work late."

She couldn't help but smile, though. Now that Alex had been cleared of all charges in Granger's death, her dad was suddenly a huge Alex fan again.

"What about your friends?" Mr. Jalali asked. "Those girls you've been hanging around with?"

Ava had received a few texts from Caitlin and Mac earlier, asking whether they should go to Nyssa's or not. Mac had decided to go, to keep track of Claire—she was the only person left on that list, after all. Caitlin had said she would go, too. Ava felt suddenly guilty—she should go with them, they'd have strength in numbers.

She nodded. "Okay. I'll go for a little bit. But Dad, if you need me, or if anything at all happens, you'll call me, right?"

"Of course." He smiled at her kindly. Mrs. Shields, however, looked at Ava as if she'd just said she was going to go out into the parking lot to smoke some meth.

She turned to leave, thinking about how she didn't have a costume and would have to shower if she didn't want to smell like hospital. Just as she reached the door, her father called out to her again. "Oh, Ava?" He reached into his pants pocket and pulled out something small and delicate. "I forgot. I found this—I think it's yours, yes?"

She crossed the room and held out her hand. He dropped it into her palm, and she studied it for a moment. It was a pretty chandelier earring of silver wire and shiny amber beads. She shook her head. "It's not mine."

Her dad looked confused. "Are you sure? It's not Leslie's, and I found it upstairs on my bedroom floor . . ."

Ava blinked hard. All at once, she got a flash of recognition—she'd seen those earrings before. Her heart stopped. Her eyes widened.

"You found this in your *bedroom?*" she cried.

He nodded, cocking his head. "Why?"

Another thought hung on Ava's lips, but she didn't dare say it aloud. *The bedroom with the balcony Leslie fell from?*

"What is it?" her father asked, leaning forward.

"N-nothing. I'll see you later. Love you." She turned and bolted for the door, her mind suddenly spinning. She needed to get to the party and find the others as quickly as possible.

The earring was Julie's.

CHAPTER TWENTY-EIGHT

ON FRIDAY EVENING, A SIX-FOOT-TWO-INCH fuzzy white bear slammed into Mac and clumsily swiped at the spilled beer on her shirt with a giant paw. "Oops, sorry!" he crowed with a muffled giggle. Mac could tell it was Sander Dennis, who was in her chem class. His girlfriend, a junior named Penelope Steward, cackled in her pink tutu, then sauntered around the DJ table toward the keg.

"Where's *your* costume?"

Mac looked up. Thad Kelly, a senior, was wearing a blue bird costume and a sash with "Insert 140 characters here" printed on it. He stared at Mac drunkenly, even though the party had started, like, five minutes ago.

Mac looked down at her boyfriend jeans, rolled up at the cuffs, and her thick cable-knit sweater. "I didn't really have time to think one up," she said.

"Lame!" He laughed and boogied away.

She sighed and scanned the room again. If only she could tell him she wasn't here to celebrate Halloween— she was here to save a life. A horrible premonition told her that tonight was going to be the night that the killer was planning on hurting Claire. It was the perfect environment: a loud, chaotic party, lots of alcohol, lots of suspects.

The exact thing they'd said when they were planning to prank Nolan at *his* party.

Mac shuddered. She *had* to find Claire. She was definitely coming to this: Earlier today, she'd posted on Facebook about her top-secret costume. Mac had also noticed a post about *her* from Claire on Facebook—a picture of her and Oliver, kissing, with a nasty caption—but she'd quietly deleted it from her page and decided not to dwell on it or on the fact that Claire had apparently snuck out of the restaurant that night and spied on her and Oliver while they were kissing. It couldn't get in the way of Mac trying to save her.

Mac had checked other people's sites, too. Ashley Ferguson's Facebook was still silent, though a lot of people had posted that they were praying for her. People had posted to Ava's account offering their condolences for Ava's stepmom, though Ava hadn't added anything in a long time.

Julie's page was just as silent. The last time she'd posted was before the whole hoarding email thing, when she'd uploaded a link to an article called "The Ten Best Pandora Downloads to Kickstart Your Weekend." There was certainly no mention that she was attending the party.

Mac closed her eyes and remembered the image of Julie driving past Claire's house. Maybe there was an explanation for it. Maybe Julie knew someone else on that street. Maybe she was driving slowly because she was looking for a particular house—just not *Claire's* house. Because why on earth would Julie be behind all this? Why would she risk so much? In fact, maybe Julie had the same reason Mac did: to check on Claire to make sure she was safe. That had to be it.

A Katy Perry song came on, and a bunch of kids screamed and started dancing. Mac took another spin around the patio, circumnavigating the pool, where a horde of juniors were playing an aggressive game of co-ed water polo, the girls holding tight to their string bikinis as they hurled themselves up and out of the water.

Then Mac saw her. There was Claire, sitting with Maeve Hurley, who played violin. Claire was dressed as a sprinkle candy from Candy Crush and holding a beer. Mac was so thrilled she almost cheered.

She marched over. When she was a few feet away, Claire looked up at Mac and narrowed her eyes. She started whispering something to Maeve. Maeve looked at Claire and giggled.

But that still didn't deter Mac from her mission. "Hey, Claire," she said, approaching her ex-friend.

Claire looked at her confusedly, then wrinkled her nose. "Nice outfit. Or *lack* of outfit. This is a costume party, dork. Or is that your costume—a dork?"

Then she and Maeve exchanged a look, stood up, and headed toward the house. "Wait!" Mac cried.

But Claire didn't turn.

Well, whatever. Mac would just tail them all night. She followed closely behind them, studying the costumed faces in the crowd to see if anyone else was watching Claire, maybe plotting to hurt her. All she saw were slutty Marilyn Monroes, disheveled rock stars, a couple of Daft Punk robots, and about a dozen of the requisite slutty cat/slutty witch/slutty nun costumes. All of them were paying attention to their drinks or taking pictures of one another on their phones.

She followed Claire and Maeve through the sliding glass doors into the kitchen, where a painfully realistic decapitated head rested on a carving platter. Next to it was a display of candy eyeballs and something that vaguely resembled human brains. A couple of giggling, red-eyed, guilty-faced jocks in totally unoriginal Seahawks jerseys bolted out of the pantry, jars of peanut butter and boxes of crackers spilling out of their hands. They careened into Mac, and she bumped into the girl in front of her. Who, actually, was Claire.

Claire swung around. "*Watch* it."

"Sorry." Mac cast her eyes down at the floor.

Claire crossed her arms, her candy-colored head cocked to one side. "What's your deal, Mackenzie? Why are you stalking me? Isn't it clear I don't want to be your friend again?"

Mac thought again of the Facebook post. This probably did seem weird. "I'm sorry. I just—"

"You just *what?*" Claire snapped. "You just are going to leave me alone now." Then she swung around and headed up the stairs.

Mac lunged forward to follow Claire once more, but then a hand appeared in her line of vision, stopping her in her tracks. Mac was suddenly face-to-face with Blake, dressed as Anthony Kiedis from the Red Hot Chili Peppers, complete with his shirt off. He had, Mac couldn't help but notice, amazing abs.

Blake looked at Mac, then at Claire, climbing the stairs. "I know you think making amends is the right thing to do," he shouted over the music, "but maybe it's a lost cause."

Mac pulled away from him. "You don't understand."

"Yeah, I do." Blake shoved his hands in his pockets. "You're trying to be a good friend. You guys have been tight forever. But she's changed, Macks. Claire isn't the girl you remember."

"I don't care about that," Mac said tightly. "I have to make sure she's *safe*."

"Safe from what?" Blake grinned. "Safe from booze? It's probably too late for that. Safe from making out with a random guy?"

Mac blinked. There was no way she could explain this to Blake. But maybe she *was* overreacting. What could really happen to Claire while she was inside Nyssa's house? After all, she had said that she would kill Claire by hitting her with a car—and that couldn't happen as long as she was indoors. She began to breathe out. All she needed to do, she realized, was make sure Claire didn't *leave*.

She turned back to Blake just as he was stepping toward her. It was weird—she'd avoided him at school for weeks now, scurrying away if she saw him in the halls or in the parking lot. And now, up close, he seemed different. Taller, perhaps, than she remembered; broader, cuter. He was standing so close to her, too, that his bare chest was almost touching hers.

He reached out gently and touched Mac's hair. "You look really pretty tonight."

Mac scoffed. Now she was sure Blake was lying, considering how un-dressed up she was.

Blake took a step closer to her. All at once, Mac could smell that sugary, bakery smell he always gave off. "I miss you so much, Macks."

She lowered her eyes. "Blake . . ."

"And I've been hoping—*praying*—you'll at least talk to me again. I've been miserable, Macks. Life isn't the same without you. Did you read my card?"

She wanted to shake her head no. She wanted to tell him she didn't care about some stupid card. But she felt her lips tremble. She couldn't get the right words out. Then he touched her chin, tilting it up. He didn't say a word, just looked deeply into her eyes, and Mac felt herself crumble. A thousand thoughts competed for attention. Could she trust him? He *seemed* sincere . . . but he did last time, too. How did she know he meant what he said?

Mac felt herself leaning toward him anyway. She wanted to trust him—she needed to trust him. And maybe she could.

The sounds of the party slipped away. She tipped her head up toward his and closed her eyes, excited to feel his lips on hers again.

"*Mac!*" Someone gripped her upper arm, snapping Mac back into the loud, raucous present. Ava stood next to her, looking both hurried and a little sheepish. "I'm so, *so* sorry to interrupt," she said, her gaze darting from Mac to Blake, "but we have to talk."

Mac had never seen Ava look so frantic. Her heart started to pound. She turned back to Blake, her lips parting. "Um, sorry, I—"

But Ava cut her off and grabbed her arm. "*Now.*"

CHAPTER TWENTY-NINE

CAITLIN ADJUSTED HER UDUB CHEERLEADER costume and tumbled out of her car, which was parked a few doors down from Nyssa's house in South Beacon, one of the prettiest areas in town. She could already hear the bass pounding inside, and a bunch of kids were standing on the lawn, drinking out of not-very-covert red Solo cups. One of the kids was Corey Travers, who was on the boys' varsity soccer team even though he was only a freshman. "Hey, ladies!" he called out. "Great game!"

Caitlin and Vanessa—whom Caitlin had picked up on the way—beamed. Corey was referring to their game against Franklin, which had taken place earlier that day. They'd totally dominated, and Caitlin felt great about it, especially since it had been her first game as captain.

Vanessa, who was dressed as a Viking—naturally, given

that "Viking" was her nickname—elbowed Caitlin in the ribs. "He's cute."

"He's jailbait!" Caitlin laughed.

"That doesn't stop *you*," Vanessa teased, her eyes glinting. Then she glanced at Jeremy, who had finally climbed out of Caitlin's passenger front seat and was walking a few paces behind them.

Caitlin blushed and swatted her head, knocking Vanessa's helmet off-kilter. Vanessa just laughed and sauntered into the thick of the crowd, tossing her long blond braids and waving around her plastic shield.

Caitlin stopped to let Jeremy catch up to her. He'd been silent on the ride over, and he looked sort of pinched and sour as he trudged through Nyssa's yard. "Ignore her," she said quickly, hoping that Jeremy didn't take offense at the jailbait comment. "She's really nice once you get to know her, I promise."

"Mm-hmm," Jeremy said.

They stepped inside, and Jeremy's lips pressed together as he surveyed the crowd. He looked uptight and annoyed. Caitlin poked him playfully with one finger, but he just stood there, looking uncomfortable in the lumberjack costume she'd cobbled together for him out of stuff in her garage. This wasn't his scene. If it were up to Jeremy, they'd be in his basement tonight, watching *Dr. Who* and making out.

"Check out that skeleton!" Caitlin crowed in an overly positive voice, pointing to a life-sized version on the porch. Then she beamed at a kid inside with a brown alien mask on. "And isn't that a character from *Star Trek: The Next Generation?*"

"A bad version of him, yeah," Jeremy said sourly.

Caitlin grabbed his hand. "Come on. Let's get some beer." Maybe Jeremy would cheer up once he was a little buzzed.

The living room was packed and sweaty, and most of the kids were already drunk. Several boys were doing keg-stands in the corner, and a huge group was toasting with neon-green Jell-O shots. Caitlin kept a smile pasted on her face the whole time, but she could sense Jeremy's distaste. Cam Washington, who was also on the boys' soccer team, came up to her and slapped her hard on the back. "Congrats on the two goals today," he slurred, his breath smelling boozy.

"Thanks," Caitlin said in a chipper voice. She gestured to Jeremy. "You know Jeremy Friday, right?"

Cam glanced at Jeremy, his eyes at half-mast. "Uh, no. Don't think we've met."

Jeremy's jaw hardened. He stared at Cam's outstretched hand but didn't shake it. Caitlin knew exactly what he was thinking: Cam had met Jeremy a zillion times. He was one of Josh's good friends and was always at the Fridays' house.

He was implying that Jeremy wasn't important enough to *remember*.

Then another voice boomed. *"Caitlin!"*

Caitlin looked across the room. Josh, dressed as David Beckham circa his Manchester United days, sat on a chair, his bad ankle propped up on an ottoman. By the look of his spinning eyes, Caitlin guessed that he'd had several beers already. She gave him a little wave, and he waved back. "Are you going to sign my cast?" he asked loudly, holding up a big Sharpie.

Caitlin balked. Out of the corner of her eye, she could see Jeremy's face growing redder and redder.

"C'mon!" Josh called out. "You said you would, remember!"

Caitlin's heart sank. Just like that, Jeremy turned on his heel and stormed away. Caitlin gave Josh a half-apologetic, half-annoyed smile, then spun after Jeremy. She wanted to kick herself. She *had* said she'd sign Josh's cast when he'd texted her about it earlier today.

Caitlin followed Jeremy into the hall, which was marginally quieter, save for the girl throwing up by the back door. "So, I guess your brother's a little drunk," she said, trying to sound lighthearted about it.

Jeremy cut a quick glance to her. "Do you even *like* me?"

Caitlin flinched, surprised by his intensity. "Why would you ask such a thing?"

Jeremy looked away. "It just seems like you'd rather have my brother back. Like maybe you're having second thoughts."

Caitlin sighed. Jeremy wasn't stupid. On the one hand, she loved that about him—that he was so tuned in, so aware of her feelings. But on the other hand, it made it hard on both of them.

"No," she said. "I don't want Josh back."

"When were you talking to him?"

She shrugged. "He texted me about his cast earlier. I agreed to sign it because I was trying to be nice."

He scoffed. "Like he's *ever* been nice to you."

"That's not fair," Caitlin said. She took a deep breath. "Jeremy, you and I are going to have to deal with your brother going forward. I'm not going to be flat-out *mean* to him. You can't get mad at me just for talking to him. We all share history. You have to try to meet me in the middle here—compromise a little. Which you haven't seemed very willing to do lately."

Jeremy's eyebrows furrowed together. "What do you mean by *that*?"

"I mean . . ." Caitlin's heart pounded. She *so* didn't want to do this. But something had been bubbling inside her— everything had felt so off. She just had to say it.

"I mean I'm proud that I play soccer," she blurted. "Yes, I'm still not sure it will be my life forever, but I enjoy it now, and it's important to me. And you just . . . well, you seem *pissed* that I'm into it, honestly."

Jeremy's lips parted. "I was pissed because you broke our date—"

"Which I understand," she cut him off. "But you made me feel so guilty. How was I supposed to know you were taking me to One Direction? It's not like you told me beforehand."

"Because it was supposed to be a surprise!"

Caitlin lowered her eyes. "I'm really sorry about that. But, I mean, I couldn't just bail on my team. Initiation is once a year. It's important that the captains are there."

Jeremy shifted stiffly. Caitlin wondered if he was resisting rolling his eyes.

She sighed and kept going. "And these people here, some of them are my friends. I *like* going to parties, Jeremy. If you gave them a chance, maybe you'd like them, too."

Jeremy made a face. "Doubt it."

"Then maybe we're too different," Caitlin said quietly. She *hated* that she was saying it—she didn't want to give Jeremy up. But she didn't want him to be miserable with her, either, and he certainly looked that way right now.

Jeremy's eyes widened. A hurt look crossed his face. But before he could say anything, Ava and Mac raced up, anxious looks on their faces.

"Have you seen Julie?" Ava said tightly.

Caitlin shook her head. Just hearing Julie's name made her uneasy. She hadn't been able to shake the feeling that something was seriously off with Julie last night. But she hadn't told the others about it, hoping that Julie had just been in a mood.

"We need to find her—fast," Ava said.

"Why?" Caitlin asked, her worry growing.

Ava and Mac looked at Jeremy. He backed up, his expression even more irritated than before. "I'll see you later," he snapped, heading for the door.

Caitlin caught his arm. "You're *leaving*?"

"There's nothing for me here," he said, and turned to cut through the crowd.

"*Jeremy!*" Caitlin bellowed. "How are you getting home?" He'd come with her, after all.

But he didn't turn back, ducking around a mummy and disappearing out the front door. Caitlin's shoulders slumped. Had she lost him forever? Just like that? She wanted to go after him, but judging by the panicked expressions on her friends' faces, something was seriously wrong.

Ava pressed something into Caitlin's hands. "I found this at my house."

Caitlin looked down. It was a dangling earring. "Okay . . ."

"It's Julie's. My dad found it in his bedroom." Ava's lips trembled. "The same bedroom with the balcony Leslie was pushed off of."

"And I saw Julie in her car," Mac broke in, "driving really slowly past Claire's house on Wednesday night. She doesn't live anywhere *near* Claire."

Caitlin's jaw dropped. "I went to see her yesterday," she admitted. "And, um, I saw something on her porch. It was—it was fertilizer. Well, it's used for fertilizer, but it's potassium cyanide."

Mac gasped and covered her hand with her mouth. "And you're just telling us *now?*"

"Anyone could have fertilizer like that," Caitlin protested, guilt flooding her. "And just because you saw Julie driving by Claire's doesn't mean anything. She could have been in that neighborhood for an entirely different reason."

"But what about the earring?" Ava insisted.

Caitlin racked her brain. She wanted desperately to find some small detail, any tidbit of information, that would clear Julie. But she couldn't think. There was just too much evidence pointing in the same direction.

"Why would Julie do this to us?" she breathed.

But Ava and Mac weren't listening. They were both looking across the room, their gazes fixed on the same person.

Julie had come to the party after all.

CHAPTER THIRTY

JULIE STOOD IN THE DOORWAY leading from Nyssa's vast double-height living room to the back hall. All around her were witches, ghouls, Kardashians, and Mileys, and even some kid who'd dressed up like the Twitter blue bird. Quite a few of them were staring at her, aghast. Others had smirks on their faces. Everyone was taking in how pale she clearly looked, how her hair was unwashed, how she was wearing a gray American Apparel tee and black Nike shorts—not exactly a costume. *Julie Redding has become a freak,* was surely what they were whispering. But it didn't matter. After tonight, she'd never see any of them again. She just had to find Parker first. But as hard as she looked, she couldn't find a pale blond girl in a dirty black hoodie.

Julie had a horrible feeling Parker had seen that post Claire had written to Mac. *She deserves it,* Parker had said that day in the woods. *She's a horrible person.* Had that Facebook post about Mac been the straw that broke the camel's back?

She'd been calling Parker nonstop since she realized she was missing, but Parker hadn't answered. Julie knew she'd come here. It was the only thing that made sense—and it broke her heart. Parker had *promised*. She was so much sicker than Julie realized. She desperately needed help, help that Julie could no longer provide. Julie just hoped she could find her friend and get her that help before Parker found Claire.

She felt someone's hand on her shoulder and turned. Ava, Caitlin, and Mac swarmed around her. Caitlin looked really cute in her cheerleader costume, and Ava looked tall and stately in a simple black flapper dress. Mackenzie hadn't dressed up and seemed a little rumpled. All three girls seemed guarded and almost fearful. "Julie, can we talk?" Ava asked.

Julie frowned. "I need to find—"

"It's really, *really* important," Caitlin cut her off.

Julie stared around at them. They were closing in on her, boxing her in.

"Okay," she said carefully, her hackles going up. "But only for a sec. I'm sort of looking for someone."

Mac visibly flinched. Ava took Julie's arm and led her through the entryway and down a long hallway toward the bedroom wing. It was quieter there, though they could hear cackles from Nyssa's room a few doors down. The faint smell of pot wafted toward them.

Julie looked at her friends, their stony expressions suddenly making her uncomfortable. She let out a nervous laugh. "What is it? You guys are freaking me out."

They stared at her for a long moment. Finally, Ava spoke. "Is there anything you want to tell us?"

Julie felt a pull in her stomach. She had a *lot* to tell them . . . but she didn't dare. "Um, about what?" she asked as casually as she could.

Ava pulled something small out of her pocket and dangled it in Julie's face. "About this, maybe?"

Julie snatched it from her fingers. "That's my earring! Where did you find it?"

Ava looked pained. "In my house. The day Leslie was attacked—in the same room."

Julie's heart plummeted, and her face crumpled into a pained expression. *Parker.* She must have borrowed it.

"And I noticed potassium cyanide on your porch," Caitlin said in a small voice. "The same thing that killed Nolan."

"I saw you driving around Claire's house," Mac added, looking just as tortured.

"Julie, what's going on?" Ava cried. "Are *you* doing all this?"

Julie blinked hard, suddenly understanding. "Wait, you think *I* did it?" she blurted. But it made sense. She'd skulked by Claire's house just to make sure Parker wasn't there. Her mom had god-knows-what on the porch, and surely Parker had known that and stolen some. And Parker had worn Julie's earrings when she pushed Leslie off the ledge.

"I know what it looks like," she said. "But honestly, guys. It wasn't me. You have to believe me."

Ava looked disappointed. "Julie, all signs point to you. What are we supposed to think?" Her face crumpled. "The question is . . . *why?* Why would you do this to us?"

"Just trust me, okay?" Julie said frantically, her eyes darting back and forth. The music's volume had been pumped up even louder, making her head swim. She craned her neck to look for Parker, worried she might be hunting Claire down. "I have an explanation for you, but I can't get into it right now."

She tried to move past them, but Ava caught her arm. "You *have* to get into it right now," she hissed. "We're not letting you go until you do."

Something inside Julie snapped. "Let go of me!" she screamed.

"No can do," Mac said, forming a wall behind Ava.

Julie struggled to get out of Ava's grip. "Let go! I have to stop her!"

Caitlin's brow furrowed. Mac cocked her head. Ava clamped even tighter on Julie's arm. "Stop *who?*"

Julie stared at them crazily. God, she didn't want to say the name out loud. As soon as it escaped her lips, she would betray Parker for good. "Isn't it *obvious?*" she cried. "Who isn't here right now? Who else knows about our list?"

"*You*, Julie!" Mac practically screamed. "*You* know! You're the one behind this!"

"No, I'm not!" Tears formed in Julie's eyes. She could practically feel Parker's presence nearby, Parker witnessing this. Hating Julie. Finally realizing what a shitty friend Julie was, something Julie had known all along. She'd *promised* Parker she'd keep the secret. She'd sworn on her life never to tell a soul . . . and here she was, telling everyone.

She pressed her hands over her face. "I didn't hurt anyone! It's Parker, okay!" She wrenched away from Ava. "I'm trying to keep her safe. And I'm trying to keep *Claire* safe. But Parker is sick, guys, and if you don't help me find her *right now*, she's going to get Claire next."

She looked up at the others, expecting expressions of shock . . . but also understanding. But Ava had gone pale. Caitlin had her hand pressed over her mouth. Mac looked almost . . . *pitying*. And it all seemed like they shared a secret, something they hadn't let Julie in on.

Her skin began to prickle. "So are you coming, or what?" she asked sharply.

Finally Ava spoke, her voice unsteady. "You want us to come look for Parker?" she repeated.

"Parker . . . *Duvall?*" Mac whispered.

"*Yes,*" Julie spat. "Our friend. Parker Duvall." She blinked at them. They all seemed to have frozen solid. "*What?*" she snapped. "Why aren't you listening to me?"

"Julie," Caitlin said quietly. She exchanged a glance with the others. Ava's eyes were filled with tears. Mac's chin bobbed.

Caitlin looked at Julie again, her expression sad and scared and very, very worried. "Julie. Parker's been dead for over a year."

CHAPTER THIRTY-ONE

AVA WATCHED AS JULIE REDDING, a girl she thought she knew, crumpled against the wall. Her whole body was trembling. *"No,"* she whispered. "That's not true. You're lying."

Mac was crying now. "Julie, Parker's dead. Her dad killed her. He . . . he beat her to death, that night she came home on Oxy."

Julie covered her mouth. "No, he didn't. She *lived.*"

Ava exchanged a devastated look with the others. "She didn't," she said softly, sadly. "We had all kinds of assemblies at school, way more stuff than we had for Nolan and Granger combined. You don't remember?" Ava could remember perfectly. Parker had been killed just weeks after Ava's mother's death. Ava had only known Parker peripherally, through Nolan—they'd been such good friends, and

Parker had been at Nolan's house a few times when Ava was there, too. After they broke up and Nolan started all those rumors about her, Parker had actually approached Ava, offering her support. *He can be such a dick sometimes,* Parker had told her. *Want me to talk to him for you?* But Ava had said she'd be fine. Still, she'd been grateful for the offer of support.

She remembered the morning she found out Parker had been killed. At first, it was disguised as a suicide: Wild girl ODs after a night of partying. But soon enough, the truth came out because of all the wounds on Parker's face and body.

"You were the one who stepped forward about her dad," Ava said in a cracked voice. "You were the one who got him arrested. Her mom didn't want to talk."

"And you went to her funeral," Mac said.

"You even *spoke*," Caitlin added.

But Julie just blinked. Ava's heart broke over and over. She'd read about post-traumatic stress disorder in psychology class last year; and they'd talked about it in more than one school assembly. It made sense, she supposed: Julie had been Parker's best friend.

But could Julie have gone this long without anyone realizing that she was delusional? Could she have lived through the funeral and the loss . . . and then blacked it all out?

Caitlin reached out and tried to take Julie's hand, but Julie recoiled. *"That's not true!"* she screamed, so loudly the voices in Nyssa's room were silent for a moment before bursting into hysterical, wasted laughter. "Parker's been with us the whole time. You're telling me she wasn't in our film studies class? She was the one who *initiated* that whole conversation!"

Ava blinked. "No, Julie. *You* did. You were the first person to say who you'd want gone."

"In fact, you said *two* people," Caitlin added. "Parker's dad . . . and then Ashley."

Julie shook her head. *"Parker* said Ashley. Not me. She started the conversation. She was with us at Nolan's party. And Granger's house!" Everyone shook their heads, but she seemed not to notice. "She's here now, too! *She's* the killer!" Her voice and face were practically unrecognizable. "She's the one doing all this, and I know it sounds crazy, but she wanted to *help* us. She was just trying to protect us. Of course it's wrong—I know that. But her heart was in the right place." She raised a trembling hand and pointed at Caitlin. "You finally have solace because Nolan's gone." She gestured at Ava. "And admit it, you would be *thrilled* to be free of Leslie. You'd have your father back."

"Shhh!" Ava hissed, her eyes widening. There were so many people around. So many people could hear.

"Parker meant well," Julie insisted, her voice strangely

calm and cold. She fixed Mac with a pointed stare. "None of those people deserved to die—not even Nolan. Which means I have to find Parker before she kills Claire. And you guys are going to *let me do that.*"

Julie burst forward, knocking Mac roughly against the wall, and dashed down the hallway before any of them could react. They scrambled after her, but she was gone, swallowed up by the crowd.

Ava paused at the edge of the amorphous mass of dancing kids. She looked at Mac. "Where did you last see Claire?"

Mac's face was pale. "In here, I think." She stood on her tiptoes, trying to see over people's heads.

Suddenly, a cry rose up in the crowd. "Cops!" a boy's voice bellowed.

Everyone screamed. Costumed kids scurried in every direction, bolting for the doors and windows, slamming into one another and pushing the crowd forward. Ava struggled to move against the tide, trying as hard as she could to find where Julie had gone.

Before Julie killed again.

CHAPTER THIRTY-TWO

MAC RACED FROM ROOM TO room, screaming Claire's name. *Please let her still be inside, please let her still be inside,* she thought frantically. People were streaming out in the opposite direction, fleeing from the police. Outside, cop cars were parked on the curb, sirens blazing. Mac heard screams and thundering footsteps, but they were fading away. Everyone was heading for the woods, desperate not to be caught. Was Claire there, too?

She stumbled into the front yard. The officers were forming a loose circle around the lawn, trying to contain the sprawling mess of running kids. One officer had a bullhorn to his lips. It echoed with feedback. "If you have been drinking or are otherwise impaired, do not get behind the wheel of your car. We will get you home. I repeat . . ."

"Claire?" Mac called out, thinking she saw her old

friend's head in a clump of kids. No one turned. More kids whooshed past. Mac looked around for Julie, too, but she'd also vanished. Her heart thudded hard.

Mac still couldn't wrap her mind around the fact that Julie thought Parker was still alive—and more than that, that Parker had been *with* them, a fifth girl in their group. She'd claimed that Parker had been the one who named Ashley in film studies that day, but Julie had said Ashley's name herself. So . . . what did that mean? Was Parker a personality of Julie's? Did Julie walk around half the time thinking she was in Parker's skin?

Mac was astonished that they'd missed something so severe right under their noses. In hindsight, there had been times where it had seemed like Julie was contradicting herself, but Mac had just thought she was arguing a problem through from both angles. And it wasn't like Julie had any parents to notice what was going on—her mom probably never even knew where she was. She could slip here and there as she pleased. If only they'd kept better tabs on her. Looked out for her more. Could they have prevented this? And worse, where was Julie now?

A shadow darted past Mac on the street, headed in the opposite direction of the cop cars. Mac took in the colorful costume and gasped—it was Claire, and now she was standing all alone in the middle of the road, staring at something on her phone.

"Hey!" Mac called out, running toward her. "Claire!"

Claire looked up, but her eyes were glassy. Her nose wrinkled at the sight of Mac. "Go *away*, already," she said in a bored voice.

"Get out of the street!" Mac screamed.

Claire made a face. "Why?"

Just then, Mac heard the rumble of a car engine. "Claire!" Mac cried as she advanced. The car revved again. An acid-like smell rose in the air. And suddenly, from out of nowhere, a car shot forward, straight for Claire's body.

"No!" Mac sprinted for Claire. Headlights blazed in the road as bright as a flashbulb, illuminating them both in the glare. The car was moving fast, seemingly oblivious to the fact that the cops were only a hundred or so yards behind them. Finally, Claire looked up. She seemed blinded by the white light. Her mouth hung open and her limbs were slack.

"*Move!*" Mac screamed. She reached Claire a millisecond before the car did, throwing herself against Claire's body and tackling her to the grass. They landed together on the other side of the street, slamming into the curb with painful force. Claire screamed. Mac momentarily couldn't breathe. The car screeched past them, just inches away, down the block and around the corner.

Mac heard a low whimpering behind her and turned. Claire had sat up, but she was hunched over, looking dazed.

She cradled her left hand in the crook of her right arm. Then she turned and stared at Mac, her eyes widening as she seemed to realize that Mac had saved her.

Wordlessly, Claire looked back at her hand. Mac looked, too. Claire's fingers were mangled, twisted over one another in an unnatural configuration. Her pinky stuck out at a horrible angle, clearly broken in more than one place.

"Oh my god," Mac said. "Claire. Your *fingers*."

Claire's face was pale. She opened her mouth as if to speak, but then her eyelids fluttered closed, and she slumped to the grass.

CHAPTER THIRTY-THREE

AN HOUR LATER, CAITLIN STOOD with Mac and Ava in the lobby of the police station. Officers were rushing here and there, and the place seemed in pandemonium, phones ringing and printers blaring and everyone talking at once. Caitlin's heart was still racing. She'd been by Mac's side shortly after Claire was mowed down by that car, but the EMTs and police officers had shooed them all out of the way, sending them home. But they couldn't go home. They had to come here . . . and tell the truth.

McMinnamin appeared in the doorway, his gaze settling over the girls. "Come on back," he said gruffly.

Wordlessly, everyone followed him. Caitlin's nose twitched with the stench of stale coffee and too-sweet pastries. She searched the officers' faces for signs of what had happened that night. Was Claire okay? No one had heard anything after she was loaded into the ambulance. Had it really been Julie who'd tried to hit her? Surely the cops didn't still suspect *them*, did they?

The officer led them into an empty room and gestured for all of them to sit. "So. Busy night, huh?"

Everyone nodded. Ava's breaths came out in little gasps.

McMinnamin put his hands on his hips. "You know something, right? Is that why you're here?"

Caitlin eyed Mac and Ava. Everyone nodded. It was time, Caitlin knew, but she still felt a pang. It felt wrong to give Julie up. They had promised to stick together.

Mac took a deep breath. "We think it's Julie Redding."

McMinnamin nodded. His Adam's apple bobbed. "Okay, then."

Caitlin stared at the floor. "She kind of . . . confessed," she admitted.

It was still hard to process what had happened . . . and who Julie was . . . and what had actually gone down in Nyssa's house. But yes, Julie had confessed. Sort of. She'd said Parker had done it, but Parker wasn't *here*.

"But then she ran off," Ava added. "We're afraid she was the one who hurt Claire Coldwell."

McMinnamin nodded. "That's what we're afraid of, too."

Caitlin whipped her head up. "Wait. You are?"

"Yes, we've been watching Julie for some time."

Caitlin squinted at the cop, still so disoriented. "I'm sorry, but how did you figure all this out?"

As if on cue, Dr. Rose, the psychological profiler, appeared in the doorway. She wore a tan pantsuit and a serious expression, and held a cup of Starbucks in her hand. "Detective. Girls." Dr. Rose nodded at each of them as she crossed the room.

McMinnamin gestured for her to sit. "Caitlin was just asking me how we knew Julie Redding was our suspect, Doctor. Would you like to fill them in?"

"Sure." The doctor sat down and collected her thoughts for a moment before speaking. "When Julie and I had our private session at the precinct the other day, I got a sense of what might be happening with her. She lives in a chaotic, abusive home. She's looking for some sort of anchor and stability. I've worked with a lot of patients who have what we call 'dissociative identity disorder,' and I recognized the signs in her immediately."

"Is that, like, when people think they're more than one person?" Ava asked.

"Yes, Ava. It's what we call it when someone—in this case Julie—believes she has two or more distinct and separate identities. And not just two names, but two separate *personalities*. It's almost like having two entirely different people living in one body. And for Julie—"

"The other person is Parker," Caitlin interjected.

"Yes. Julie is Julie, *and* she is Parker, at different times— and sometimes at the same time, too."

Caitlin swallowed hard, the antiseptic smell of the hospital suddenly making her sick. She'd hoped there was another explanation besides this. But here it was. And in a way, it made sense. She recalled that strange, sullen, totally un-Julie-like Julie she'd met in Julie's front yard yesterday. Had that been "Parker" she'd met? Caitlin had *known* something was wrong. Should she have done something about it? Alerted someone? Then again, how was she to know it was something so . . . *extreme?*

Dr. Rose shifted in her seat. "When she told Detectives McMinnamin and Peters the other day that her alibi the night of Ashley's disappearance was hanging out with Parker, well, that basically confirmed my suspicions," she said. "Julie most likely hears Parker in her head—and probably sees her as sort of a hallucination. She's as real to Julie as I am to you right now. And I'm guessing," Dr. Rose went on, "that if you girls think about it, you'll remember incidents when you thought you were talking to Julie, but you were really with Parker—or, the Parker identity of Julie."

Caitlin nodded reluctantly. Then Mac. Then Ava. They all looked so guilt-stricken. Caitlin sensed they felt as duped as she did.

"Why do you think this happened to her?" Mac asked quietly.

Dr. Rose sighed. "Julie didn't help Parker the night Parker's father killed her. My guess is that she assumed Parker's personality soon after Parker was killed because she couldn't handle the guilt. *Becoming* Parker was a way of keeping her alive—and Parker served as an outlet for the angrier parts of Julie's personality. It's my understanding that Julie was a very popular, high-achieving—dare I say *perfect*—student at Beacon Heights High. Is that correct?"

Everyone nodded mechanically. "That's an understatement." Caitlin let out a dry, sad laugh. "She was amazing."

"Smart, pretty, friendly . . . everyone loved her," Ava said.

Dr. Rose took a sip of coffee. "Well, that fits. Julie couldn't break the rules, because she was protecting her own secrets—about her mother, her house. So she needed to keep a very pristine exterior. She couldn't skip school or mouth off or otherwise step outside the lines. Everyone needs to let off steam, but Perfect Julie could never allow herself to do such a thing. She had too much at stake. Parker, on the other hand, was free to do and say whatever she wanted. Including get her revenge on people who hurt her or those she is close to." She looked around at the girls. "Nolan Hotchkiss, yes, but also Ashley Ferguson, who was ruining her life—police haven't found her yet, but we fear the worst."

"She hurt my stepmother, Leslie, too," Ava said in a choked voice. "I told her how awful Leslie was. But I never thought she'd . . ."

"And Claire, obviously." Mac pressed her hands over her eyes. "Claire tried to sabotage my Juilliard audition. But I would have never wanted to *hurt* her."

Rose exchanged a surprised look with McMinnamin, then nodded. "She was acting out your frustrations because she could," she said. "For 'Parker,' there were no rules. She crossed the line many times, broke all kinds of boundaries. I'm sure you can think of things that Julie said that seemed a bit . . . out of place, perhaps?"

Caitlin flashed back to that day in film studies. It had probably been "Parker" who'd started the conversation, not Julie—because Julie wouldn't have dared. But Julie had backed "Parker" up quickly, she remembered, adding Parker's dad's name to the list almost instantly. It was disturbing to think that every time she'd sat across a table from Julie, there were two people looking back.

She shifted in the uncomfortable interrogation-room chair. "Does Julie realize she has two different personalities?"

"Do you think there are *more* personalities besides those two?" Ava said at the same time.

Dr. Rose cocked her head, considering this. "As far as we know, it's just Julie and Parker. But I'd have to work with her over a significant period of time to say for sure."

Everyone fell silent. A phone rang loudly outside. An officer passed by, muttering to himself.

"Okay," said Ava, leaning closer to the detective and the doctor. "I get why Julie—or Parker—would kill Nolan, Parker's dad, even Ashley. But, assuming all this is true, then why did she kill Granger? Because he was picking on me and all those other girls?"

"We think it had something to do with this." McMinnamin pulled a mud-caked envelope scrawled with *JULIE REDDING* from his folder. "We found it in Granger's yard Friday night."

He slipped a finger under the flap and tugged out a stack of papers. It was a report, handwritten by Mrs. Keller, Beacon High's counselor, during grief counseling after Parker's murder. "Ms. Redding displays a worrisome, fragmented personality," he read aloud. "She seemed to conduct a conversation with someone else who wasn't in the room. When asked about it, Ms. Redding became very agitated and secretive."

Caitlin shut her eyes. "Why didn't Mrs. Keller report this to a doctor at the time?"

"I don't know," McMinnamin said. "Maybe she didn't recognize what was happening. Or maybe she just thought Julie was being dramatic."

Mac's head shot up. "If you found this at Granger's house, then that means . . ."

"He knew." Ava's eyes were huge. "About Parker, I mean. Or, well, maybe not that Julie's other personality was *Parker*, per se, but that something was going on."

"That's right." McMinnamin rubbed his eyes with his hands. "This report is highly confidential and should have been carefully guarded. But, given what we know now about Lucas Granger's questionable ethics, we believe that he noticed something off about Julie and stole the report from the counselor's office. What he was going to do with it is anyone's guess."

Caitlin squinted, trying to put the pieces together. "So this is why Julie—or Julie as Parker—killed Granger? To keep the secret safe?"

McMinnamin nodded. "Julie's fingerprints are on the envelope, so we know she handled it at some point—whether as Julie or as Parker, we don't know. We figure she found it at Granger's house the night you ladies were there."

"Julie was afraid Lucas Granger was going to out her, and then she'd be forced to seek treatment," Rose added. "You see, most of my previous patients with dissociative identities are *very* resistant to treatment. They've created these other personalities to survive and fill some significant holes in their lives. The tiny little lucid part of them that still exists inside their original personality knows that losing one of these *other* identities would be like a death. In Julie's case, if she were forced to get help, then Parker, as Julie understands her, really *would* die. Julie would lose her best friend—again. It would be absolutely devastating for her."

Everyone nodded calmly, but inside, Caitlin's feelings were raging. On the one hand, Caitlin thought they should be angry—Julie had murdered three people *and* set the rest of them up to take the blame. But on the other hand, how could she hold Julie responsible when she was so sick?

McMinnamin cleared his throat. "I'm sorry we kept you girls as suspects for so long. But there are still some holes we need you to fill. Like what you really were doing at Granger's house. *And* what was happening the night of Nolan's party? I know you girls were involved. Too many signs point to you."

Caitlin felt a dart of nerves, and she lowered her eyes. Her friends shifted, too. "It was meant to be a prank," she eked out.

"We never thought he'd die," Ava whispered.

"It was a terrible thing to do," Mac added.

And Caitlin looked at the detective pleadingly. "Will this get us in trouble?"

McMinnamin crossed his arms over his chest, heaving a sigh. "After everything that's happened, all I want is a confession. And I need you to help us find Julie. She's very sick. She needs to be in custody before something else happens." He coughed into his hand. "It's why we came to the party tonight. We suspected Julie might be there. And we've just confirmed that she isn't at her residence. Can you girls think of anyone else she's close with, somewhere she might be?"

Ava frowned. "Well, she went on a few dates with a new boy at school, Carson."

McMinnamin shook his head. "Carson Wells. We already checked with him. He hasn't heard from her in days, and he's worried—especially when he found out that the friend Parker she kept referencing died last year. We have our guys looking for her everywhere. But until we find her, she's on her own."

Hot tears flooded Caitlin's eyes. Julie was out there somewhere, with no one—no one real, anyway—to help her. How would she take care of herself? Did she even have any money for food or a place to sleep? "We have to find her," she whispered.

"You don't have to hunt me down," said a small, choked voice.

Everyone's head shot up. Julie stood in the hall; who knew how she'd gotten past the front desk? Caitlin stifled a gasp. Julie wore a dirty hoodie. Her hair was matted and messy around her face. Her skin was pale, her makeup smeared, and there were deep hollows under her eyes. Caitlin couldn't help but wonder who was staring back at them—Julie or Parker. She felt sorry for both.

"I'm here. And—you're right. I'm sick. I need help." Julie choked back a sob. "But I have one request, okay?"

"We'll try and honor it," Rose said quickly.

She looked back and forth, her jaw trembling. "I want to talk to *my* therapist—and only him. His name is Elliot Fielder."

CHAPTER THIRTY-FOUR

"PASS THE MUFFINS, WOULD YOU?" Ava mumbled through her already-full mouth.

Caitlin snatched the basket off the coffee table and passed it across, leaving a trail of gluten-free Paleo morning glory crumbs across Ava's sprawling L-shaped couch. "Thanks," Ava said gratefully, stuffing one in her mouth. "These are my favorite." She was about to wax poetic about how the muffins were both decadent *and* fairly healthy when Caitlin shushed her, pointing to the TV across the room.

"An update!" Caitlin cried.

Mac grabbed for the remote and turned it up. A chipper blond reporter stood in front of Beacon High. They caught her in mid-sentence. ". . . Miss Redding has confessed to three confirmed killings—Nolan Hotchkiss,

Lucas Granger, and Ashley Ferguson, whose body was dis-covered by police divers in a river behind Ferguson's house yesterday, just where Redding told them it would be. Three of Redding's classmates at Beacon Heights High near Seattle have admitted to pulling a prank on state sena-tor Hotchkiss's son, Nolan, involving OxyContin, but they have been cleared of any involvement in his death and given a slap on the wrist."

Ava shifted nervously, weirded out that their secret was finally out in the open. Not that the reporter called them out by name . . . but still. They'd negotiated to keep other details of what they told the police a secret, too. Like how they'd made that list in film studies of people they wanted dead . . . and how that list wormed its way into Julie's head until she felt it necessary to avenge all their enemies. Ava hadn't wanted to tell the police about the list, but it was probably right to come absolutely clean. Still, she hoped that the police would never, ever tell anyone about it. She couldn't imagine what her father would think of her if he knew.

The reporter continued. "Redding herself said they had nothing to do with the murders. It is assumed the high school senior will likely try for an insanity plea, as her case of split personalities is, according to experts, 'extremely severe.'"

The screen flashed to a shot of Julie's dilapidated house,

where crime scene techs in full-body biohazard suits swarmed in and out, carrying filthy box after filthy box. They cut to Julie's mother standing on her porch, greasy hair pushed back from her face, her torn, shabby housecoat and crazy eyes on display for the world to see. "Julie was never right. Never right. Her father knew it from the start."

And back to the reporter, her hair blowing in one solid piece in the breeze: "Join us tonight at eight, when our own Anderson Cooper finds out what goes on inside the mind of a teenage killer. He sits down with Redding's mother for a one-on-one interview you won't want to miss. Now back to you in the studio, Kate."

Caitlin muted the TV again, and the girls sat in silence. "Why don't I feel any better?" Mac asked miserably.

Caitlin tossed the remote onto the couch between them. "I don't know if it's better or worse that we don't have to go to school this week."

Suddenly, Ava's phone buzzed in her pajama pants pocket. She had a text from Alex. *Are you okay? What can I do?*

She smiled and tapped out a quick response, asking if he'd come over later. She was so glad everything between her and Alex was okay. He made her feel protected and safe.

Then a shadow appeared in the doorway. Ava looked up. It was her father, wearing a rumpled sweater and corduroy pants. Ava shot to her feet. "Dad?" she asked worriedly. "Is everything okay? Is it Leslie?"

Mr. Jalali looked conflicted. "Do you mind if I speak to you alone for a moment, *jigar?*"

"Sure," Ava said, shrugging to her friends and disappearing into the hall. Her father leaned against the railing, worrying his hands together. Ava's heart pounded hard. Maybe there *was* something wrong with Leslie. Or—and maybe this was worse—maybe her father had found out that Julie had shoved Leslie off that balcony because *Ava* wished her dead. What if he hated her now? What if he wanted her out of the house? Maybe she deserved that, though. Once people started dying, once they'd gotten an inkling that this might not be a coincidence, she hadn't done much to keep Leslie safe.

Finally, her dad took a breath and looked up. "Leslie awoke from her coma this morning."

Ava's mouth dropped open. "She . . . *did?*"

He nodded, but strangely, he didn't look that happy. "Yes. And she started saying immediately that you did this to her."

Ava's heart plummeted. "I didn't," she squeaked. "You know I never—"

"Ava, why did you never tell me the truth?"

She blinked, silenced. Her father looked so sad. "The truth about what?" she asked in a small voice.

Mr. Jalali shut his eyes. "I installed security cameras in the house a few months ago when Leslie started saying that she thought the cleaning lady was stealing from us. They're in the living room, dining room, kitchen."

Ava frowned. "You . . . did?" She hadn't known about that.

He nodded. "And just now, I watched some of them. Watched how Leslie interacted with *you*. Always when I was out of the room, out of earshot. But the things she said, *jigar*. Horrible things. Things that weren't true. They were the same sorts of things she said when she awoke from the coma this morning. I'd never heard her talk like that— I was so surprised. That's why I went and looked at the cameras." He leaned closer to her, plaintive. "Why did you never come to me with any of this?"

Ava blinked, astonished. "B-because I didn't know if you'd listen." A look of heartbreak crossed his features. "You started dating Leslie so fast after Mom," Ava said quickly. "And she came in and just . . . *changed* everything about you. I just figured she changed how you thought about me, too." She lowered her eyes. "I thought you wouldn't believe me."

Mr. Jalali opened his mouth as if he wanted to protest, but shut it again. Tears silently welled in his eyes. He pulled Ava close and wrapped her in a huge hug. "I'm sorry. I'm so, so sorry," he whispered.

Ava started crying, too. And they stood there, the two of them, father and daughter, locked in an embrace for what seemed like forever. Ava didn't know what the future would hold, but something told her that Leslie might not be in it—or, if she was, that their lives would be very, very different. It felt like her father was *back*. Truly hers again, truly looking out for her. Which, somehow, just made her cry harder.

Suddenly, she flashed back to Friday night at Nyssa's party, when Julie had told them that "Parker" had killed all those people. *Admit it, you would be* thrilled *to be free of Leslie*, she'd said to Ava. *You'd have your father back.*

It was a horrible thought, but it was true: Now that they were free of Leslie—or at least, the distrust she'd created in their family—Ava had her father back. But just because she'd wished for it didn't mean it should have happened that way. Just because someone was a jerk . . . or a child-beater . . . or a bitch . . . that didn't mean they deserved to die.

She shut her eyes. She wasn't sure what she deserved these days, but one thing was for sure: She was never, ever taking anything for granted anymore. Not Alex. Not her father. Not her freedom.

And she was never saying anything that she might live to regret.

CHAPTER THIRTY-FIVE

SEVERAL MUFFINS AND SOME LEFTOVER pad Thai later, Mac stepped out of Ava's house, debating whether or not to head straight home. She stood with her hand on her car door handle, staring up at the bright blue sky, the first clear, sunny day they'd had in weeks. The air felt thinner, crisper, cleaner. The leaves on the trees swaying in the light wind were saturated with greens, yellows, and oranges richer than any colors she'd ever seen. Even the sky seemed more endless, the small puffs of clouds softer. It was as if all her senses had been reawakened and reinvigorated. But she still felt unsettled. Unfinished. There was something she needed to do.

Screw it, Mac thought.

Ten minutes later, she pulled into the Coldwells' driveway. Claire's car sat near the garage. Mac took a deep, steadying breath and strode to the front door. She prepared herself for a cold reception—even a door slammed in her face. But she knew she had to try.

She rang the bell, listening to the familiar tone. After a moment, she heard a soft shuffling sound as someone approached on the inside. She held her breath as the door swung open.

Claire wore flannel pajamas decorated with dancing musical notes. Her curly hair was pinned back on either side of her face, and her feet were ensconced in giant, fluffy bunny slippers. The left sleeve of her baggy top was rolled up to the shoulder, and below it her arm was bent at the elbow and encased in the thickest, sturdiest, most alarming cast Mac had ever seen. It extended from just below Claire's shoulder all the way down to her fingertips.

The two girls stared at each other for a beat. "Oh my god," Mac burst out. Which was totally not the tone she was going for to break the ice.

But when she looked up, Claire was smirking, not crying. "I know. Pretty impressive."

Mac blinked hard. Claire hadn't kicked her off the porch yet. "Um, I was thinking more like *terrifying*."

Claire sighed. "It's like a medical device and a weapon all rolled into one. And it itches already. Like, really, really bad."

"That sucks."

An awkward silence fell. Claire shifted. "Do you want to come in?"

Mac wouldn't have been more surprised if Claire had pulled out her cello and conked her over the head with it. "Um, are you sure?"

"Well, actually, I need a favor." Claire turned and started down the hall. "Maybe you can open a frozen pizza for me? It's amazing what you can't do with only one hand."

They headed for the kitchen, where Mac busied herself with the freezer and the oven. She'd been in this kitchen hundreds of times, heated up a gazillion pizzas over the years. She turned back around and found Claire watching her, a curious look on her face.

"So was that why you were following me around all night?" she asked.

Mac swallowed hard. "Well . . ."

"Did you know Julie Redding was coming after me? I mean—I barely *know* her. And yet you were following me around like you were protecting me."

Mac stared at the floor, her stomach churning with guilt. *Because I put you on a list of people we wanted to die.* How could she explain to Claire that what she had thought was an innocent—if totally harsh—conversation turned out to be a serial killer's instruction manual? That it was all her fault that Claire's fingers were totally crushed, her musical career probably over for good? Mac wondered if she should crush *her* fingers, too—maybe that would be a punishment that fit her crime. It didn't seem fair that she would get to go to Juilliard unscathed after all this.

But she couldn't tell Claire the truth. Not now. Maybe not ever. "Um, Julie said something that made me realize you were her next target," Mac muttered. It wasn't exactly a lie. "And I couldn't let that happen to you."

Claire shook her head. "It's terrifying she even had targets at *all*."

"I know," Mac said wearily. "Sorry I followed you around like a freak, though. I know it was probably weird."

Claire smiled, and for the first time in a long time, there was no trace of the conniving or competitiveness that had defined their friendship for what seemed like forever. It was just a genuinely grateful smile, and it filled Mac with warmth and happiness. She realized how much she had missed Claire. "You saved me," Claire said simply. "You totally didn't have to."

Mac shrugged. "Of course I did."

The smell of warming pizza filled the kitchen. Mac found her eyes drawn to Claire's cast again. She had saved Claire's life, but what about everything else?

"So will you ever be able to play again?" she said quietly.

Claire looked down. "The doctors say it doesn't look good. Or at least I'll never be up to my old level."

Mac shut her eyes. "I'm so sorry."

Claire sat down at the kitchen table and started fiddling with a cello-shaped salt shaker. "I've had a lot of time to think. And I realized . . ." Claire looked up at her, almost seeming embarrassed. ". . . I'm not sure I even *want* to go to Juilliard."

Mac frowned. Surely Claire was just saying that to make herself feel better. Or maybe she was just high on the pain pills the doctors had given her.

Claire clacked the cello salt shaker with a violin pepper shaker. "It sounds crazy, I know. But I think I've realized that I only wanted to go because"—she let out a sheepish little chuckle—"because *you* did. I just wanted to beat you. But then I thought about what *I* really wanted. And you know what? Oberlin sounds cool. Maybe I'll study music. Maybe not. I have all these choices now, which I never had before when it was always just *cello cello cello*, you know?"

Mac wasn't sure whether to laugh or cry. After all the stress and sacrifices, all the years of band camp and orchestra, the endless practicing, the deception and lies, the heartbreak with Blake . . . Claire didn't even want the final prize. It was like a bad joke with a stupid punch line.

Mac was astonished, too, how willingly Claire had admitted that she'd wanted to beat her. Then again, if she thought about it, wasn't she the same way? For as long as she could remember, Mac had been intensely, blindly driven to be the best cello player, to practice more than Claire, to nail every performance when Claire fumbled, to snatch back first chair when Claire had it. She did truly want to go to Juilliard, but that was almost beside the point. Mac had been equally as competitive, equally as willing to go to the ends of the earth to get what she wanted. Hadn't she proven that by putting Claire's name on the film studies list?

Suddenly, and probably inappropriately, Mac burst out in a fit of hysterical giggles. "I'm sorry," she blurted. "It's so not funny. I don't know why I'm laughing."

Except that Claire started laughing, too. At first it was tentative, but then her shoulders shook, and tiny squeaks came out of their mouths.

"I'm really sorry," Mac said again. "I have to stop."

"Me too," Claire gasped.

But they both kept laughing. It was like the old way they used to laugh together: doubled over, clutching their stomachs, cackling so hard there were tears streaming down their faces. Mac laughed so hard her glasses fogged up. It brought back so many good memories: of Claire and Mac at music camps, or of weekend sleepovers after orchestra practice, or of the colossal giggle fit they'd had in the orchestra pit at Carnegie Hall over the conductor's open fly. Mac never thought she'd share this sort of moment with Claire again—or that she even wanted to. But it felt so *good*.

Only after Mac had cleared their pizza plates, sliding them into the dishwasher, did they manage to maintain a straight face. "So I wanted to tell you," Claire said, squeezing the fingertips of her left hand, which were just barely exposed at the bottom of her cast, to get some circulation going. "I'm really sorry about that Facebook post of you and Oliver. It was shitty of me. I was just so jealous."

Mac just shrugged. It felt so in the past now. "Whatever," she said softly.

"What *actually* happened with Oliver? I lied when I said I wasn't into him. Are you together?"

Mac could tell she genuinely wanted to know. The question rang so familiar in Mac's ears—it was the way they used to talk about boys, long before Blake changed everything between them. "No," Mac replied, feeling a little sad for how she'd just let Oliver dangle for so long. "We didn't . . . click."

Claire nodded, a knowing look suddenly on her face. "Of course you didn't."

"He's nice, though." Mac gave her a genuine smile, too. "You should go for him. I'll put in a good word."

And then, as if on cue, Mac's phone began to vibrate in her pocket, and before she could silence it, it began to play a Bruno Mars song—a very *familiar* Bruno Mars song. *Shit.* She had never changed the ringtone she had long ago assigned to Blake. And Claire knew it.

She quickly covered the screen with her hand and looked up at Claire, suddenly panicked that all of this laughing and being honest and feeling close would all come to an end. But Claire was grinning. "It's okay. You can answer it." She tilted her head toward the phone in Mac's hand. "He always loved you, you know."

Mac sucked in her breath and went very still. The phone kept ringing.

Claire lowered her eyes. "I knew it that first day at Disneyland, but I lied when he asked me and told him you weren't interested. Then, before the auditions, I told him to hang out with you and distract you. I just—" Her voice cracked. "I had no idea how far it would go. It's not his fault, Mac. I made it so he would feel guilty if he didn't do it. He didn't want to."

Mac took a few breaths, trying to process this. It felt good that Claire had come clean. And it felt good that Blake had really been telling the truth. She shot forward and hugged her friend tightly, feeling so relieved. "I love you," she said.

"Huh?" Claire gave her a strange look. "I just told you that I'm basically a bitch, and you say you love me?"

But that was the thing: Mac did love her, despite everything. Not that this made them equal. Mac would always feel guilty for naming Claire in that conversation. It would always linger in the back of her mind, the one thing in life she wished most she could take back. "I just want us to be friends again," she said softly.

Claire groaned and rolled her eyes. "Okay, cut the cheesy stuff. Call him back!"

Mac looked at her appreciatively, then swiped at the phone with one finger. "Hi," she said, a little shyly.

CHAPTER THIRTY-SIX

CAITLIN SLAMMED HER GYM LOCKER door shut. She was off school for the week, but there was no way she was abandoning her soccer team. Especially not tonight, when they played Bellevue. It was also their first game with the new freshman recruits.

"Let's go, Caitlin!" Her teammates filed past her, tightening their hair bands and slapping one another with their towels and jerseys. Ursula let out a loud *whoooooop!* and started a call-and-response cheer as the team jogged through the field house door and into the courtyard. She shot Caitlin a smile over her shoulder, and Caitlin smiled back. It was funny—not long ago, Caitlin had suspected Ursula of being her ultimate enemy. Killing Nolan and framing them. Eavesdropping on their awful conversation in film studies and forming some sort of master plan. It seemed so ridiculous now.

Then again, the truth was pretty unthinkable, too.

Her thoughts turned to Julie. Last she'd heard, Julie had been checked into a high-security mental facility about twenty miles away. It was the type of place where she couldn't have visitors for a while, as she would be in round-the-clock, incredibly intense therapy. Caitlin tried to picture what her days were like. At least she was in a cleaner, less-cluttered environment. At least there were no cats. Would she be sad to part with Parker? Had that even *happened* yet? Maybe it was the type of thing that took months, even years. *It's like a death,* Dr. Rose had said. Caitlin felt so sorry for Julie, despite everything. She couldn't imagine having to go through losing Taylor twice.

A whistle blew outside, snapping her back to the present. Caitlin adjusted her shin guards, popped in her mouth guard, and followed the rest of her team. As she crossed the parking lot to the field, she caught sight of her moms on the bleachers and smiled. Things were okay with them again, for the first time in a long, long time. Last night, she'd had a serious heart-to-heart with them, and though they were still upset with her for pranking Nolan—especially because it had been her Oxy—they were on her side again. Caitlin had finally admitted to her moms just how much rage she'd felt toward Nolan, and how much she directly blamed him for Taylor's suicide. She'd told them how she reread Taylor's journal a thousand times in the past six months, trying to figure out the exact moment when he had decided to go through with it . . . the exact moment when she had missed the most important clue of all.

Her moms had just gazed at her, their eyes spilling over with tears, their mouths squeezed shut to hold back the sobs. Then they had all cried together, and it was like they had finally acknowledged that . . . *thing* . . . the shared pain that was there with them every moment of every day but was too great to even speak of. Just knowing that they were in it together made it hurt a tiny, microscopic bit less.

Caitlin was the last one on the field. She closed her eyes to absorb the cool evening air, the clatter of the crowd, the opposing team's coach calling out warm-up drills, the tooting of air horns. There was only one thing that still wasn't right, that hadn't been put back into place. Jeremy. They hadn't spoken since Nyssa's party. Even *Josh* had called her the next day, apologizing for drunkenly calling her out about signing his cast. "Was that why my brother left?" he'd asked.

"Not really," Caitlin said. And it was true: Jeremy had left because of *her* feelings, *her* conflict. She didn't want Josh back. And Josh probably didn't want her back, either. She understood that even better after his phone call—but it was nice that they'd come to some kind of peace.

Caitlin pulled off her warm-up jacket and threw it onto the grass behind the bench. She had to focus on the game.

She bent down to tighten a shoelace on her cleat, and suddenly something caught her eye up in the stands. Jeremy was sitting all alone, his face painted in Beacon High maroon and white. He held a giant poster board sign with *GOOOOO, CAITLIN!* handwritten in big, sloping letters.

Caitlin's mouth fell open. Despite the fact that the game was going to start in only a few minutes, she dashed off the field and up the bleacher steps, straight toward him. "Look at you! Oh my god!"

Jeremy smiled sheepishly. "I had to come and support my girl."

Caitlin felt tears appear in her eyes. "Really?"

"Well, yeah." He grinned at her, but then his face grew serious. "I thought about what you said, and you were right, Caitlin. I should love you for *exactly* who you are—and that's a soccer player. A girl who goes to parties. A really *hot* girl who plays soccer and goes to parties, by the way." He touched her arm. "And you know what?" he went on. "I love that girl. Every inch of her."

Caitlin thought her heart might burst. She broke into a gigantic smile and jumped into Jeremy's arms. She squeezed him as tightly as she could, breathing him in. It felt so good—so right—to be with him, then and there.

Caitlin could have stayed there all night, just holding him, but she needed to get back to her team. Just as she pulled away from Jeremy, she saw Mary Ann running across the soccer field, headed straight for them. For a millisecond, Caitlin thought her mom was angry about her Jeremy PDA, but as Mary Ann got closer, the look on her face was tense and weird—even worried. It was, Caitlin realized, the same look she'd had when she'd found out Taylor was dead.

Mary Ann reached her side and, winded and panting, grabbed Caitlin by the arm and pulled her away from Jeremy. "What is it?" Caitlin cried. "What's happening?"

Mary Ann caught her breath and locked eyes with her daughter. "It's Julie. She broke out of the mental hospital. She's . . . *gone.*"

CHAPTER THIRTY-SEVEN

FLAT, BRIGHT SUNSHINE ILLUMINATED THE landscape outside Julie's hotel room window. Palm trees dotted the horizon, and cars glinted on the freeway overpass as the afternoon rush hour swung into full gear. Julie leaned back in the stiff upholstered chair and gazed into the cloudless blue sky. Her whole body—arms and legs, fingers and toes—was relaxed. Her mind was still for the first time in as long as she could remember. The absence of stress, of fear, was beautiful and invigorating.

The last twenty-four hours were a blur. Julie had no idea exactly how far she'd traveled, but it didn't matter. All she needed to know was that she was as far from the secrets and cruelties of Beacon Heights as possible, where no one would find her. She had left them all behind, shaken them all from her trail—even the doctors and nurses at the facility, even the cops. They were smart, there was no denying that, but she had still executed her plan to perfection. There was no way she was going to stay in a mental institution, for god's sake—there were limits, after all, to how far she'd go for Parker.

Julie felt no remorse for lying to the hospital staff. She did the right thing, telling the doctors and cops and attorneys that she was sick, letting them work themselves into a tizzy over her very rare, very severe case of dissociative identity disorder. After all, escaping a mental hospital was a hell of a lot easier than escaping from prison. How else would she have been able to get away? Lying to them, telling them that Parker was a figment of her imagination, was her only choice. And she had done it for both of them, for herself and for Parker. But Julie knew the truth: Parker was as real as she was. And *Parker* was the one who had committed those crimes. Not her.

It had been Parker, though, even before she'd turned herself into the cops, who'd laid the groundwork for the plan. Julie had found her in the woods when she'd fled from that party, and Parker had taken her shoulders and said, "It's going to be okay. For both of us. I have an idea. We should use Fielder."

"Fielder?" Julie had frowned. "I thought you hated him."

And then it was Parker who'd come clean: She'd been seeing Fielder, both as a patient and, sort of, as a friend (she'd lowered her eyes when she said this, though). She told Julie that she'd really bonded with him, and it seemed that he had a soft spot for her, considering what had happened to his mom. "He'll come and see you in the hospital, I promise," Parker had said. "And then . . ." She whispered the rest.

Julie had been hesitant, but she'd taken Parker's word. So she'd turned herself in to the cops. Let them cart her off to the hospital, tie her down, sedate her—but they promised, from the start, that they'd try to track down Fielder. Finally, he'd arrived, all flushed and freaked out, his hair flying every which way around his head, and his shirttails hanging out over his pants. He heard her out. She gave him the same spiel about Parker not being real. Fielder had nodded, tears in his eyes. "I want to get better," Julie had urged. Fielder had placed his hand over hers. "I want that for you, too."

It was when he'd grabbed his coat that she'd snatched the visitor's pass off his jacket. He didn't catch it at all, smiling at her sadly when he left, promising to return the next week. Twenty minutes later, when she was sure he was gone and the nurse shift had changed—she was still so new that most of the nurses didn't recognize her—Julie changed clothes, pinned the badge on her shirt (luckily, it only said *E. Fielder*, so she could be an Elizabeth, or an Elsa) and walked out of there. Easy as that.

Did she feel bad she'd used Fielder? Not really. He'd stalked Parker, and that still made him a weirdo in Julie's book. And anyway, it had been Parker's idea: *We have to take extreme measures to get free,* she'd whispered to Julie that night in the woods. Fielder would be fine: Guards might suspect him of assisting in her escape at first, but once they talked it out, this wouldn't hurt his career. He'd just look like a dupe.

Julie's stomach growled as she watched the cars slow to a standstill on the off-ramp. She'd need to get some food soon. Traffic inched forward. *So many people,* Julie thought, *stuck in their cars, stuck in their lives, just waiting for someone else to get out of their way. But not me.*

It was better this way, Julie knew. There was nothing for them in Beacon Heights anyway—not anymore. She felt a shot of longing for Carson, who had been so good to her, but then she reminded herself that he most certainly thought she was nuts, just like everyone else in town. Just like her own mother, according to the horribly awkward interviews she'd given on CNN, MSNBC, *60 Minutes.* It was better to have a clean break. She should have thought of doing this years ago.

There was a knock on the door, and Julie hopped out of her seat. She skipped across the room, past the two queen beds, past the tiled bathroom, and opened the door slowly. When she saw who stood there on the thick carpet in the hall, she let out a little cry of joy.

"Oh, thank *god!*" Julie exclaimed, shooting forward and wrapping her arms tightly around Parker's thin, hunched, hoodie-clad frame.

Parker stood outside the door, grinning broadly. Julie looked so grateful, as if she'd feared she might never see her again. "Can I come in?"

"You don't need an invitation." Julie laughed, opening the door wider.

Parker stepped over the threshold, a plastic bag bursting with Chinese takeout boxes dangling from one hand, spilled sauce beginning to pool in a corner of the sack. "Hungry?"

"Starving." Julie smiled, a smile big and broad and full of sunshine. "Thank god you're okay," she gushed, holding out her arms and pulling her friend into a hug.

"Oh, please," Parker scoffed, brushing her off. "I'm a fighter. I'll always be okay, Julie. You know that."

"I know, but you risked so much."

Parker shrugged. All she'd done, really, was hide while everything went down with Julie. While Julie turned herself in, while Julie spent those days at the hospital, while Julie narrowly escaped, carefully adhering to Parker's plan. She'd known where to find Julie afterward, traveling far to get here, always in disguise. After all, Julie was the one who'd taken the heat—for everything Parker had done.

340

And Parker would always be in her debt.

Then she pulled away and looked her friend squarely in the eye. "I'm always going to be fine, you know. As long as I have you."

Julie beamed. "Same here."

Then they sat down and divvied up the food. Parker ate and ate and ate, suddenly hungrier than she'd been in years. She felt . . . *alive* again. Revived. Everything about this moment was right. They were alone, but they had each other. In a teeny, tiny way, Parker regretted using Fielder—they really *had* made a connection, she thought. But she couldn't dwell on that. The important thing now was Julie. Finally, they were together, with no one to threaten their bond again. The closest of friends forever.

And Parker and Julie swore to themselves in a singular thought, communicated through that uncanny telepathy they sometimes had, that they would never, *ever* be apart again.

ACKNOWLEDGMENTS

HUGE THANKS TO KATIE MCGEE, Lanie Davis, Sara Shandler, Les Morgenstein, Josh Bank, Romy Golan, and Kristin Marang for their creative brilliance on this project. Also kudos and hugs to Jen Klonsky, Kari Sutherland, and Alice Jerman at Harper for making the project even better. A big shout-out to Jen Shotz: I couldn't have done it without you.

Also, though this is a work of fiction, I want to emphasize that there is nothing glamorous about laughing at the expense of others, much less what these characters do in the books. Everyone, be good to each other. Kisses!

Read on for a sneak preview of

Pretty Little Liars

Aria Montgomery burrowed her face in her best friend Alison DiLaurentis's lawn. "Delicious," she murmured.

"Are you smelling the grass?" Emily Fields called from behind her, pushing the door of her mom's Volvo wagon closed with her long, freckly arm.

"It smells good." Aria brushed away her pink-striped hair and breathed in the warm early-evening air. "Like summer."

Emily waved 'bye to her mom and pulled up the blah jeans that were hanging on her skinny hips. Emily had been a competitive swimmer since Tadpole League, and even though she looked great in a Speedo, she never wore anything tight or remotely cute like the rest of the girls in her seventh-grade class. That was because Emily's parents insisted that one built character from the inside out. (Although Emily was pretty certain that being forced to hide her IRISH GIRLS DO

IT BETTER baby tee at the back of her underwear drawer wasn't exactly character enhancing.)

"You guys!" Alison pirouetted through the front yard. Her hair was bunched up in a messy ponytail, and she was still wearing her rolled-up field hockey kilt from the team's end-of-the-year party that afternoon. Alison was the only seventh grader to make the JV team and got rides home with the older Rosewood Day School girls, who blasted Jay-Z from their Cherokees and sprayed Alison with perfume before dropping her off so that she wouldn't smell like the cigarettes they'd all been smoking.

"What am I missing?" called Spencer Hastings, sliding through a gap in Ali's hedges to join the others. Spencer lived next door. She flipped her long, sleek dark-blond ponytail over her shoulder and took a swig from her purple Nalgene bottle. Spencer hadn't made the JV cut with Ali in the fall, and had to play on the seventh-grade team. She'd been on a year-long field hockey binge to perfect her game, and the girls *knew* she'd been practicing dribbling in the backyard before they arrived. Spencer hated when anyone was better at anything than she was. Especially Alison.

"Wait for me!"

They turned to see Hanna Marin climbing out of her mom's Mercedes. She stumbled over her tote bag and waved her chubby arms wildly. Ever since Hanna's parents had gotten a divorce last year, she'd been steadily putting on weight and outgrowing her old clothes. Even though Ali rolled her eyes, the rest of the girls pretended not to notice. That's just what best friends do.

"I'm so glad this day is over." Alison moaned before gently pushing Spencer back through the gap in the hedges. "Your barn."

"I'm so glad seventh *grade* is over," Aria said as she, Emily, and Hanna followed Alison and Spencer toward the renovated barn-turned-guesthouse where Spencer's older sister, Melissa, had lived for her junior and senior years of high school. Fortunately, she'd just graduated and was headed to Prague this summer, so it was all theirs for the night.

Suddenly they heard a very squeaky voice. "Alison! Hey, Alison! Hey, Spencer!"

Alison turned to the street. "Not it," she whispered.

"Not it," Spencer, Emily, and Aria quickly followed.

Hanna frowned. "Shit."

It was this game Ali had stolen from her brother, Jason, who was a senior at Rosewood Day. Jason and his friends played it at inter-prep school field parties when scoping out girls. Being the last to call out "not it" meant you had to entertain the ugly girl for the night while your friends got to hook up with her hot friends—meaning, essentially, that you were as lame and unattractive as she was. In Ali's version, the girls called "not it" whenever there was anyone ugly, uncool, or unfortunate near them.

This time, "not it" was for Mona Vanderwaal—a dork from down the street whose favorite pastime was trying to befriend Spencer and Alison—and her two freaky friends, Chassey Bledsoe and Phi Templeton.

"You guys want to come over and watch *Fear Factor*?" Mona called.

"Sorry," Alison simpered. "We're kind of busy."

Chassey frowned. "Don't you want to see when they eat the bugs?"

"Gross!" Spencer whispered to Aria, who then started pretending to eat invisible lice off Hanna's scalp like a monkey.

"Yeah, I wish we could." Alison tilted her head. "We've planned this sleepover for a while now. But maybe next time?"

Mona looked at the sidewalk. "Yeah, okay."

"See ya." Alison turned around, rolling her eyes, and the other girls did the same.

They crossed through Spencer's back gate. To their left was Ali's neighboring backyard, where her parents were building a twenty-seat gazebo for their lavish outdoor picnics. "Thank *God* the workers aren't here," Ali said, glancing at a yellow bulldozer.

Emily stiffened. "Have they been saying stuff to you again?"

"Easy there, Killer," Alison said. The others giggled. Sometimes they called Emily "Killer," as in Ali's personal pit bull. Emily used to find it funny, too, but lately she wasn't laughing along.

As they reached the barn, the girls heard giggles coming from inside. Someone squealed, "I said, *stop* it!"

"Oh God," Spencer moaned. "What is she doing here?"

As Spencer peeked through the keyhole, she could see Melissa, her prim and proper, excellent-at-everything older sister, and Ian Thomas, her tasty boyfriend, wrestling on the couch. Spencer kicked at the door with the heel of her shoe, forcing it open. The barn smelled like moss and slightly burned popcorn. Melissa turned around.

"What the fu—?" she asked. Then she noticed the others and smiled. "Oh, hey guys."

The girls eyed Spencer. She constantly complained that Melissa was a venomous super-bitch, so they were always taken aback when Melissa seemed friendly and sweet.

Ian stood up, stretched, and grinned at Spencer. "Hey."

"Hi, Ian," Spencer replied in a much brighter voice. "I didn't know you were here."

"Yeah you did." Ian smiled flirtatiously. "You were spying on us."

Melissa readjusted her long blond hair and black silk headband, staring at her sister. "So, what's up?" she asked, a little accusingly.

"It's just . . . I didn't mean to barge in . . . ," Spencer sputtered. "But we were supposed to have this place tonight."

Ian playfully hit Spencer on the arm. "I was just messing with you," he teased.

A patch of red crept up her neck. Ian had messy blond hair, sleepy-looking hazelnut-colored eyes, and totally gropeworthy stomach muscles.

"Wow," Ali said in a too-loud voice. All heads turned to her. "Melissa, you and Ian make the kuh-*yoo*-test couple. I've never told you, but I've always thought it. Don't you agree, Spence?"

Spencer blinked. "Um," she said quietly.

Melissa stared at Ali for a second, perplexed, and then turned back to Ian. "Can I talk to you outside?"

Ian downed his Corona as the girls watched. They only ever drank super-secretively from the bottles in their parents' liquor cabinets. He set the empty bottle down and offered them a parting grin as he followed Melissa outside. "Adieu, ladies." He winked before closing the door behind him.

Alison dusted her hands together. "Another problem solved by Ali D. Are you going to thank me now, Spence?"

Spencer didn't answer. She was too busy looking out the barn's front window. Lightning bugs had begun to light up the purplish sky.

Hanna walked over to the abandoned popcorn bowl and took a big handful. "Ian's *so* hot. He's, like, hotter than Sean." Sean Ackard was one of the cutest guys in their grade and the subject of Hanna's constant fantasies.

"You know what I heard?" Ali asked, flopping down on the couch. "Sean really likes girls who have good appetites."

Hanna brightened. "Really?"

"*No.*" Alison snorted.

Hanna slowly dropped the handful of popcorn back into the bowl.

"So, girls," Ali said. "I know the perfect thing we can do."

"I hope we're not streaking again." Emily giggled. They'd done that a month earlier—in the freezing frickin' cold—and although Hanna had refused to strip down to less than her undershirt and day-of-the-week panties, the rest of them had run through a nearby barren cornfield without a lick on.

"*You* loved that a little too much," Ali murmured. The smile faded from Emily's lips. "But no—I was leaving this for the last day of school. I learned how to hypnotize people."

"Hypnotize?" Spencer repeated.

"Matt's sister taught me," Ali answered, looking at the framed photos of Melissa and Ian on the mantel. Her boyfriend of the week, Matt, had the same sandy-colored hair as Ian.

"How do you do it?" Hanna asked.

"Sorry, she swore me to secrecy," Ali said, turning back around. "You want to see if it works?"

Aria frowned, taking a seat on a lavender floor pillow. "I don't know. . . ."

"Why not?" Ali's eyes flickered to a stuffed pig puppet that was peeking out of Aria's purple sweater-knit tote bag. Aria was always carrying around weird things—stuffed animals, random pages torn out of old novels, postcards of places she'd never visited.

"Doesn't hypnosis make you say stuff you don't want to say?" Aria asked.

"Is there something you can't tell us?" Ali responded. "And why do you still bring that pig puppet everywhere?" She pointed at it.

Aria shrugged and pulled the stuffed pig out of her bag. "My dad got me Pigtunia in Germany. She advises me on my love life." She stuck her hand into the puppet.

"You're shoving your hand up its butt!" Ali squealed and Emily started to giggle. "Besides, why do you want to carry around something your *dad* gave you?"

"It's not funny," Aria snapped, whipping her head around to face Emily.

Everyone was quiet for a few seconds, and the girls looked blankly at one another. This had been happening a lot lately: Someone—usually Ali—mentioned something, and someone else got upset, but everyone was too shy to ask what in the world was going on.

Spencer broke the silence. "Being hypnotized, um,

does sound sort of sketch."

"*You* don't know anything about it," Alison said quickly. "C'mon. I could do it to you all at once."

Spencer picked at the waistband of her skirt. Emily blew air through her teeth. Aria and Hanna exchanged a look. Ali was always coming up with stuff for them to try—last summer, it was smoking dandelion seeds to see if they'd hallucinate, and this past fall they'd gone swimming in Pecks Pond, even though a dead body was once discovered there—but the thing was, they often didn't *want* to do the things that Alison made them do. They all loved Ali to death, but they sometimes hated her too—for bossing them around and for the spell she'd cast on them. Sometimes in Ali's presence, they didn't feel real, exactly. They felt kind of like dolls, with Ali arranging their every move. Each of them wished that, just once, she had the strength to tell Ali no.

"Puh-*leeeeeze*?" Ali asked. "Emily, you want to do it, right?"

"Um . . . " Emily's voice quivered. "Well . . . "

"I'll do it," Hanna butted in.

"Me too," Emily said quickly after.

Spencer and Aria reluctantly nodded. Satisfied, Alison shut off all the lights with a snap and lit several sweetly scented vanilla votive candles that were on the coffee table. Then she stood back and hummed.

"Okay, everyone, just relax," she chanted, and the girls

arranged themselves in a circle on the rug. "Your heartbeat's slowing down. Think calm thoughts. I'm going to count down from one hundred, and as soon as I touch all of you, you'll be in my power."

"Spooky." Emily laughed shakily.

Alison began. "One hundred . . . ninety-nine . . . ninety-eight . . ."

Twenty-two . . .

Eleven . . .

Five . . .

Four . . .

Three . . .

She touched Aria's forehead with the fleshiest part of her thumb. Spencer uncrossed her legs. Aria twitched her left foot.

"Two . . ." She slowly touched Hanna, then Emily, and then moved toward Spencer. "One."

Spencer's eyes sprang open before Alison could reach her. She jumped up and ran to the window.

"What're you doing?" Ali whispered. "You're ruining the moment."

"It's too dark in here." Spencer reached up and opened the curtains.

"No." Alison lowered her shoulders. "It's got to be dark. That's how it works."

"C'mon, no it doesn't." The blind stuck; Spencer grunted to wrench it free.

"No. It does."

Spencer put her hands on her hips. "I want it lighter. Maybe everyone does."

Alison looked at the others. They all still had their eyes closed.

Spencer wouldn't give in. "It doesn't always have to be the way you want it, you know, Ali?"

Alison barked out a laugh. "*Close* them!"

Spencer rolled her eyes. "God, take a pill."

"You think *I* should take a pill?" Alison demanded.

Spencer and Alison stared at each other for a few moments. It was one of those ridiculous fights that could have been about who saw the new Lacoste polo dress at Neiman Marcus first or whether honey-colored highlights looked too brassy, but it was really about something else entirely. Something way bigger.

Finally, Spencer pointed at the door. "Leave."

"Fine." Alison strode outside.

"Good!" But after a few seconds passed, Spencer followed her. The bluish evening air was still, and there weren't any lights on in her family's main house. It was quiet, too—even the crickets were quiet—and Spencer could hear herself breathing. "Wait a second!" she cried after a moment, slamming the door behind her. "Alison!"

But Alison was gone.

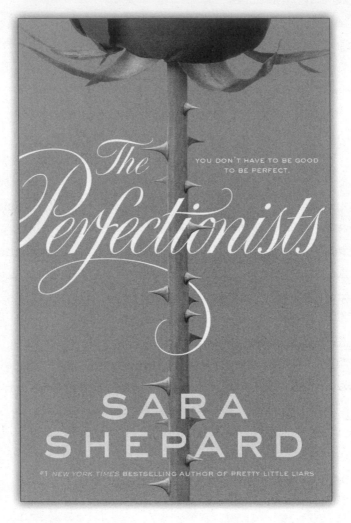

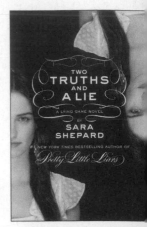

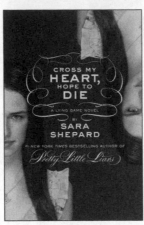

THE HIT ABC FAMILY ORIGINAL SERIES

Pretty Little Liars

all new • tuesdays 8/7c

abc family
a new kind of family

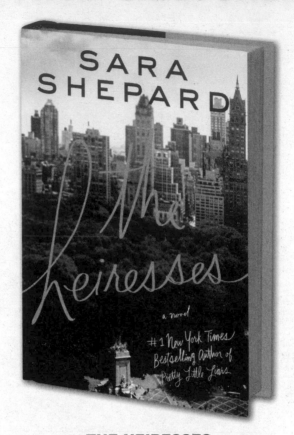